Farawayer

Billy DeCarlo

Published by Wild Lake Press, Inc, 2022.

FARAWAYER

First edition. May 28, 2022.

Copyright © 2022 Billy DeCarlo.

ISBN: 978-1732066984

Written by Billy DeCarlo.

Table of Contents

For Jenn

and

For Dawnen Thomas, an unknown legend in his time - June 19, 1956 - March 29, 2022

"I consider myself neither poet, composer, or musician. These are merely tools used by sensitive men to carve out a piece of beauty or truth that they hope may lead to peace and salvation."—Gil Scott-Heron

1 Bivouac

The old Bivouac Tavern pulsed with roadhouse music and held its regulars like chicks in a nest. Lake Sussex vacationers avoided the place. It was dangerous for strangers, especially tourists. Rows of black motorcycles in the war-zone parking lot and its battered log cabin exterior served as a warning to stay away.

Shayne signaled the bartender to bring us another round.

I coughed and glanced up at the formerly white cork drop ceiling, now stained brown with nicotine. The fans above whirled the dense smoke in rivers above us.

"It'll take old Slow Joe a while to fill those. Let's get some air," I said. Neither of us smoked, so we made a habit of ducking out often to breathe. Shayne hopped off his barstool and led the way.

He decided early in life that he wouldn't let his height be a liability. In high school, he never signed up for a sport but spent every day after classes in the weight room. It showed, and he swaggered when he walked, a signal that he wasn't taking any shit—a necessary attitude to survive in a place like the Bivouac. It was always full of working-class dudes with chips on their shoulders, ready to vent their frustrations

1

and impress a biker chick by pounding the snot out of some poor bastard.

We had been best friends since first grade and knew each other instinctively. His motor was always running, and his brash comedic style never suffered a frown on anyone's face. I still owed him $300 from money he'd chipped in for a drug deal I'd gone into the city for and gotten robbed. He never brought it up, but it nagged at me every day.

Shayne popped the door open, causing smoke to billow out into the dusk. It clanged shut behind us, muffling the music that came in a torrent from the half-lit neon jukebox inside. We leaned on the front porch railing. The lake was visible through the trees, sparkling with the last of the day's sun. Speedboats thrummed along the surface, leaving white foam wakes to disperse behind them. Disco crews from the city parked in the lot across the street and walked past on their way to the Lightship Club, a fancy place right on the water.

"What the fuck is happening to music, man?" Shayne asked.

"I dunno. Everyone was playing Led Zeppelin when I went into basic training. When I got out a few months later and could listen to music again, all I heard was that crap. It was like the world went away and I emerged on a different planet. *Twilight Zone* shit. Maybe we're turning into the old people, complaining about the young people's music." The thought was depressing.

"Looking good, fancy boys," Shayne called out to some dudes wearing polyester pants, brightly colored open shirts, and excess jewelry. "This is what a man wears to the bar," he shouted, flexing in his tight black wife-beater.

"Cool it, bro," I said. "Those fucking New Yorkers carry guns. I don't want to get shot before I leave in the morning. I've been planning this trip for too long."

He laughed. "Look at those pussies. They've got tight pants and socks crammed in their crotches. Where the hell are they going to hide a gun?"

"In the car, maybe. Why are you looking at their crotches?"

He looked at me and laughed. "Oh, hilarious, Levi."

"Fuck you, shorty," one of them yelled back.

Here we go, I thought, and immediately grabbed the back of his belt as he started toward the steps to the street. "Come on, man. No fights. I'm leaving tomorrow, not sitting in a jail cell. Let's catch a buzz and go back inside. I think that girl playing pool had her eye on you. Your quarter is probably up soon, and there's a Jack and coke waiting for you on the bar by now."

He hit me on the arm. "You used to like a good scrap. What happened? Turning soft, Levi?"

"I had enough of that in the military. I don't like hurting anyone. Besides, we're adults now. People just want to sue the shit out of you."

"You didn't have to be such an animal."

"You know the deal, Shayne. Once someone pushes you into a fight, it's do or die. No rules. There is no *fair*. Anyway, that part of my life is over. My Catholic guilt can't take it."

We laughed as I pulled out my wallet, extracted a flattened, half-spent joint, and fired it up. We passed it back and forth as we talked.

"Speaking of hurting someone, what are you going to do about Sarah?" he asked.

"It's bullshit, Shayne. You know that. I'm not going back up north. Fuck that. It was a setup, what she did."

"I thought you said it wasn't your..."

I cut him off before he said it. "Look at those poor bastards in that bar behind us. Same shit every day—get up early, go to your miserable job, get bitched at by your miserable boss, stop in there and have a quick couple of beers to take the edge off, go home, get bitched at by your miserable wife, yell at your miserable kids for whatever stupid shit they did that day in school. Then the next day, you get up and do it all again. It's a fucking hamster wheel. For what? There's no freedom. You're a slave to everyone in your life, all of them, until the day you die."

"Damn, bro. I only asked about Sarah."

"I'm not falling for her trap. Listen. I fucked up right out of high school by not going on that cross-country trip with you. I didn't want to enlist, but I never told you why I did it."

He hit the joint, causing the tip to flare orange, and spoke as he held the smoke in. "I'm all ears."

"It pissed me off when my old man laughed at me for wanting to go to college and said there was no money for it. Plus, I wanted to make my grandfather proud. 'Every generation has served,' he kept saying to me all my life. Then he goes and dies right before I leave for basic training."

"You sure fucked that up, getting bounced after three years."

"Yeah. Well, I'm glad Grandpa wasn't around for that part. He was like a father to me when my father wasn't. The point is, I'm in my twenties now, and I've never been free, always having to answer to someone. End of subject, new subject. Did you think about coming with me on this trip?"

"I'd love to. Job, though. Next time."

"Fucking slave," I responded. "There are plenty of jobs in Tulsa with the oil boom. Better ones. It's cheaper to live there than here in Jersey. Sarah's brothers are already there. They said they'd put me up for a bit, and their boss already said he'd hire me. I figure it'll take three days to hitchhike down there. It's all set up. My pack is ready at home. First thing tomorrow, I'm out. Gone."

"Sarah's brothers? Are you kidding? They're likely to beat your ass or shiv you in your sleep, bro. Let me know how that works out for you. Her old man said he wanted to kill you. The dude is a fucking prison guard. He knows people. Those are his sons. He's only got to say the word."

"I think they're hoping I'll get settled down there and then send for Sarah and the kid."

"They'll kick you out as soon as they figure out you have no plans to do any of that. You taking I-80 across?"

"Nah, I'm going the southern route, I-78 to I-81 to I-40. It'll be warmer, more scenic."

"How're you set for cash, Levi? Need me to front you any?"

"I'm good, for now, thanks." I never liked to talk about how much money I had because it usually wasn't much. It was also a thing with my family. Nobody talked about money. It scared me, having watched my mom cry at a kitchen table covered with bills many times late at night. Since my discharge, I had busted my ass installing chain-link fencing with my uncle and cousin. I had enough dough for now. *Money corrupts.*

"Cops," Shayne said, palming the joint. A black and white slowed as it rolled past. The officer flipped on his multi-colored light bar, blipped his siren briefly, and wagged his finger at us.

"He's cool," I said. "He'll probably be in here after his shift and smoking one out back later. Let's get back inside."

We settled back into our seats at the bar, sinuses cleared and fresh drinks at the ready.

"What's with the cops?" Joe, the bartender, asked. "I thought I heard a siren."

"It was Randy, just saying hello," I answered.

"Good. I worried you two were messing with the disco rubes again."

"That too!" Shayne shouted. "You know it!"

I checked the pool table and saw that Shayne's penny-topped quarter was up next. Grey-haired Jimmy was at his usual con—acting drunk and sloppy until someone put up big bucks, then running the table.

"Hey, don't put any money up against that old guy," I said, nudging Shayne. "He's a hustler."

Jimmy leaned back on his cue and made a point of staggering backward as his opponent came out of the restroom, a big red-headed guy wearing a denim jacket with the sleeves cut off.

"Oh, hell," I said. "That's Quinn. He's with the Pagans, not wearing his colors. I run weed for them sometimes."

Shayne turned to watch.

"Whose shot is it?" Jimmy called out to the bar, slurring his words.

Quinn pointed his cue at Jimmy, then at the table. All Jimmy's solids remained, and Quinn was down to just the eight ball.

"Watch this," I said. "This shit's going to get ugly."

Jimmy approached the table and slammed a solid home on a bank shot. Then again, and again. He straightened up after each achievement, admiring it before bending to the table to continue his work with precision. After cleaning up the solids, he called a difficult bank on the eight, forgoing the easier straight shot, and dropped it clean.

Jimmy stood and bowed to the audience, smiling, then put his hand out, palm up, toward his opponent to collect his winnings. A few of the old rummies at the bar clapped for him.

Quinn walked up to the table and threw his cue on it, sliding it across the green felt.

"Easy on the table there," Slow Joe called from behind the bar.

Jimmy walked up to Quinn, palm still out. Quinn reached toward the leather biker wallet chained to his belt and protruding from his back pocket. Instead, he grabbed the cue ball from the table and slammed it into Jimmy's forehead, knocking him to the floor, out cold, then walked out the door.

"That didn't go well," Shayne observed, as a few of Jimmy's friends pulled him up and into a chair.

"Table is open. Care for a game?" I asked.

THE NIGHT WORE ON, and we commandeered a table, filling it with empty shot glasses and beer bottles.

"Lots of dead soldiers. We're doing good work here tonight," Shayne shouted, gesturing at them over the shoulder of the girl on his lap.

John Barrack sat next to me, guzzling the remains of his mug. He was much older than us, late forties, maybe, and had a sketchy past. He'd been to prison, but he never said for what and got pissed if anyone brought it up. I usually kept my distance from him, but he had joined us. I wasn't in the mood to argue and didn't want a problem with him. He could be unpredictable and violent, especially when drunk. By this time in the evening, he was usually looking for someone to fight if he hadn't hooked up with some skank. He was a thick-armed longshoreman who liked to wear tight white T-shirts with a cigarette pack rolled up into one sleeve, and he still lived in the 1950s, his black hair greased into a DA. He drove around in a battered and faded '57 Chevy he called the Bozo-mobile.

"So you're leaving, huh?" Barrack slurred. "Big adventure tomorrow?"

"Yeah," I answered. "Just heading south to make some money and avoid the cold up here for the winter." I let him know I was broke. He was always looking for money, and had probably come to our table looking for free drinks and to skim any unattended cash into his pocket.

"What if I want to go?" he asked.

I paused, considering how I could put him off. He was likely bluffing, talking shit, but I didn't want to take a chance. I shouldn't have mentioned the jobs down there in front of him. My excitement had gotten away from me.

"I dunno, John. My friends are down there in a cramped efficiency apartment. There's barely room for me on the floor. And just that one job is open," I said. "How about I call you after I'm settled and in a place of my own?"

He nodded, seeming to buy it. "I need to get the fuck out of here. I got trouble coming with the law," he said.

I escaped him by going to the bar for another round of drinks. Steve Gianis was there, drinking alone. He was a grade ahead of me in high school, a real smart-ass who kept after my girlfriend Carla relentlessly, until one day I broke his nose in the hallway between fourth and fifth period. He had grabbed her ass as we walked hand-in-hand, so he had it coming, and I earned a two-day suspension. Since he was on the basketball team with a big game coming up and all, he got nothing. I hoped to ignore him as Slow Joe shuffled behind the bar, placing our drinks on a platter for me.

"Hey, Levi," he said cheerfully. "I ran into your old flame Carla the other day in the mall. She was asking if I'd seen you."

He had my attention. "Really? What did she say?"

"She said nothing was working out for her and she missed you. She asked if I'd seen you with anyone. Said she made a mistake by dumping you when you were gone.

Sounds like you have a real shot to get her back. You should go for it. You guys were inseparable. Cute couple."

Joe placed the platter of drinks in front of me, and my heart swelled with hope. I brought the tray to our table and put it down, fishing in my pocket for change.

"What's up?" Shayne asked. "You're smiling like you just got laid."

"I might stick around after all. Maybe this isn't the right time for this trip."

"What?"

"Be right back. I've got to call Carla."

"Oh Jesus, bro. Not again. Please don't do this to yourself."

I ignored him and went to the phone booth at the back of the bar, closing the shutter door behind me. I pushed a dime through the slot and dialed the number to the pink Princess phone in her bedroom, messing up the first time with a shaky index finger, and having to do it all over again.

I let it keep ringing until she finally answered in a sleepy voice.

I tried to conjure my most mature and confident tone. "Hey, it's Levi. How's it going, Carla?"

"What? What time is it?"

"Um, I dunno. Late, I guess. Sorry. Steve Gianis told me what you said to him at the mall, so I called right away. I miss you, Carla. I love you and want to try again."

There was a long pause, and I hoped she was considering my offer, and hadn't fallen back asleep. The waiting was agony. I imagined her lying in that bed, in the room where we had both made love for the first time, two long-ago virgins fumbling with each other's bodies.

"Levi, you're drunk. Again. I don't know what you're talking about. I haven't seen Steve since we graduated. Good night." The click of the handset as she hung up resounded in my ears. I left mine dangling at the end of its cord.

As I left the booth, I glanced over at Gianis. As I expected, he had swiveled on his barstool to enjoy the whole thing, and was laughing at me. I started toward him and he put his mug down, preparing. This time Shayne saved me, grabbing my arm and guiding me back to the table. "Leave it alone. Put him on the list."

I blamed myself. I drank too much and should have seen through it. *Carla too, for writing the letter that broke me, instead of telling me face to face.*

"What happened?" Shayne asked.

"Nothing. Fuck it."

He pushed a shot toward me, and I threw it down my throat. "I have plans. On the road tomorrow. I don't need her. I don't need *anyone*."

Bobby Russo and his girlfriend, Gwen, came over and sat down. He had moved to Jersey from Brooklyn a few years ago, and took every opportunity to remind everyone he was from there. It was pretty annoying, and I hoped he wouldn't agitate Barrack. Russo was an insecure braggart, but a nice guy, and I often felt sorry for him.

I tried to steer the conversation to safe harbor. "What's new, Bobby?"

He looked at Gwen and smiled. "We're celebrating too. I just got my black belt at the Tae Kwon Do place I train at in the city." It surprised me he didn't wear it to the bar, and didn't doubt it was under his shirt or something.

Barrack perked up at the comment. "Oh, everybody look out! Kung Fu man might kick our asses!" He stood up and simulated some karate chops, stopping just short of Russo's nose, and laughed. Then he paused, as if an idea had popped into his addled brain.

"Last call!" Slow Joe yelled from behind the bar.

I turned to Shayne and noticed the girl on his lap was gone. "Well, I've got a long day tomorrow," I said.

Everyone got up to leave, and I cleaned the table, bringing the empties and shot glasses over to Joe at the bar.

"Thanks, kid," he said. "Sorry to see you go. You're the only decent fucker in the place." He pushed a free shot of Wild Turkey at me and I downed it.

"See you next summer maybe, Joe. It gets hot as shit down there, so I'll likely be back then."

Our group reached the parking lot, and I thanked Shayne again for giving me a ride on his motorcycle, since I had no vehicle at that point in my life, and didn't want one.

"Uh, oh," he said, looking toward the Bozo-mobile. Russo's car sat next to it, and Barrack was in a fighting stance, challenging him.

"Come on, Bruce Lee. Show me what you learned," Barrack egged him on.

"I don't want to fight you," Russo said. "You're drunk. Go home."

"Let it go, John," I called out. "Cops will be by on patrol any time now." I knew Barrack wouldn't give up.

"Because you're a big pussy Russo, aren't you? Big city pussy," Barrack continued.

Gwen guided Russo toward the passenger seat. Barrack stepped closer. "And that ugly bitch you're with, she thinks you're a pussy too. Big black belt New York City pussy, right?"

Russo pulled away from Gwen and came at Barrack, who stepped back into his fighting stance. He was drunk, but I knew this was one thing he could do naturally, like functional alcoholics that can get wasted all day and go to work with no problem. It was his thing. It was what he lived for and all he was good at.

"Let's go, pussy," Barrack urged. He was smart enough to wait for Russo to come at him. I knew what he'd do—deflect the blow, fake with his right, then land a hard left cross. I'd seen it before. It was his go-to move. I always took notes about how people fought in case it ever became my turn.

And that's what Barrack did. Russo went down hard, and Gwen screamed as she ran to him. Barrack moved in, urging him to get up and fight like a man. He never wanted to finish quickly, always yearning to inflict more pain.

Shayne and I moved between them as Gwen helped Russo up. "John, he's finished. Let it go," I urged. "I have some good weed. Let's stop at your place and fire one up before we call it a night." I knew he could never turn down free stuff, especially booze or any type of drugs. He nodded, and Shayne and I guided him toward his car.

We pulled into the gravel driveway at Barrack's little shack by what used to be an old tourist mini-golf place. Barrack stepped up to his front door, fumbling for his keys.

"Hey, I'm gonna head out," Shayne said.

"Come on, dude. Don't leave me here with this psychopath," I answered. It was close enough to walk to my parents' place, so I wasn't worried about that.

"Why did you come here, then?"

"I had to separate him from Bobby before he killed the guy. It's just for a few minutes."

"Well, I'm gonna get going. I have to work with the landscaping crew bright and early. Be careful on the trip. Send some postcards and ring me up when you get to Tulsa."

"Alright. Thanks for hanging out tonight, brother." We embraced, and I watched him get back on his Harley, rev the throttle, and disappear over the bridge across the lake. I wished I still had my bike and could take it on the trip instead of hitchhiking. Suddenly, I felt alone and looked at Barrack's shack with foreboding. He appeared at the door and motioned me in. I knew if I left without getting him high, I'd have to hide from him for a long time. He loved to carry a grudge.

We settled into his living room full of musty, broken furniture and I fired up quickly. I wanted to get it over with. He brought me a beer. I noticed the cap was loose, and it wasn't quite full. He had probably started drinking it earlier and put it back in the fridge. After discretely wiping the top with my shirt, I tasted it, and it was flat.

We passed the joint back and forth wordlessly. Barrack grabbed a roach clip and attached it to the stub, then offered it.

"Go ahead, man. I'm set," I said. He looked at me funny, and I felt something bad was coming.

He exhaled a long stream of smoke at me. "I'm still thinking about going with you, Levi."

Terror struck me at the thought. "We talked about that at the Bivouac, John. There's no room, there's no job waiting for you there. I said I'd get set up and call you, right? You have a job here. You have a nice place."

He disclosed he had lost his job at the city docks, was three months behind on the rent, had gotten busted for shoplifting at the mini-mart last week, and was out on bail.

He persisted, so I gamed it out as best I could, given I was now pretty wasted. I had sworn I'd take it easy and leave rested and ready in the morning. Hitching is a bitch when you're hung over. A ride for at least part of the trip would be nice. Taking my experience with the guy into account and what I knew about him, I decided he'd bail at some point and head back home. I called his bluff.

"OK, sure, John. Pack some shit, but keep it light. Remember, there's no room. You might have to sleep in your big-ass car when we get to Tulsa."

He laughed. "Bozo-mobile's tank is empty. We have to fill it up."

"John, I've been out of work. I don't have money, just enough to eat once a day on the road. That's why I'm hitching it." I thought I had found a way out. It got quiet as he tried to find a solution—a dangerous thing for such a small mind.

He stirred and smiled. "OK, Levi. Here's the deal. Taylor's service station is just across the street. I've got a bunch of five-gallon gas cans and some hose on the back porch. Grab a few cans and fill them by siphoning out some cars waiting for repair in his lot. Ferry them back here and I'll fill the Bozo-mobile, and we'll take a few full ones to refuel along the way. We do the same thing the whole way down. Let's leave in an hour and be on our way to Tulsa. We'll drive and sleep in shifts."

It was something I'd done before, but I didn't want any trouble. I just wanted to be free. Exhausted, I relented and stood up to get started.

I crouched next to the first car and sucked the end of the filthy hose. In my compromised state, I drew too hard and got a mouthful of gasoline. Retching, I then vomited, the bile spewing from my nose and mouth—a full night's worth of beer and stomach acid. I thought about leaving, just walking home and being done with it. I'd sleep in my bed, say goodbye to Mom, Dad, and my sisters in the morning, sling my pack on, and be on the road alone and free.

The can overflowed, and I swapped the hose to the second container. I looked across the street and saw Barrack standing by his car, smoking a cigarette. *Great, he'll get us blown up.*

Sitting against the car as the second can filled, I dozed off, then startled awake to bright, multicolored lights bouncing off everything around me. A siren sounded. *Cops.*

I scrambled to my knees, and crawled between cars as fast as I could, feeling the gravel pierce my skin through the holes in my jeans, then the ooze of blood and fierce pain. Making it to the side of the garage just as the black and white was pulling in, I peered around the corner. A second police car had driven up onto Barrack's lawn, and John was resisting as a big cop tried to pin him against his car. Another cop was inspecting the gas cans and hose I had left behind.

"He's been siphoning gas," the cop yelled to his partner at John's house. "Cuff him up."

I felt bad, but it was John's idea. I also knew he'd throw me under the bus immediately. Ducking around the back, I crouched and ran up the wooded hill behind the service station. I'd been to Bobby Russo's house on the road behind it. As I made it to the top, I heard Barrack screaming, "I'll fucking get you for this, Levi! You motherfucker!" The big cop was loading him into the first car. The second cop car was gone. I started toward Russo's house and saw it creeping up the road toward my position, the spotlight searching.

I made it to Bobby's place, breathing hard and sweating. I banged on the door as softly as I could in my panic. Gwen answered, wearing next to nothing. I knew her a little and had a crush on her. She was too good for Bobby, a real sweetheart, and petite, which was what I liked. Her nipples poked through her sheer mid-drift silk top and her tight white bikini briefs exposed the shadow of her pubic hair. She ushered me in. "Keep it down, Bobby's sleeping. Thanks for helping him tonight. What the hell happened, Levi? Why are you here?" She sat against me on the couch.

"Listen, the cops are looking for me. Can I crash here?"

"Sure," she said, putting her hand on my knee.

The searchlight hit the house, and I heard the cop car pull up outside. "Oh, shit. Where can I hide?"

"I guess under the bed is best," she said, guiding me into the bedroom. Bobby was sprawled naked on their bed, face down, snoring. I crawled under it just as a knock sounded at the door.

I heard her answer, and the cops asking questions as Russo snored above me. She handled them well. They were likely as distracted by her appearance as I had been.

The door clicked shut. She came back into the room, got on her hands and knees, and looked under the bed at me. "Goodnight, Levi," she said, leaning in to kiss me.

"Goodnight, Gwen. Thanks."

Before I lost consciousness, I wondered if Barrack knew where my parents lived, and thought about how stupid I'd been to get tangled up with him.

2 On the Road

Dawn's light attacked my eyes through broken and missing window blinds. My back ached and my knees were throbbing. Gas fumes filled my nose and mouth, and I held back from retching under Bobby Russo's bed. I slid out carefully, taking one last look back at Gwen, longer than I should have, before leaving the house.

Taking the off-road trails I explored as a kid, I made my way home, avoiding the roads. I wished I could go back to those days, and do so many things differently. It was too late, time to play the hand life dealt me. *That I had dealt to myself.*

Mom greeted me as I came through the door. "Jesus, Levi. What happened to you?"

I sat on our old comfortable couch, exhausted. "It's a long story, Mom. I don't want to revisit it."

She sighed and gave me a disapproving look. I knew I had let her down again. I hated disappointing her; she always had such high hopes for me. "Well, the police were here a few hours ago looking for you."

"Oh no. Was Dad upset?"

"No. Thank God he passed out by then. He had too much to drink at the beach club last night."

"Of course," I said. "Look Mom, I have to go. I'm sorry. I'll get things together in Tulsa, you'll see. There's work there. It'll be good for me. I'll be back."

She paused and looked down at the worn carpet. "That's not all, Levi. Sarah's mom called me last night."

"Great." I didn't want to talk about it any more.

"Levi, is there any chance they're right? I have to know. You might not be thinking clearly."

Feeling sick and tired, I got agitated quickly. "No, Mom. We've been over this. I told you. She was in Oklahoma with her brothers for most of last year, after we broke up. She was dating someone there. Her brother Don told me. She came back just before I got my discharge."

She looked at me uncomfortably. "Did you..."

"Yes, Mom. We got drunk a few times before I left. It was a mistake. But the timing's off. There's no way that kid is mine. Do the math yourself. We were guessing before, but now we know when the baby was born. Go nine months back."

"Leah, Levi. Her name is Leah. These things aren't precise, you know," she said, placing her hand on my shoulder. I knew she wanted to be a grandma, and wanted me to settle down, and stop getting in trouble, stop trying to be different, to be free. She wanted to brag to her friends about me, as she had when I wore a uniform. I felt sorry for her, and just wanted to die for always hurting her.

"Right. Well, it's not close, Mom. You know how these things work. You've seen the movies. The girls around those desolate military bases, those little podunk towns, they all use the same game plan. They get some dumb ass boot to knock them up, and that's their ticket out of town."

"Honey, you know Sarah's not like that. She's very nice and honest. Besides, don't you think they're looking at it like another old story—military guy gets a local girl pregnant and leaves?"

She had a good point, and it stung. "You're right, but that's not what happened. She got pregnant in Tulsa, probably got dumped, whatever, and she's trying to pin it on me, to get out of the north country."

"That's not true. Her mom said she'd like you to live there. The whole family would."

"Sure Mom, and do what? Get a job at that damn mill and die from the cancer it gives everyone? Or go back to work at the base as a civilian, after all the trouble I got in? I don't think so. It's damn cold up there on the Canadian border. I want to be somewhere warm. I want to be *free*, Mom."

She was about to cry. "Oh, that again," she said under her breath. "Then why did you go into the military?"

"Because I had no options, Mom. I wanted to go to college and become a writer. I needed the GI Bill to do that. And I always remembered when that older neighborhood kid got killed in Viet Nam. I was mad about it. I liked him."

"Sal Finnuci..." she said wistfully.

I stood up, pain shooting through my raw knees. "I've got to get cleaned up, Mom, and hit the road."

She stood and hugged me. "OK, Levi. I'll get some coffee ready and send you off with a nice breakfast. And yes, you stink, son. I don't even want to know why."

"Well, that's unusual, you not wanting to know something," I said, forcing a smile. We both laughed, and I headed downstairs to my bedroom and the shower.

I cleaned up quickly and emerged from the basement to the familiar smells of her breakfast special, the one I'd enjoyed my entire life, except for the years lost to the military. She watched while I devoured the plate full of her love for me.

"Why don't you stay and enroll in county college?" she asked, baiting me.

"That ship sailed when Dad laughed at me. 'Oh, fancy boy wants to go to college,' he said. Remember?"

"So you're punishing yourself by punishing him for that?"

I chewed and talked. I wanted to get on the road. "It's not just that, Mom. Look how people live—you're subservient to your parents and teachers for the first eighteen years of your life. After that, to professors or sergeants for another bunch of years. Then to some moron boss at work, and someone you thought you loved and who you thought loved you, until they became completely different. Then to the kids. You finally get rid of the kids, and by then your parents are old and you have to take care of them. It's an entire lifetime of subservience. I want to be free, and enjoy my life. We only get one, as far as we know, right?"

"Levi, you can have a good life by settling down."

"Oh, please, Mom. I know all your friends. Name me one couple married longer than five years who aren't miserable and screwing around on each other, or wanting to."

She countered and appealed to me by quoting our favorite movie to watch together. "There's no place like home."

"Ever since whatever alien race cast us out and deposited our species on this planet like a failed experiment, we've spread out like a plague. We're wired to roam. From all the nomadic tribes of the caveman days, to the heroes of the Bible, to the Vikings and great explorers, to Jack Kerouac, it's what we do. I'm just fulfilling that natural compulsion, that destiny."

She sighed. "Oh, brother, Levi. You need to stop seeing yourself like you're in some dramatic movie." I laughed, and she changed the subject. "Your father will be up soon. You two should talk before you go."

"No. I've got to go. The cops will be back soon. Can I get a ride out of town?"

She nodded, and we began cleaning up the dishes.

I LOADED MY BACKPACK into the trunk in case we got pulled over. My knees ached and my head was splitting. I wished I'd just stayed home, spent my last night with my family, and rested instead of going to the Bivouac. *Stupid.* While I was behind the car and out of Mom's sight, I bent down and raised my right pants leg to adjust the bayonet I kept in my boot in case of trouble.

We headed down familiar roads in her huge old Buick LeSabre. I tried to slouch down as much as I could, but couldn't help watching as memories flowed by the window. The bus stop where Carla and I had walked to and from, hand in hand, making so many promises to each other, ranking on each other, busting on everyone else, gossiping, dreaming, promising, young and in love.

The Buick rolled over the ancient steel bridge I had fished from, dove from naked on a dare, and once crashed my motorcycle on in the rain, after drinking too much and trying to show off my peg-dragging skills to Carla's friend Doris, who was on the back.

The car itself was a part of me. I flashed back to my first driving lessons—Mom pressed up against me on the bench seat so she could interfere with the pedals and steering wheel. That didn't go well, and I learned instead from an alcoholic gym teacher who had me run cases of beer to his bar during driver's education class.

I looked at the back seat where Carla and I had spent many nights at the local drive-in, leaving spent from the beer and passion back there, often not even bothering to notice what movie was playing. She was the only one who had ever left me, and I still missed her badly. *I should never have gone away.*

"How's this?" Mom asked, jolting me back to reality.

We were on the county road, a beautiful area near the huge state park that the city folks swarmed to every summer day, not too far from the Pennsylvania line. "Yeah, this'll work. Thanks, Mom."

"Wait, Levi." She pulled her purse from the floor and dug through it, producing a small gray box. She handed it to me and I opened it to discover a pewter Saint Christopher medallion on a silver chain. "He's the patron saint of travelers, Levi," she said, crying.

I held the length of it across my hands to admire its beauty and promise, then slipped it over my head.

"Thank you, Mom. I love you very much." I removed my dog tags on their simple beaded chain and handed them to her. "Guess I don't need these anymore." We looked at each other with tears in our eyes for a moment, clutching our gifts.

"Just be safe, Levi. That's all I ask, son."

"I will, I promise." I hugged her and stepped out to grab my military-issue pack, chosen for its ability to gain sympathy and a ride from fellow vets, or maybe from a cop that might pull over to harass me because of my long hair. We said our I-love-yous, and I watched the white Buick go down the road, back toward home.

I tucked my hair up under my favorite traveling hat. It was a low black Stetson made of beaver fur with a black leather band studded with silver diamond-shaped emblems. It helped me out with the truckers and pickup truck rednecks. Everything had to have a strategic purpose in order to be in the road kit.

Placing the pack in front of me as an "open for business" sign, I pulled my Rand McNally road atlas out and sat against the cold steel guardrail to consult my planned route. *Man plans, God laughs.* Turning the pages with one hand while sticking my thumb out with the other, I was already breaking a fundamental rule of hitching—stand straight, look the drivers in the eye, and smile. I dressed comfortably, yet presentably, in nearly new jeans and a light flannel shirt. Holding up signs with your destination written on them was corny and too much clutter.

After confirming my intended route, I stood proper and smiled, eager to see who fate would dispense for me from its human vending machine. The fresh air and greenery around me washed away the fear, stress, and hangover from the night before. I felt alive again, happy to be going somewhere, adventure ahead. It was the same type of exhilaration as emerging into the sun from a stifling classroom after the dismissal bell on the last day of school.

When I was a kid, my grandfather took us on a summer road trip to Michigan to see family members. It was my first time out of the childhood bubble in New Jersey and I felt like a true explorer. The road signs to strange towns and new states fascinated me. There were people who spoke differently in the wonderful roadside diners we ate at, and sparkling clean motel rooms each night with pools to swim in, brand-new tiny bars of soap in wrappers, pinball machines and vending machines fed with a constant stream of coins from my grandfather's bottomless pocket of change. Someone came by to clean the rooms so my mother didn't have to. We got in the car each day and woke each morning somewhere new. I was a real-life intrepid traveler; *Robinson Crusoe* and all my treasured book heroes come to life. It was only the Rust Belt, but to me, it was Tahiti.

I heard a vehicle slow down and looked up to see an old Volvo with Pennsylvania plates pull over just ahead. *Here we go, the first customer of the day.* I peered in first to assess the risk. An old couple sat in the front seat, smiling at me and waving me in. Bushels of apples sat in the back. I swung the door open and climbed aboard.

"How are ya, young man?" the wife asked with a smile. "I'm Hazel and this is my dearly beloved Herbert."

He jumped right in. "Did she say dearly beloved or dearly departed? And it's Herb, damn it! Don't mind her. She's gonna yap your ear off. You'll be wanting to jump out by the next red light!"

"We're in the country, Herb," she scolded. "There's no dang red lights until we get back to PA."

I hadn't answered yet, but was excited to hear that it was going to be a ride across the state line. "I'm Levi. So, you came to Jersey to get apples? Aren't they good in PA?" I asked.

"C'mon boy, you know this here's the Garden State. What are ya, a dang New Yorker or somethin'?" the husband asked.

"Heck no. I'm a Jersey boy, sir."

The wife reached back and slapped me on the knee. "Well, go ahead, son. What're you waiting for? Have one of them Red Delicious beauties. Have two!"

I thanked her, found a nice plump ripe one, and bit into it with a crunch. I slid another into my pack.

"Ain't that a great sound, boy?" Herb asked. I wondered who the real excess talker was.

"Yes, sir, almost as good as the taste. By the way, I'm trying to get to I-78 West, if you're going that way. But anywhere in that direction is fine." *Never be afraid to ask.*

This time she slapped his knee, and hard. "Herb! You never asked the young man where he's going! Why, he's probably worried he's being kidnapped by a couple of old geezers!"

"Yeah, that's us—a couple of old serial killers," he said. They both laughed at the idea. I wasn't so sure. I'd seen weirder things on the road. "But sure, son. We were taking the country roads across, but we'll swing south toward I-78 for ya."

"Thank you, sir." I pulled my book out of my pack, hoping for some time to read while I ate the rest of the apple. It was nice catching rides, but sometimes you ended up captive in one way or another. *There's a price for everything.*

They had the windows rolled up, and I was sweating under the hat. I pulled it off and Herb glanced at his rear-view mirror.

"Well, hell's bells, Hazel. We got us a bona fide hippie right here in the car."

Uh oh. The ride is over.

I expected her to turn to me and scowl. Old people often did. Instead, she gave me a wide smile. "Don't mind him. He's a right-wing neo-con. I'm with you, Levi. I'm a hippie at heart, and I'm sorry I was too old for all that and already married to this right-winger."

I threw them a distraction to get back to my reading. "So, I guess I don't have to ask where you each stand on the election coming up in November?"

It was like throwing a match in a gasoline-soaked house, and I kind of felt bad about doing it. They immediately went at each other, damning and praising Carter and Reagan. It went on forever, with one or the other throwing back a "Right, Levi?" I'd take a moment to compose a neutral response and let them get back to it, so I could get back to Steinbeck.

Road signs caught my eye as we made progress through the last of my home state. There were signs for towns with nice names like Liberty, Harmony, and Hope. We hit Phillipsburg and then crossed over the Delaware River to Pennsylvania's beautiful Lehigh Valley.

I felt a sense of achievement at crossing my first state line and nodded out at some point, despite the racket of their ongoing political dispute, and woke to the crunch of gravel as the Volvo pulled over.

Herb looked at me through the mirror. "I figured this truck stop would be a suitable spot for you to grab another ride," he said. "I-78 is just up ahead."

"Perfect. Thank you so much. I really enjoyed meeting you both, and I hope you both vote for Carter."

"I knew it! Should've dropped you off long ago. Dang hippy!" Herb shouted, smiling. They asked me to take more apples, and I did before saying our goodbyes. The last thing Herb said to me, before rolling his window back up, was "Nicely played, son," and he winked when he said it.

I was ahead of schedule and took a break to use the bathroom at the truck stop. I pulled two squished hard rolls and my road atlas from my pack and sat at a table to figure how far I might get before dark, and where I might find a place to stay.

Surveying the nearby tables, I spotted a trucker that looked semi-friendly. Asking if I could bother him, I moved over with my atlas and asked about the road up ahead and my planned route. I already knew the answers and was just fishing for a ride. The plan worked—he offered to take me as far as Martinsburg, West Virginia. *Bingo.* The rush of a success like that was something that kept me going, despite how hard it could be on the road.

We settled into his rig and roared off down the highway. He worked the double-clutch and gearshift like a maestro, the engine in perfect pitch as it moved from gear to gear like a 12-bar blues progression.

His name was Rebel. He had his own tall Stetson and complimented my hat, asking if I'd like to trade. I was glad he was only joking. He exuded toughness, wearing battered but comfortable looking cowboy boots, jeans, and a T-shirt with some faded country idol on it. His pock-marked face wore about a week's worth of salt and pepper beard. A plastic Jesus stood rigidly on the dashboard, arms out in a welcoming gesture, right alongside a dancing plastic hula girl with a green grass skirt and huge boobs barely covered in coconut shells. I liked trucker rides because they talked little, at least to me. He was active on the CB radio, though, speaking an alien language to others unseen out there on the road, their home away from home.

"Breaker, Rebel here. Doctor Love, do you have your ears on? I just left the choke & puke, fueled up on go-juice, and back on the super slab 78, just outside of Allentown. Heading for Martinsburg. Hammer down."

"Affirmative, Rebel. Doctor Love just ahead of you, 10-73 be alert, full-grown bear ahead, Kodiac with a Kodak, just shot me in the face. Better back it down."

"Did that bear bite you, Doctor Love?"

"Negative, Rebel. I kept right on going, no gumball lights from Smokey."

They were free men, more or less, modern stagecoach drivers, their own closed society with their own rules. They weren't chained to cubicles, suffering crass coworkers, stuffy office buildings, or windowless factories.

Often, when allowed to crash in the front seat while the trucker slept in the sleeper cab, I watched at night as sad, shadowy figures in miniskirts, tube tops, and fishnet stockings crept from truck to truck, down the line of parked rigs at any rest stop in America.

But yet, the truckers had to live within a framework, and their master was the mileage they had to accrue at the risk of their health and safety. It drove them to push their body and mind with barbiturates, and to abuse alcohol. They were semi-free, but they still had their own form of the hamster wheel to deal with.

Very few people ever get to experience absolute freedom. It's always been the same. You could read this a hundred years from now and it will probably be the same damn thing. Corporate greed, making working people cogs in a wheel, using them up, casting them aside, replacing them with a younger, newer cog when they've finally broken down.

That's what I saw coming, and I wanted no part of it. That's why I was sitting in the cab of a big-ass tractor trailer, next to some guy I just met named Rebel, writing all this down, completely free, not a damn care, on a late summer day, watching America roll by with soft country music. I was trying hard not to think about Sarah and Leah, trying hard not to think about Carla. I had all their pictures in my wallet and resisted pulling them out. *It would do no good at this point. Forward.*

A sign for Hamburg whizzed by. When I was ten, and got my First Communion, my mom asked what I wanted as a gift. They thought I'd say some kind of plastic crap they could just go buy at the store. I remember the look on my dad's face when I said I wanted to see the FBI headquarters in Washington. I had just read a book on the subject. Mom made him say yes, but our car broke down in Hamburg, and we retreated to home after a night in a motel, the money tapped out, another dream unrealized. I still wonder if the old man had anything to do with that car problem, because I saw him and the repairman laughing together the next morning.

I was pious when I was young, breathing in all the Biblical stories, the magic and wonder of miracles, the inspiration and goodness of it all. It was my nature. Being an avid reader even at that age, I read the entire Bible cover to cover. That was before an awful experience as an altar boy turned me away from organized religion. Anyway, the hypocrisy was already becoming clear. Our next-door neighbor was a big deal at the church, often called up to do readings during mass. His wife sometimes had bruises on her face, and I heard her scream a few times in the dark of night when I was out later than I should have been.

I gave up going to mass. Ricky Thompson and I began taking the money our parents had given us for the collection basket and heading to the local mini-market instead. We'd buy packs of hot dogs, go out into the woods behind the church, make a fire, eat a grand outdoorsman meal, and check the Hav-A-Hart traps we'd always set to catch squirrels, rabbits, and raccoons. When I got home, my old man would ask if I'd been to mass, and spot-check me by asking what color the priest's robes were. I'd make up a color, as I knew he had no damn idea what color the priest's robes were.

Rebel and I kept rolling inside the enormous machine, through Central Pennsylvania and places like Harrisburg and Hershey. I had circled the latter on my map, meaning to stop there and see what that big chocolate factory was like, and maybe see how something fresh off their line tasted. I thought about asking Rebel to drop me nearby, but the chance to get through to Martinsburg was too much to pass up. *Next time.* You have to be flexible on the road, change plans as the wind blows, and let fortune and fate guide you along your journey. Sometimes, it was like drifting along a lazy river, feeling good that you only had so much control over things.

An invitation to take 15 South down into Gettysburg passed by as well and I thought that would be cool to stop and visit. Instead, Rebel and I talked about the Civil War and everything that happened back then. He was a well-read, smart guy. Most people misjudge working people that way. They're not stupid—they mostly just had more difficult circumstances and backgrounds, and didn't have the wheels greased for them like rich kids do. They went to public schools in towns that couldn't afford to pay the best teachers.

Even though I was passing up these opportunities, despite being a free man, I was doing it on my terms, making my own decisions, not having to beg permission for anything. *And that's the way it should be*, I reminded myself.

Since we were about five years old, Shayne and I were going to be truckers, share a rig, driving in shifts, and make big money on the road. We agreed it would be the most bad ass rig on the road, all painted up in flames and naked babes with sparkle-paint and have cool sayings on it like "The road is life." We'd blow our horns when little kids in nearby cars demanded it, and laugh at the stiffs going to their shitty office jobs in their stupid fancy cars and uncomfortable suits and ties. Maybe run a few off the road, just for kicks.

But that never happened. Not yet, anyway. Despite all our plans, Shayne and I had a thing where one of us or the other was usually in some stupid relationship and tied by the shackles of some insecure girlfriend demanding we not discuss such silly ideas. They would say things like *'grow up'* or *'you can't have a good marriage and nice things in a job like that.'* I drove big rigs in the military, sometimes loaded with huge bombs. As I sat next to Rebel, I wished I'd have gotten my commercial truck license to take a shift at the wheel and let him get some rest. He seemed damn tired.

We broke through into Hagerstown, Maryland, and the state went by in a shot, passing us into West Virginia in just minutes. The clock of seasons had reversed itself, with the gray leafless trees of the north now becoming green and full again. Rebel pulled into a truck yard near Martinsburg, and we said our goodbyes. I scouted for any other drivers or rigs that might be helpful, but it was pretty empty. Rebel went into the dispatch office to file his paperwork, and I trudged off toward the road. It was well into the afternoon by then, and I thought about bunking up in the woods, or the cab of an empty tractor if I could find an open one. I didn't want to get Rebel in trouble, though.

I was now officially in the south, an area of the country I never much cared for. I didn't get along well with the southerners in the military. They cared little for Yankees, and especially me, since my two best friends were a black dude named Damon Green and a Mexican named Diego Takata. Diego's last name was a story in itself. He was born in Acapulco, part of a cliff-diving family. His divorced Mexican mother had married a Japanese-American man, who then adopted Diego, which later allowed him to enlist since he was officially an American citizen.

I felt somewhat tired, despite catching some cat-naps on my two rides, and should have called it a day, but I pushed on. I'd regret that decision later, for sure.

3 Tennessee

My earlier good luck ran dry in Martinsburg, West Virginia. Maybe it had something to do with my attitude about the place, and being in the south. It's interesting how your frame of mind can influence the things that happen to you, or at least your perception of them. I tried to have a better attitude, but it wasn't working.

I picked up a few short rides from the locals, mostly rednecks in pickup trucks, and for just a few exits. I felt some relief crossing back into Virginia proper, even though my rides took me south along the West Virginia border. Signs for Charlottesville reminded me of the big, prestigious university there. It was on Carla's wish list. Her estranged father had money, and she'd always hoped he'd come through for her. I wondered if maybe she was there, and how she was doing. I pictured myself there as well, attending classes in ivy-covered old buildings, learning how to become the writer I'd always aspired to be. Maybe we'd have a sparse off-campus apartment, enjoy simple dinners with a flickering candle on the table, and spend our nights studying and making love. *Stop. Just stop.*

A dude in a new BMW picked me up around Lynchburg. It was a rare treat to spend some time in a comfortable luxury car. We sped down the highway with the top down, enjoying the gorgeous day. He was a pharmaceutical salesman, and happy to talk about his success and income. Everything was perfect about the guy—manicured nails, skin, crisp blindingly white dress shirt, sparkling shoes beneath the dash, working the pedals. My hair broke loose from the worn elastic tie I'd stolen from my sister and whipped around in the wind, while his hair never moved a whit.

We shouted to each other over the road noise and annoying pop music blaring from the sound system, even though we had almost nothing in common and not much to talk about. He worked hard to impress me with his knowledge of an assortment of things in order to establish superiority. I had a feeling he did that a lot, and was probably disliked very much by his family, friends, and coworkers. I felt bad for the guy. He didn't seem to be happy at all. *What things in his life had led him to be this insecure, despite his success?*

I usually placated people like that just to keep the ride going, but it was hard to do. The good thing was that he said he'd take me all the way to Knoxville, and I didn't want to blow it by making my disdain for him known.

"Damn shame what happened to all those people there," he shouted as we passed the Roanoke exit, turning the radio down to better display his historical knowledge. I got the sense he was hoping to tell me the entire story, assuming I was ignorant because I was hitchhiking and looked like I did.

I couldn't resist any longer. "It wasn't here," I shouted back.

"What?" he responded, appearing shocked that I contradicted him.

It was too late to backpedal out of it, and I didn't much feel like it, anyway. I was getting sick of the guy's condescending attitude. *Freedom.*

"The Lost Colony was on Roanoke Island in what's now North Carolina," I said, "not Roanoke, Virginia." I made that last point a bit severely and shouldn't have smiled at him.

He yanked the wheel and pulled the Beemer onto the shoulder with a screech of tires and a loud crunch as it slid in the gravel. "You can get out here, smartass," he said.

I grabbed my stuff and thanked him for the ride. I was kind of happy to be rid of the guy and vowed to never be like him. He peeled out, spraying road debris on me.

The area was spectacular—we'd been driving along the Blue Ridge Mountains and one of the great American roads, the Blue Ridge Parkway, was just to the east. It tempted me to head that way and enjoy it, but I didn't have the luxury of leisure on this trip. The opportunities that waited for me in Tulsa might be fleeting, and I depended on them.

I took the time to head into the woods to relieve myself and eat a few more crushed rolls and an apple. Lying on the soft forest floor, I smoked a half-joint, and read Whitman's *Song of the Open Road*, before noting the time and heading back to the highway. I wanted to hit Knoxville, Tennessee, before the end of the day. It would get me more than half-way to Tulsa. It bothered me again that I was allowing myself to become a slave to time and passing up opportunities.

A few nondescript trips took me to my goal as the sun set. The last one dropped me off just past Kingsport, TN. I felt exhausted from the long day, much of it in the sun, and not making the best decisions. Almost getting arrested the night before had scared me, and I wanted distance from my mistake, John Barrack, and the cops that were likely still looking for me. I fantasized about catching one last ride, perhaps an overnight trucker, and I'd wake at or near Tulsa.

I stood at the edge of the highway with my thumb out. Passing cars and trucks buffeted me backward. Something felt off. I had a sixth sense developed from my time on the road. I persisted, sticking my outstretched hand out a little further, offering a smile. *Listen to your instincts*, I had always told myself.

The highway emptied, and I stood alone. I thought about pulling back into the woods behind me, to regroup, maybe take a nap, get out of the dusky heat and humidity. A big sedan approached from the distance, moving slower than normal for the interstate. *Old-timer*, I thought. I pushed my hair behind my ears and tried to appear pitiable.

The blinker came on, and the car glided into the shoulder, still a few dozen yards ahead of me. It was strange, since most rides pulled over after passing by. I processed what I could, trying to push through the fog of the earlier joint.

The vehicle rolled to a stop just ahead, tires ominously crunching the gravel. *Don't be paranoid*, I told myself. *It's likely just another old-timer.* I reached down to pick up my rucksack and head toward my ride. *Single rider. No passengers. Male. Big.*

I waved as I approached. The driver didn't reciprocate. I slowed, sensing trouble. Veering toward the left and the passenger side, I stopped as I noticed him reach toward the seat next to him. He pulled up an enormous hat and fixed it on his head, leaning into his door to push it open. I stopped short of his bumper as he emerged from the car and slammed the door shut. He towered over the car and strode toward me in his crisp uniform. *Tennessee state trooper, unmarked vehicle.*

I dropped my backpack and put both hands out, palms facing him. I thought about breaking for the woods and remembered the stories of those who had run from the cops in the south. "Good afternoon, sir," I offered.

He stopped just close enough to glare down at me through his aviators, sunlight glinting off his five-point badge, right hand resting on his sidearm. "What the fuck are you doing on my highway, son?"

"What?"

"Here in TEN-nessee, we like our highways nice and clean. No trash. No long-hair druggies. You aware that hitchhiking is illegal, boy?"

I looked around before realizing I was the trash he referred to. "Sir, I'm on an interstate, not a state road. I think I'm OK..."

"Shut the fuck up. You got drugs in the backpack?"

"No, sir. I'm a vet and I'm clean." *I definitely have drugs in the backpack.*

He took his hand off the sidearm. "What branch?"

"Air Force, sir. Strategic Air Command. Plattsburgh Air Force Base, New York." I knew it was a mistake as soon as I said it.

He smirked. "Fuckin' Yankee. Air Force pussy. Marines wouldn't take you, huh?" It was a statement, not a question. I remained silent. *Don't push back. Respect his authority. Pick your battles.*

He glanced at the backpack.

"The Marines were my first choice," I lied, attempting to distract him. "But Dad wanted me to follow in his footsteps. Rest his soul," I added, shooting for some sympathy.

"Dad was an Air Force pussy too, then." I kept my discipline and didn't take the bait, holding his steady gaze. "My dad was a good man, sir."

We waited each other out for a bit. A long strand of hair cut loose from behind my ear and blew across my face. It seemed to annoy him.

"Listen, boy. I'll cut you a break since you're a vet. Do yourself a favor and get a fucking haircut. There's plenty of barbers in town that'll fix you up good, high and tight. Get your self-respect back. Be a man. But like I said, we don't like trash on our highways here in Tennessee. I strongly suggest you get your ass a half-mile down the road to the off-ramp and make some other arrangement to get where you're going."

He spun on his heel military style, removed his hat, and got back into his car. Glaring as he crept past me on the shoulder, he gunned it and sprayed hot gravel, just as the last ride had.

A truck approached, and I didn't dare stick out my thumb. I grabbed my pack and began walking. Reaching the highway ramp, I crossed over to the entrance side and sat on the guardrail to wait for oncoming traffic. Vehicles came and went, their drivers averting their eyes as they passed by my outstretched arm. I noticed a diner at the adjoining state road and wondered what delicacies waited inside.

A car turned onto the base of the entrance ramp toward me, and I stood, trying to appear respectable. I put out my thumb as I looked through the windshield and recognized the vehicle and driver at once. The trooper hit the gas and aimed straight for me. I arched back and flipped myself over the guardrail. His chrome fender grazed my boot and threw me sideways, tumbling down into a ravine.

I lay in a small stream, ice-cold water drenching my back, listening to the vehicle roar off, until I felt it was safe to rise. My backpack and hat lay nearby, thankfully out of the water and dry.

I limped to the diner in agony. Taking a seat at the counter, I ordered a large mug of hot water. The pretty, older waitress stared at me for a moment. *Oh hell, what next?*

"Honey, you look like hell. And you're about to cry, ain't ya?"

"Yep," was all I could offer. She walked away, shaking her head.

After she brought my water, I grabbed the ketchup and poured an ample amount into the steaming mug when she wasn't looking. I drank my makeshift tomato soup quickly, burning my mouth and throat, and headed to the pay phone.

"Collect call," I told the operator, and gave him the number. I listened as he asked my mother if she'd accept the charges. The sound of her voice took me home. She was likely on the kitchen phone, cord all stretched out and cooking something amazing, just one floor above my basement bedroom, where I grew up and didn't have a worry in the world. If it were just a few years earlier, Carla and I would be down there, high school dreamers madly in love, promising each other the world.

"Mom, I think I want to come home," I blurted out, surprising myself. I didn't want to go back to New Jersey. I wanted to go back to Carla if she hadn't moved on yet.

I waited for her response, imagining her standing there by the stove, by the table we'd all sat around for years, the family petri dish that cultivated me. "You'd have money and a job if you hadn't left the military early," she said, mostly to herself. She knew she'd hurt me, and added, "Your uncle would hire you back on the fence crew," she said, and then in a more hopeful tone, "You could go to college."

I thought about it for a moment. *Security*. I'd be like everyone else on that hamster wheel of life. Work, television, mortgage, wife, boss, kids, eat, sleep, death. "Mom, I just need to get to Tulsa. There's lots of work. Oil's booming, they're paying good wages. I'm halfway there, but I can't hitch here in Tennessee. I almost got locked up. Can you just wire me some money to get a bus the rest of the way?" I asked hopefully. "Fifty bucks. I'll pay it back."

The line was quiet. *Hang up. Don't beg, don't give in.* She spoke. "You know your father would raise hell with me. He watches the money, and he said if you do this, you do it on your own, sink or swim." She paused, and I thought I heard her muffle a sob. "Levi, what are you doing? You've got a child."

"No mom. She's not mine. It's not possible. It's a trap. We talked about this. I'm not falling for that, sorry. I shouldn't have called. Love you, mom."

She repeated herself. "You know your father would raise hell if I sent you money after the things you said to him. You said you didn't need us—you didn't need anyone..."

I wiped away tears and held my voice steady. "I'm OK, just had a bad day. Call you when I get to Tulsa. Love you, Mom. Tell Dad I said hi, and I'm sorry."

I stretched out my time at the diner, chatting up the waitress, shamelessly hoping for an invitation back to her place to spend the night. *Husband and kids, no dice.* As the sun went down, I broke a cardinal rule and headed back to the highway to hitch after dark. I had to get out of there.

The passing cars were anonymous headlights in the dark. It was the sign I'd always promised to obey. *Hitchhiking after nightfall is an invitation for trouble.* A pickup truck slowed down and moved to the shoulder. I thought I might have a ride. *Salvation in the dark.* I reached down for my backpack, just in case it was for real.

I made eye contact with the Tennessee rebel behind the windshield as he leaned and peered, probably trying to make sure the long hair that caught his attention belonged to a female. He closed in, noticed my Fu Manchu mustache, and quickly jerked the car back onto the road, speeding past me, gravel spraying for the third time that day.

I set my backpack down and turned to survey the woods up on the hill behind me for a decent place to crash and ride out the darkness. *Fresh start in the morning, at first daylight.* The sultry night wind came and almost took my beloved hat away. Only the lanyard around my neck saved it.

A car was there when I turned back around, idling just up ahead in the dark, taillights bright like an amusement ride on the Jersey shore boardwalk. I hadn't heard it pull over. I turned back toward the woods, prepared to take the safe choice, then I thought about the chance to be further down the road by the next day, maybe all the way to Tulsa.

It was late and, because of my exhaustion, I got sloppy and skipped my safety check protocol. As soon as I entered the car, I knew I had made a mistake. The grease shone off the fat man's black hair in the moonlight. The car reeked of body odor and booze, but it was spotless. *Too clean. Crime scene.* If I felt unsafe, I usually tried to sit in the back seat, although it would often upset decent, innocent people who were kind enough to give you a ride. "You think this is a taxi?" they'd say. The ride would be off to a rough start and often be short. Here, I knew right away that I should have been more careful.

"How are you this evening, young man?" he asked in an oddly proper tone.

"I'm OK. Heading to Tulsa," I answered in a flat voice. He pulled away from the shoulder onto the empty highway, and didn't speak.

Down the road we went, wordlessly, with no radio. I dozed off and shook myself awake a few times until I lost my fight and slept. His grip on my thigh jolted me back from a dream. I checked the window—we were off the highway, on a country road.

"You're a good-looking kid, sweetheart," he said, leering at me and smiling.

Pushing his hand away, I reached for the door handle, calculating whether our velocity would shred me or save me if I ejected. He gassed it, making it unsafe to bail out.

"Pull the car over, motherfucker," I yelled as I pulled up my right pants leg.

"It'll be OK, sweetheart. This won't take long, and I'll drive you to wherever you want to go. It was Tulsa, correct? We'll go. Calm down, these things happen. It's no big deal. It's just a human transaction."

His huge hand again clamped on the soft part just above my knee. He was incredibly strong.

"I'm warning you, pull over," I shouted as I pulled at his hand.

"I will, I will, sweetheart," he said. "I'm looking for a nice, quiet place for us."

He jerked the car to a stop and cut the lights. I fumbled at my pants leg, digging in my boot for the bayonet. He shoved over toward me, grabbing my belt.

I found the leather grip of the bayonet just in time, and pulled it, digging the point into his fat, sweaty neck. "Back off or I shove this motherfucker all the way in," I said with authority. He pulled away instinctively at the pain and relaxed his grip. I yanked the door handle and tumbled out, grabbing my pack from the floorboards just in time.

I ran up a hill and into the woods. No way that fat fuck was going to catch me. I made it halfway up and looked back.

He had exited the car and stood watching me as it idled between us.

"See you later, sweetheart," he said, waving and smiling as he got back into the car. *Fucking psychopath.*

After he pulled away, I sat and collected myself. The moon was full and lit the floor of the woods through the overhead canopy of trees. The ground was soft with old leaves, rustling with a breeze, welcoming me. I put the pack under my head and fell asleep, the bayonet still in my hand.

I remember dreaming about good things. There was a love scene with Carla, and another where I was ocean fishing on a boat with Dad back when things were good. I had caught a big fluke and was trying to bring it in when a shark came and took it. Dad dove into the water and there was suddenly a lot of blood. I woke, startled by the violence of it, upset about my father, and thought I had heard a sound.

I sat up and surveyed the surrounding forest. Insects whirred and chirped to each other in the night symphony. *Are they warning me?* I decided I was being paranoid and went back to sleep. It was still the middle of the night, and I wanted a fresh start at first light. I tucked the bayonet under my leg and dozed off again.

This time, the sound was definitive. It was a fast, steady crush of leaves and twigs, like an enormous animal closing fast. I thought I was dreaming again and felt a shock of terror when I realized I wasn't. *It's him.*

I leaned up and saw the fat man coming at me. "It's OK, sweetheart," he kept saying, out of breath and wheezing. I grabbed the long knife from under me and pulled it up just as he leapt to contain me under his weight.

Instinctively, I put the bayonet between us. As he came down on me, the butt of the handle jammed against my sternum. I felt a definitive pop as the point drove through his skin and into his chest. A warm rush of blood spread over me. He made a guttural sound and rolled off, laying face up on the bed of leaves with his hands over his chest, on either side of the protruding leather handle. Blood soaked his yellow T-shirt, spreading fast like a paper towel laid down on a wet counter top.

"What did you do, sweetheart?" he whispered, as his eyes rolled back in his head. "Help me out, kid, will ya?"

My heart raced, and I felt the rush of panic mixed with compassion for the man. *Who knows what circumstances in his life led him to this?* I remembered where I was, and the state cop who had tried to run me down the day before. Blood covered the front of my shirt. *How do you leave a man to die?* I decided his actions had led him to his fate, and there was nothing I could do. *You may save others from him who aren't as resourceful. This is his sentence.* Scenes from the altar, Communion, Catechism, priests in robes giving fiery sermons all flashed through my mind. *Guilt.*

He was quiet. I yanked the bayonet out of his chest, grabbed my pack, and ran down the hill, tumbling and almost impaling myself with the knife as well.

Catching my breath, I realized in that moment that what had just happened would never leave me until I took my last breath. No matter what I was doing, making love, eating, dreaming, it would always lurk there, under the surface, asking me what right I had to enjoy myself. At the moment, it was making me sick. I leaned over and vomited the little food I had in my stomach, wasting the makeshift free soup.

I ran down the country road for a while, as long as I could before my body stopped me. As I walked, panting, I saw the first glimmer of car headlights way down the road behind me. I pushed back up into the woods to let it pass.

I caught my breath and calmed myself using the meditation I had learned by reading Buddhist texts after my discharge. The bloody bayonet was still in my hand. I dug into the soft ground with it, and kept digging and digging, angry at circumstances, angry at myself, venting on the soil, until I had a big enough pit. I pulled off my shirt, wiped myself off, wrapped the knife in it, and buried it, hopefully for some future wanderer or archaeologist to find and wonder what it was all about. Small flashes caught the corner of my eye and I realized it was the moonlight glinting off the shiny new Saint Christopher medallion. Blood speckled it. *Please help me. I'll be good.*

Holding my breath for quiet, I listened and heard water running. A short walk later, I found a stream and washed the medallion, my hands, arms, and bare chest again and again. I smelled the iron scent of the blood, and Shakespeare's Lady Macbeth ran through my head—*A little water clears us of this deed. Out damned spot.* I didn't like to hurt people, and now I feared I had done the worst. I kept wanting to go back and help him; it pulled at me relentlessly. *You put him out of his misery.*

I pulled a clean shirt from my pack and checked my jeans and boots to make sure they were clear of blood. Back on the road, I spotted a traffic light in the distance and began walking toward it, fighting the urge to go back and at least bury him somehow.

Just past the intersection and down a long grade sat a truck stop, with several rigs idling in the parking lot and at the fuel pumps. I made my way to it and entered the small attached restaurant. Confederate flags adorned cheap souvenirs, T-shirts, hats, mugs, and bumper stickers. Even the barstools at the counter had them. I took a seat in an unused section, a few empty stools down on each side from truckers silently eating, and ordered another mug of hot water.

"What happened to you, dear?" the elderly waitress asked.

"I'm sorry?"

"There's blood on your face." I felt the others on each side of me looking, and my heart raced.

"Yeah, I get nosebleeds. I'll be right back." I rose and headed for the neon sign pointing toward the men's room, wiping my face and checking my hand.

The mirror showed it wasn't too bad, just some speckling and a small streak on my cheekbone. I removed my hat and washed up with cold water to wake myself. It felt good, and I kept going, losing myself in the brace against my skin. When I finished up, I checked my watch. It was almost five in the morning.

I made my way back to my seat and didn't even try to hide the act of pouring ketchup into the steaming mug.

"Bum soup, huh?" the trucker to my right asked.

I looked over and he smiled at me through his gray beard. He looked like my lost, beloved grandfather, and he had a huge Celtic cross tattooed on his hand.

"Yeah, breakfast of champions," I replied.

"Where're you heading, son?" he asked.

"I'm going to Tulsa. Got some work and a place waiting for me there." I paused. "If I can make it alive, I guess."

"Well, I've dropped my load and I'm heading home to Muskogee. I can take you that far, if you'd like."

For the first time since the old folks with the apples picked me up, I smiled and felt happy. "I'd really like that, sir. Thank you." I thought maybe I was dreaming it. The ride would take me almost all the way to my destination. *No more danger, no more cops. Don't blow it.*

"An Okie from Muskogee, huh?" I asked with a smile.

He laughed at the phrase. "Yep. Someone knows their country music. Good old Merle Haggard. *We like livin' right, and bein' free.*"

He seemed to detect my stress. "Don't worry, I'm a good redneck. I might chat you up some about the good Lord, is all. Be forewarned, it's the price of admission."

Maybe I could use that. Better than attempted rape, I thought.

He bought me a delicious fried egg sandwich with sizzling bacon strips and I slathered it with ketchup, replaced the toast lid, and devoured it. We made our way out to his rig, adorned with scripture from Matthew and airbrushed scenes from the Bible. One depicted Jesus adorned in light and holding his hands out as if to deliver compassion to those in need. *That's me. Thank you, Jesus.*

Jeb was his name, and he wasn't persistent, but he was convincing. I crashed, and he graciously let me sleep. When I woke, we talked about religion, racism, politics, and America. As each milestone passed, we taught each other about historical context and things we'd like to do someday if we had time. He gave me the silence and privacy to write in my journal when I pulled it out. As I recounted what had happened when writing it all down, I became distraught. I need to write it, to reconcile it with myself, always my form of therapy. I felt myself becoming emotional, filled with guilt and fear, and distraught.

"Son, I can feel it from here. You're carrying a heavy weight, besides that backpack, aren't you? Care to talk about it?"

I vowed I would tell no one. Maybe someday, long in the future, past the statute of limitations or whatever, I'd write about it if I couldn't take the guilt anymore. I vowed to help people in need, and thus maybe make up for it many times over as my penance, and receive that compassion from Jesus, if he was really with us and all the stories were true.

"Yeah, not really. Not yet. I'm sorry, sir."

He tried to help me by talking about forgiveness for sins. He disclosed he was former drunk and now an ordained minister, and turned the truck cab into a confessional, where I gave mine in loose, vague terms.

"Pray with me, Levi. Will that be OK?"

We recited the Hail Mary, Our Father, and kept going and it felt little by little that I was being filled with some level of absolution and felt cleansed. But I knew it was temporary, and the guilt would never leave me until I took my last breath, because I'm wired that way. I thanked the Lord for connecting me with Jeb.

We passed Nashville, and I talked about how I loved music. "Even country music," I added. I told him about how my father was a big fan of Johnny Cash, Waylon Jennings, and Willie Nelson. Jeb laughed as I told him about how Dad would sit on the living room floor with a six-pack, put on headphones connected by a thick jack to the massive piece of new furniture he was so proud of, our cheap family entertainment center. He'd play 8-track tapes of his favorites, and sing along louder and louder as the beer kicked in, not realizing how off-pitch and horrible it was, thinking he was making the sounds that were coming into his ears. I sometimes watched while I read on the sofa, waiting for the hilarious moment when he had to piss and forgot about the headphones.

"Sounds like me," Jeb said. "I think I like your old man."

"He's alright, I guess. We never got along much, but he works hard and I think he didn't have exemplary parents to learn from. His dad, my grandfather, was a Korea vet and mean as cat shit."

"It's why we have to never be quick to judge," Jeb said, "and think about what folks have been through to make them the way they are."

I thought about my would-be rapist again and thought about making an anonymous call so someone could find him. *Maybe he didn't die.* I let myself think maybe Jesus would raise him up as he did with Lazarus. I fantasized he would rise, realize his good fortune, and find Christ and turn his life around, making me his forever unknown hero and savior. *Or maybe he'll show up someday and return the favor by putting a dagger in your heart.*

Memphis came later in the day, and I told Jeb about Damon, my black roommate in the military barracks. When I put on my Led Zeppelin or Cream albums, he'd always listen patiently and appreciatively, then pull out his old Muddy Waters and other blues records and play me the original versions of those songs, which were copied by my heroes. I had thought mine were originals, and it was eye-opening. He had enlightened me about slavery, and how the call-and-response mantra of the songs had kept those folks going, allowed them to sing veiled insults to their masters, share their misfortunes, and give them hope that there would someday be a better life. I told Jeb about it all, and how Memphis was such an important part of that history. We decided we'd like to visit it someday, but right now, there just wasn't time.

We crossed over into Arkansas and through the sprawling beauty of the Ozark Mountains and national forest late in the day. As dusk settled, we hit Fort Smith and crossed into Oklahoma. It had been 24 hours since the nightmare, and I still wished that somehow, it was a bad dream and had never happened.

Oklahoma became flat, but I didn't mind. I was almost there, and the worst was behind me. We reached Muskogee early at night, in the dark.

"You can drop me anywhere," I said. "I'll camp and head out in the morning."

"Tell you what, Levi," he said. "My old lady has a rule against me bringing home strays—sorry for the reference.

Let's just say it hasn't worked out before. But I'll tell you what. I'll leave the rig out by my barn and you can sleep either there or in the sleeper cab."

"Thank you, sir. That would be nice."

We pulled up at his place and I watched him go into his warmly lit ranch house. I saw his wife give him a long embrace and kiss as if he'd been off to war for years. His kids ran to him and hugged his legs as he and his wife kissed again and again, as a dog ran around them in circles, vying for his attention. I wondered what it was like to be loved like that. *Settling down might not be so bad after all.*

I crawled back into the sleeper cab and turned on the dome light to do some reading and journaling. As it became harder and harder to keep my eyes open, I gave in, doused the light and fell back to sleep.

THE NEXT MORNING, I woke to a sharp rap on the side of the cab and sunlight streaming through the windshield. Jeb climbed in with a steaming hot plate of pancakes, eggs, toast and a huge cold glass of orange juice.

"Oh, Lord, thanks Jeb," I said, grateful and starving.

"I like to hear you talk that way, son. Maybe I got through after all," he laughed. "Eat up. I told my wife all about you. She's standing by the no strays rule, but we agreed we'd buy you a bus ticket from the Muskogee station to Tulsa. I'll drop you off in about an hour."

He left me to the miraculous plate of food and I savored every bite, mixing it up with careful sips of the juice to stretch it out. My journey was almost at an end. I had survived. *You're not there yet,* I admonished myself to not jinx it.

4 Tulsa

M uskogee seemed bland, like pretty much all of Oklahoma I'd seen so far. I wasn't there for the scenery. The bus station was small but well appointed. I'd been in so many of them; there were always rows of wood benches, cigarette machines, racks of various pamphlets, and ticket windows.

Oilfield workers milled about, probably on their way home with their paychecks for a brief break. A few bums wandered around, scrounging for loose change or cigarette butts. There were also real, live Native Americans—the first time I'd encountered the people I'd always read about and respected.

I clutched the paper ticket that Jeb had bought me before we said our goodbyes. The road life is hard, but full of brief, beautiful, and sometimes violent encounters. It's primal, especially when you're out in the dregs, surrounded by people who are barely surviving and desperate. Anything can happen, and there are no safety nets. For every horrible thing that happened, though, there was always a beautiful act of kindness, like someone buying you a bus ticket or a meal. I hoped to be the giver more often than the receiver someday. *Penance.*

I thought about Tennessee. Every time I did, I felt that pop of skin again, along with a psychosomatic sharp pain in my own heart. It always brought me down immediately, into a dark place within myself. I never wanted to hurt anyone. I'd sulk for days after a fight, and now I'd likely done the worst thing one person can do to another. *He may have survived.*

I watched as a Native American girl about my age walked up to the ticket window. She was beautiful, with high cheekbones and dark eyes. We were on the border of the Cherokee and Creek jurisdictions, and I wondered if she were of one of those tribes. She wore baggy sweats and a backpack that was way too big and overloaded for her. Her long, jet black hair, shining under the harsh florescent lights, tumbled over the pack. Bright, woven dream catchers and symbols adorned its canvas exterior.

The load became too much as she argued about something with the clerk. She let it slide down her slim back and onto the floor behind her. I realized I wasn't the only one watching her. The military had drilled situational awareness into my being. An old bum leaning against the wall to her right was eying the pack as he stabbed his cigarette out against the painted concrete. *Don't do it, buddy. I don't want trouble.*

She gestured with her hands at the clerk as the bum pushed himself away from the wall. I looked around for a cop to alert, but there were none. He sauntered toward her, looking around the station, probably for the same thing. I released my grip on my backpack and nudged it under the bench with my boot.

I saw the exit door to the left and guessed that was his planned route. He closed to within a few feet of her, then reached down and snatched her pack, struggling with its weight, pulling it up and cradling it like a baby while running for the door.

Using the trajectory skills I'd learned as a failed defensive back on the high school football team, I angled quickly to intercept him just before the door and took him down hard. We landed face-to-face, the backpack between us. The impact knocked the wind out of him in a torrent of stale wine and smoke, right into my face, gagging me. This time, I was on top.

"I'm gonna get off you now. Just get up and leave," I said. "Just let it go before someone calls the cops. I don't want trouble, and I'm guessing you don't either."

"Fuck off," he said, wheezing and trying to get his breath back.

From the corner of my eye, I saw her rush up and swing her leg back to dig a pointy-toed, red-fringed cowboy boot into his ribs. I reached out to catch it by the ankle just before making contact.

"Don't," I said. "He's leaving." Her face twisted in anger, brows furrowed down and toward each other, and still beautiful.

I released her leg and rolled off the bum, grabbing her bag. He made his way to a sitting position as she grabbed the pack away from me and went back to the ticket window. The bum moseyed toward the exit, smiling at me, as I went back to my seat. He stopped, pointed at her, and yelled, "Fucking squaw!" on his way out the door.

She resolved her ticketing conflict and came over to sit next to me. "Thanks for the help," she said.

"No problem. My name's Levi." I put out my hand.

"Mary Jefferson," she said, taking it in a firm grip. It was a grip that told you someone's life had been hard, and her eyes seemed to say the same as they looked into mine.

She must have noticed some reaction on my part to her name. "Yeah, I know," she said. "You expected Running Bear, Little Feather, or some shit, right? Problem is, your people decided they didn't like my people's names, so we all got new ones."

"I know the history, and I'm sorry, Mary."

"Too late for that," she said. "Where were you in 1890?"

I decided a change of subject would be a good thing. "Where're you heading?"

"Back to Tulsa. I work at the junior college in the computer room."

"Wow, that's cool. Computers are the thing now, I guess. What do you do, programming?"

She laughed. "Nothing that glamorous. I load tapes onto machines and decks of punch cards into the card readers. But I get free tuition, couldn't afford it otherwise, and I'm learning to program. COBOL. Beats the oil fields. Tulsa is trying to modernize and leave all that shit to Texas. It's a rape of the land, a rape of our planet. I won't take part. What's your story?"

I avoided mentioning my oil field job. "I'm from up north. There's not much work up there, and some friends invited me here to find something. I'm a vet, so I have the GI Bill. I'd love to start classes. Maybe I'll see you there."

She smiled, finally, revealing brilliant white but uneven teeth that worked well for her. We compared tickets and verified we were on the same bus, and settled back to leave each other alone for a while. While we waited for departure, we established trust by watching each other's bags during bathroom trips, and I bought us both a sandwich and soda. We ate in silence, stealing glances at each other.

Finally, the intercom announced our bus was boarding, and we made our way to the massive Greyhound, at the front of a long line of ragged, tired travelers. "I like the back," she said, and I concurred. We passed the long rows of seats and spread our things out across the rear bench, hoping to each other that we could keep it to ourselves.

She pulled a device from her pack. A long wire connected it to a headset with orange ear covers, which she slipped on over her hair.

"What's that?" I asked.

She pulled the headphones off. "What?" she asked.

"What is that?"

She pushed a button, then another, and a cassette tape popped out. "It's called a Walkman. It's a new portable music player."

"Wow," I responded, leaving her to it. I noticed the tape was Neil Young, my favorite. I felt like I liked her a lot and wondered if she liked me. *Don't fall in love, again, stupid. You promised.*

As soon as the bus pulled out of the station, she dozed, her head nodding forward and then jerking back up. She shifted and leaned against me. I was never an initiator, shot down and embarrassed the few times I had dared to ask pretty girls to dance, or thinking it was OK to steal a kiss, misjudging, and getting slapped or laughed at.

I moved my arm around her as she nuzzled against my chest. The headphones slid off one ear and onto her cheek. I pulled them off, gave the device a short listen, then put them on her lap and turned it off to save her batteries. The ride was only an hour, but it was quiet bliss, peaceful, with the roar of the engine beneath us droning on mile after mile. I enjoyed her against me, watching the landscape roll by through the window, while passengers slept and bums grumbled, holding empty bottles of cheap Ripple wine up to the light to check their progress with it. I wished we were on a long cross-country trip, not just a quick hop. Maybe we could have an idyllic life together, me and Mary Jefferson, fighting prejudice and social injustice together forever.

I saw a fellow hitchhiker through the bus window, standing by the roadside. He looked tired, and I felt guilty in my indulged pleasure.

Mary stirred as the bus pulled into the station and jerked to a stop. I wondered if the driver had done that to wake everyone, along with the overly loud intercom announcing our arrival in Tulsa.

"We're here?" she said groggily, looking up from my chest. It was a moment of simple beauty I wished I could preserve forever. It was one of those seemingly innocuous moments in one's life that somehow perseveres in memory over more significant but forgotten ones.

"Guess so," I said. "Unfortunately."

We took our time as the other passengers shuffled off in tiny steps, packed against each other in the aisle, moving on to whatever awaited them in Tulsa. As we exited the bus, a tall, thin Native American guy about our age waved excitedly from the nearby parking lot, calling her name. My heart dropped instantly.

"OK, well, it was nice meeting you, Mary. See you around, I guess." I put my hand out in case it was her boyfriend waiting.

She laughed and said, "What a gentleman." She took a step forward, grabbed the front of my shirt, and pulled me to her. Her mouth was warm and wet and soft. I closed my eyes to enjoy it and put my arms around her, not wanting to let go. Wisps of jasmine came from her and I breathed them in eagerly.

We broke off, and I checked to see if our embrace upset her friend. "That's my brother, silly," she said. She rummaged in her pack and pulled out a journal and pen. Ripping a page out, she scribbled on it and handed it to me. "Here's my number, Levi. Call me."

I took it, and she ran toward her brother. They hugged, and she turned one more time and waved goodbye to me.

Their car pulled out, and I stood alone next to the bus, the other passengers all having had their joyous reunions and on their way to comfortable homes, at least as I imagined it. I realized I didn't have a welcome reception, but I now had Mary's phone number.

I entered the terminal, found a seat, and dug out my little black book. I thumbed to the 'J' page and put in Mary's number. Then I looked up the phone number for Sarah's brother Don and fished a dime out of my pocket.

Leaving the phone booth door open because of the stench of urine, I dialed excitedly, the long trip over and ready for the next chapter to begin. I couldn't wait to get my first paycheck, and have money to blow on greasy cheeseburgers and put into a savings account. I reminded myself to save enough to take Mary on a date at some great Tulsa steakhouse. Yellow taxis idled nearby, and I decided to splurge and take one to Don's place if it wasn't too far away.

The receiver was filthy, so I held it away from my face after I dialed, and hoped he'd be home and would pick up. I wanted to start work the next day, if I could. The wait for the connection to complete seemed forever. Finally, there was a click, then "We're sorry, the number you are attempting to dial has been disconnected..." I hung up and my dime rattled down into the coin return. I stuck my finger in and pulled it out, and found it coated with what was obviously saliva. Some bastard had spit in there. *Some joke. What drives people to be so mean?*

After wiping my finger off on my pants, I dialed more carefully, but yielded the same result. Panic set in. I had no backup plan. They were always bragging about the money they were making, so I thought maybe they'd moved to a better place nearby or closer to a new field assignment. I sorted through my alternatives until realizing I had only one option.

I'll have to call Sarah.

I took a moment to reach inside my shirt and hold the medallion for luck before dialing and inserting the extra coins demanded by the phone company recording. She picked up on the first ring, of course. Hearing her voice brought back a flood of memories, and a wave of guilt and remorse. I heard the baby babbling in the background and my heart hurt in an entirely different way. I tried to make it stop and focus on the business at hand.

"Hey, Sarah. Listen. I just got to Tulsa. Remember Don told me that those guys were down here, making good money, and I could crash at their place and they had a job for me?"

She hesitated, a moment of just the baby cooing. "Well," she started, "Don called a few days ago. They said an oil bust was happening—work was drying up, so they headed to Wichita, Kansas, for some jobs there."

"Damn, Sarah. Nobody called me. I let them know I was coming."

"I don't think my family is happy with you, Levi," she said. "So, I'm not surprised."

"Great. Now what do I do?" I asked, really to myself. I didn't expect her to be helpful.

"I heard the mill up here might hire again soon. My dad might get you in at the prison as a guard. It's good work and has wonderful benefits. You could stay here with me and my folks. Maybe we could get our own house after a while."

I pictured myself being arrested for murder and having the bad luck to be guarded by her father. He worked at the maximum security Dannemora prison, called "Little Siberia." It was a former asylum for the criminally insane. "No, Sarah. I'm here and I'm broke. I need to find a place to stay and a job."

"Well, my sister Jean is there, working at the hospital as a nurse's aide. She's staying with Barry. I'll give you his number. Please don't be mean to him."

Her older sister Jean was a drunk who ran around a lot, and Barry was Sarah's childhood best friend, a gay dude that I had taunted and teased the few times he'd come around. In Jersey, we learned to do that as young men to confirm our masculinity, and show that we were straight and disgusted by such behavior. But really, I don't think anyone particularly gave a shit. I felt bad about how I'd treated him, mostly when I was drunk and trying to be funny, and doubted either of the two would now welcome me.

"The baby has your eyes, Levi. Did you get my latest pictures?"

"Yes, my mom gave them to me, since you made it a point to address them to her," I said, annoyed that she had done it.

"I didn't know if you'd still be in New Jersey. You're always gone somewhere, Levi, always running from something. You're a farawayer, that's all. I think you're just afraid. You want to be far away from any responsibilities. I'm a stayer, and you're a farawayer. Come back and stay with us, Levi. Leah, and you, and me."

I cut the conversation short, said goodbye, and hung up, depressed, everything I'd hoped for, everything I'd made the trip for, gone in a flash. I wondered if I'd have to get back on the highway and go home, hat in hand, defeated.

I thought about Mary and then made the call to Jean and Barry. It rang until I gave up, moving the handset toward the cradle, and then heard someone answer. It was Barry, in his high, effeminate, cheerful voice.

I gave him a quick description of the situation, and semi-pleaded for him to let me stop by to crash at least for a night, and figure out my options.

"Who's that?" I heard Jean's familiar slurred squawk in the background.

"You'll never guess," he called out. "It's Levi, begging to come over."

They both laughed hard, and I guessed they were drunk and high. I had to think to figure out what day it was, and realized it was Saturday, so they were likely off from work.

"Fuck that asshole," she yelled, loud enough for me to hear. "Hang up on him, Barry."

Fortunately, he didn't. He asked me a few questions, seeming to enjoy having the upper hand. I gave him that and apologized for my past behavior. He had moved to Tulsa before anyone else, as it was a town that was well known to be gay-friendly.

"I guess you could come over for a while," he finally said.

"No!" I heard Jean insist from the background.

"Shut up bitch, it's my place," he hollered back at her. They both laughed at his attempt to talk tough, and I couldn't resist doing so myself, the problem now being solved.

I took down the address and hung up. Opening my atlas to the city map of Tulsa, I traced the route from the bus station to their block, then headed outside to stick out my thumb again. Hopefully, for one last time on the long trip.

5 Barry and Jean

A few friendly Okies got me to the right block. I walked through the flat neighborhood, searching for the house number. Eventually, I found it—a ramshackle duplex with a front porch that was leaning to one side and looked ready to fall over.

I heard music inside and knocked on the door. The shabby curtains in a window moved slightly and a single eye peered out.

"We don't want any," I heard Jean yell from inside. I could have predicted she'd say that.

The door creaked open and Barry held it for me, wordlessly. I stepped inside.

"Well, look what the cat dragged in," he said triumphantly. I was already sick of their cornball expressions. It was their far-upstate New York country way.

"You look like shit," Jean added.

"Thanks," I responded from my position of humility.

"Turn that hillbilly crap down, Jean," Barry said, turning to me. "She thinks she's a native cowgirl now. Big shit."

He offered me a seat and a beer. The furniture was sparse, but after what I'd been through the past few days, it felt like heaven to be in an actual home. The cold beer tasted somewhat off, but delicious. I felt bad for the way I'd treated him in the past, and how nice he was treating me.

"It's three-two beer. They only sell beer that's 3.2% alcohol, can ya believe that?" Jean protested. "I've got to drink twice as much to get my buzz on." It was a good thing for her. As long as I'd known her, she carried a prominent beer belly on her slight frame, and she was, in fact, proud of it.

"Which is every day, you alcoholic," Barry added. "Sorry for the furniture. It's rental stuff. We weren't sure how long we'd be here, especially when the others started talking about Kansas. Tulsa is too gay-friendly, and this ho over here is digging the cowpokes too much for us to leave. We have pretty good jobs at the hospital down the street. I guess we should buy our own furniture now that we're sticking around. But we're pretty much paycheck-to-paycheck, just making it."

"Because we spend half our paychecks drinking and partying," Jean added.

"As it should be," he answered. "We're young and single. We have the rest of our lives to be responsible with money."

We all laughed together, then spent time catching up. I watched Jean slug down beers, wary of my experience with her after she'd had too much. I knew she'd bring up the topic I didn't want to discuss. Between that, and what happened in Tennessee, I was having a hard time. I realized how physically and mentally exhausted I was and just wanted to sleep for a while.

"So, when will you be sending for my sister and that beautiful baby of yours?" Jean eventually demanded.

"I won't," I said, my answer already decided and prepared. "That baby's father is here, somewhere in Tulsa. You know that, and I'm sure you knew him. Do the math yourself."

"Don't go there. Math is not her best subject," Barry said, giggling.

We bickered for a short while until it was time for her to get ready to go out partying. Barry puttered about his place, tidying up her empty beer cans and emptying ashtrays. I sank back into the ratty, soft lounger and fell asleep.

The setting sun caught the blinds at just the right angle to hit me in the eyes like a far away laser, and I woke. Barry had covered me with a blanket and put the lounger into the recline position, and Jean was, thankfully, already out for the night.

I was starving, but didn't want to ask for food. He'd been kind enough already. "Hey, Barry, is there a store nearby? I'll grab something for us to eat."

"Yeah, there's a convenience store two blocks away. Go left out the door, you can't miss it."

I left my pack behind and headed out the door. Inside the store, I surveyed the possibilities. Shiny, greasy hot dogs rolled and rolled behind a glass rotisserie window and the smell was overwhelming. They looked delicious, and I wanted to eat each one of them, regardless of bun or condiments. It has been forever since I'd had one.

I noted the clerk behind the counter, reading a celebrity gossip rag, and walked the aisles looking for something cheap but not insulting to bring back. There were some sandwiches in a rack, all past the expiration date. I passed boxes of crackers, and normally would have gone with the Saltines, which were pretty good and filling for just a buck.

Coolers lined the back of the store, filled with multi-color sweetened beverages and food that needed to be kept chilled. I spotted packs of plump hot dogs, including my favorite brand from the days of skipping mass, and pulled one from the cooler while glancing back at the still-distracted clerk. I slid the package into my back pocket and pulled my shirt tail down over it.

On the way out, I grabbed a bag of buns and paid for those to ease my guilt a little. When I had to resort to means like this, I always kept the amounts and addresses in my journal and vowed to return the money someday. I also grabbed handfuls of small ketchup, mustard, and relish condiment packets and dumped them into the sack.

Back at Barry's, I produced my bounty, having put the hot dogs in the bag with my other items to hide the fact I had stolen them. We boiled up the dogs and sat down to our feast. He ate three, and I devoured the remaining five, picking at the crumbs on my plate and enjoying the cans of beer he brought as soon as I emptied one.

"Thanks for the beverages," I said.

"Oh, no problem. Those are Jean's." We both had a good laugh, and he got me another. "There'll be hell to pay tomorrow, so enjoy," he added.

They were kicking in, too. I hadn't had a beer buzz since the night at the Bivouac. It had only been a few days ago, but felt like an eternity. I wanted to tell him all about it, but I also liked to keep quiet about things. I caused many of the problems in my life to date by saying too much after too many drinks. The days on the road, enjoying nature and waking with a clear head were my favorite times, not the drunken nights.

He had showered and changed, getting ready to go out as well. He wore a fancy, frilled polyester shirt that I tried not to laugh at. I was pretty high, and wondering if there was a bar nearby I could check out to celebrate the end of my trip. *Maybe I'll run into Mary.*

"You want to come with?" he asked.

The question made me take pause. "To a gay bar?"

"It's not all gays. There are curious straights, and some that are just there because the drinks are damn cheap. It's fun."

"Thanks, Barry. I don't think it's for me."

He reminded me about all the proselytizing I'd done earlier, saying how important it was to be free to experience new things in the big world around us. "Are you afraid, Levi? That doesn't sound like you. Listen, I'll put the word out and guarantee that nobody will hit on you. I'll also guarantee that you'll drink for free all night. Give it a shot."

He was right. I was being a hypocrite. I thought about it a moment, and agreed, grudgingly. "Do I have time to clean up?"

He stared at me. "You're not going unless you do. You reek."

I took a long hot shower, using ample amounts of the array of great-smelling bath products in the rack that hung from the shower head. Days of sweat from the heat and stress streamed away from me. *And blood, probably.* I emerged feeling cleansed, full of energy from my nap, and resolved to not think about anything bad for the rest of the night.

Back in the living room in just my jeans, I rummaged in my rucksack for the one good button-up shirt I traveled with, just in case. It wasn't there. *Damn.* I thought to ask Barry to borrow one, but he was much smaller, so I imagined it would be tight, and likely delicate, and I didn't want that.

He came down the stairs from his bedroom with my shirt on a hanger, freshly pressed. It also smelled nice, but not too nice. "Thanks!" I said, relieved to see it.

We headed out in his beat-up, huge green jalopy. He rode with one frilly arm out the window in the cool night, to constant taunts and insults as rough riders drove by. Even the women were merciless. Some pulled around the other side and yelled the same things at me, to which I responded with a single upraised middle finger.

Aside from the shirt, I wondered how they could tell he was gay. I looked at him. His features were small and feminine, pale skin and pink lips. Sarah had told me that, as a child, he preferred girly things and spending time with her and her friends rather than the boys. I realized for the first time that people really were born that way, and I felt shame for treating them as if they had a choice, and if they did, that this would be a wrong one. I felt even worse as I imagined the hell his life must be, day in and day out, especially as a young kid with horrified, ashamed, and disappointed parents.

"Does that bother you?" I asked.

"Not anymore. I stopped letting it. It was hell in New York, but believe it or not, despite these idiots, it's way better here. You'll see what makes up for all this."

I wished I'd just stayed back, played some music on his stereo, and rested. I needed to hit the ground running to find some work and a place to stay. He hadn't told me if I had to leave, but I knew staying there with Jean wouldn't work.

We pulled into the club parking lot. It was hard to miss, brightly lit with neon borders around the sides and roof, and an enormous neon sign. Some bulbs were broken, probably by haters. As we got closer, I noticed pockmarks from bullets on the exterior. The place was pounding with overly amplified-bass disco. *Great, revenge of the Light Ship back on Lake Sussex.* I could hear the laughter and shouting from within.

We entered swirls of tiny lights from a plethora of overhead disco balls. It was crowded, the dance floor full of squirming, twirling bodies hustling and fist-pumping into the air with joy. A ripped, tough-looking doorman stopped us in the vestibule. His dark hair cropped high and tight, he peered suspiciously at me and my driver's license through reflective aviators. As he held it up to the light to see better, his biceps seemed to grow as if there were some invisible air pump connected to them.

After we passed scrutiny, we stepped into the main hall. Barry cupped his hand and shouted into my ear, "Wait here." He headed off to a group that was waving at him from the corner of the room. They embraced him as he arrived, and he began speaking to each friend and pointing over at me. Some of them smiled, gave me a thumbs-up, and waved me over.

I made my way through the crowd, getting smacked on the ass once, and almost turned and left. A drag queen stepped in front of me and shimmied, taking my arm to guide me to the dance floor. I shook him off and continued to the group.

Barry's friends pulled me into the center of their mass at the end of the bar and handed me a drink. "You're safe with us!" one of them yelled. "Stay in the middle! We're your protectors, Levi!" shouted another.

I got to know them all. You wouldn't know most of them were gay, other than the way they behaved while in their safe space. They laughed a lot, told me jokes, teased me a little, and we got on well. The night wore on and Barry was right; I hadn't paid for a single drink.

About half the group had migrated to the dance floor, giving me more room to create my own space. I leaned back against the wall, observing, not wanting to pull out my small pocket notebook and risk upsetting them, but documenting everything to memory. I marveled at the circumstances that had put me in this place. It was a huge contrast from the Bivouac just a few days ago. That's one thing about the road—every day is different, every day a new adventure, for good or bad. It was freedom, and it was real life.

I realized I hadn't pissed yet, and was perhaps avoiding it, but couldn't any longer. I looked for the neon marker and headed that way. "Want me to watch your back?" Barry asked, arriving sweaty from the dance floor.

"I don't need an escort."

He laughed. "Don't use that word in here, brother," and I continued on. Wanting to hurry and get back to my safe space, I started unzipping on my way in. It was nearly empty. Pictures of naked men in various poses and states of undress lined the walls. I picked a urinal in the middle of an empty group, and the other dudes took little notice.

It might have been the environmental stress, or just one of those things when you're in a real hurry and that causes things to not work right, but I had trouble starting the stream, despite feeling like I was going to bust. The guy to my left took notice.

"Having trouble, sweetheart?" he asked.

The word brought me back to that terrible night. I felt panic and anger at hearing it. I wanted to knock him out, but he didn't know. He was smiling, and I decided he meant nothing by it. *How could he know?*

The distraction had done the job. I felt relief as the hot urine rushed out of me, my bladder feeling like a balloon deflating.

"There you go, touchdown!" the dude yelled. I continued to ignore him. He zipped up and stopped on his way past. "Care to dance later?" he asked.

"I'm not gay," I responded.

"Honey, we're all gay. Some of us just don't know it yet." He lifted and then dropped my pony tail on the way out.

I made my way back to the group, which was thinning out with the rest of the bar. Checking the clock up high on the wall, I saw it was well past midnight.

"Last call," the bartenders started shouting.

"What's the deal with that?" I asked Barry.

"It's a private club, not a bar," he answered. "Rules are different down here. It's weird."

He rounded up his crew and urged them all to head back to his apartment for an after-party. We all left the place, everyone still raving and giddy with Saturday Tulsa night euphoria, and piled into just a few cars, each one stuffed with revelers.

I sat up front in Barry's car, squished between him and two skinny, perfumed dudes, and we left the parking lot in a happy queer parade of vehicles. As we moved from stop light to stop light through the outer city to his place, they were oblivious to the hate surrounding them. The honked horns and shouted redneck insults couldn't pierce their veil of pure joy. They blew kisses, and it only made the haters more angry.

After we got inside and everyone had chosen a seat (I had rushed to my comfortable and familiar reclining lounger), they passed beers around and there was a cacophony of flip tops popping and initial guzzling. I produced a joint and became the hero of the moment.

One of them knelt at the stereo system and cranked up much of the same music we'd heard all night. I was out of gas and getting pretty sick of it. I thought about going into the yard, pulling the bedroll off my backpack and crashing out back under the Oklahoma stars.

A car sounded outside, a loud, muscular engine, headlights flaring the windows as it bounced up onto the lawn. Barry's friends had taken all the street parking.

"Here comes trouble. Incoming. Everybody buckle up," Barry announced to the room.

Jean barged into the room followed by a tall, lean, mean looking guy in a cowboy hat. His mustache was trim—too trim, and it felt like he was military. He immediately reminded me of all the sergeants and officers I hadn't gotten along with during my abbreviated stint. He surveyed the room that way as well, scanning laterally and taking in each person, each detail. Someone turned down the music, and it became quiet. A few of Barry's friends put their hands to their mouths to suppress laughs.

"What the fuck is going on here?" Jean demanded. "Barry, you know our deal. No gay parties. And what's Levi still doing here?"

"It's my place, Jean,"

"And I'm paying half the rent. We had a deal."

Her companion wore an angry scowl. "I smell dope. You fags been smoking dope?" he asked in a country drawl.

"Better be straight with him," Jean added. "Buck's a state trooper."

"Ooh, state trooper. Me likey," one of Barry's friends whispered, kicking off more giggles.

I sensed I wasn't the only one in the room feeling panic at her statement. Nobody answered, but everyone began shifting nervously.

"Hey, aren't you driving around drunk tonight, state trooper?" another of Barry's friends asked. They all began giggling again, further enraging Buck.

He reached down and picked up my pack, inspecting it. "Is the dope in here, pony boy?" he asked me. I stared at him without answering. He looked at it closer, turning it over, likely hoping something incriminating would fall out. He pointed out a spot on the bottom edge. "What's this, pony boy? Looks like blood to me."

Fear struck me, but I refused to look and struggled to remain calm. I knew how to deal with his kind and ignored the question. "Got a warrant, Buck? Because my brother's a fancy ACLU lawyer. This won't look good on your record, along with driving drunk tonight.."

He threw it down and turned to Jean.

"We're going to the after-hours club for one more, and we'll be back in an hour. Everyone better be gone," she said, guiding Buck out the door. The car roared back down the road.

"Oh my God, that was awesome," one of Barry's friends exclaimed, high-fiving me.

The music resumed, and Barry returned from the kitchen with an armful of beers. "Good thing she didn't look in the fridge," he said. "This is the last of her beer."

I was now too worried about Buck spotting blood on my pack to get back into a festive mood and allowed myself to drift off in the chair.

When I woke, it was still dark. I could make out the shapes of empty cans scattered around the room. Someone had covered me again. I checked immediately to make sure my pack was next to the chair and pulled my toothbrush from the side pocket.

As I fumbled my way to the bathroom, trying to be quiet, I passed a closed door and heard a noise inside. It was Jean moaning softly. I stopped to listen. There was a quick succession of thumps, and then a male grunt.

"That's it?" I heard her say. "Goddamn, Buck. I told you to take it easy on the shots."

He gave a muffled, angry retort. I went into the bathroom and brushed my teeth quickly, and encountered him leaving the room on my way back to my chair. He kicked my pack aside and sat on the sofa to pull on his cowboy boots.

I settled back into the recliner and pulled the blanket back over me. "What's the deal with you cops?" I asked. "Why all the hate and anger?"

He gave me an annoyed look. "What, you talking about the queers? It ain't right. Says so in the Bible, what they do is a sin."

"So is what you just did. Do you go to church, Buck?"

"Nope. Too busy."

"What about the blacks? You like them?"

"Nope. They don't want to work. Lazy. Dishonest. All I do is chase one or another around for stealing stuff."

"Maybe because it's way harder for them to find work and feed their families? To get a good education?"

"Where there's a will, there's a way, Levi."

"How about the Mexicans?" I was enjoying taunting him.

"Some of them work hard. They need to speak fucking English, though. This is America."

"So, what you're saying is that you're against anyone who acts differently, looks different, or talks differently from you. Do you understand that what's made this country great is its diversity? That we're a nation of immigrants? Do you think that maybe you're just afraid of people who're different? I thought you state cops were all about virtue."

He stood up, having finished with his boots. I had succeeded in angering him, and it helped bring out the truth. "Look, Levi. Forget the fairy tales. Grow up, put your long-hair hippie idealism aside, and join the real world. Lots of cops are basically the jocks and bullies from high school that didn't want to go into the military but wanted a way to keep kicking ass, because that's what we like to do. The job provides the opportunity for that. The sooner you realize it, the better for you. But when your life is in danger, we're the ones you want protecting it. You'll be happy we're kicking ass."

"Night, Buck," I said as he slammed the door behind him. *Don't poke the bear. You never learn.*

I tipped the recliner back. It had been a pretty good night. I wondered what Mary Jefferson was doing and if she was nearby. I imagined her sleeping soundly in a nice warm bed, her dark hair splayed around her pillow. I wondered if she was dreaming about me and hoped I could dream about her.

6 Village of Prayer

I woke at first light, as was my habit after having it drilled into me during basic training. My head throbbed, and I felt shaky, still exhausted after just a few hours of sleep. I cursed myself again for not moderating my intake and searched for some aspirin. I found a vial, gulped two tablets down with cold tap water, and began cleaning the place up.

After I'd finished, Barry and Jean were still sleeping. I didn't want to be around when either of them woke, so I took a quick shower, dressed, and took a walk to the mini-mart.

I bought a large black coffee, newspaper, and a thick roll that I hoped would fill me. On the way out, I stopped by the condiments area and loaded up on more packets of mayo, ketchup, mustard, relish, and whatever else was free.

I stole nothing this time, as I'd taken too many chances lately, getting sloppy, and when I did, I always paid a price. I was already envisioning Buck back at the state police barracks looking up background on me, with the help of Jean, and asking some corrupt Okie judge for a warrant. There were items on my record from northern New York and New Jersey I was sure he'd find. *And maybe something about me having been in the vicinity of a murdered guy.*

Outside, I sat against the building and spread out my feast and the paper. There were less help wanted ads than I had hoped for, but some excellent possibilities. I circled them, then read the rest of the news, focusing on the local section in case they tested me on my knowledge during any interviews. The coffee and aspirin kicked in, and my headache was fading.

The walk back to Barry's in the clear, crisp morning helped to invigorate me. By the time I got there, I was feeling energetic and optimistic. A few of my calls yielded interview appointments and requests to come in to fill out applications. *Pretty good for a Sunday.* I left to follow up on those before Barry and Jean got up.

THE DAYS THAT FOLLOWED were all the same. Summer had transitioned into fall, although it wasn't as noticeable in Tulsa. I came to an agreement with Barry and Jean, paid what I could, and made earnest promises for when I'd have an income. I tried to be invisible, cleaning up after myself (and them), and kept my head down, staying away when I knew they were there.

I called Mary a few times, and she offered to take me out, but my pride wouldn't allow it. I told her we'd celebrate after my first paycheck. Often, when downtown, I'd hang out around the junior college, hoping to see her.

Shayne and I had been trading letters. Occasionally, he'd call Barry's phone, and we'd talk a little. He'd saved some money, and wanted to take a motorcycle trip down for a week with his friend Tim before it got too cold. I told him it should be fine, maybe around Thanksgiving, as I expected to have my own place by then.

The oilfield jobs had mostly dried up, as others had said. It was the Great Tulsa Oil Bust of the eighties. That also meant that the laid-off workers were competing for other jobs. As a long-haired Yankee, my odds weren't great competing with local Okies or their brethren from neighboring states like Texas. Yankees were the worst in the eyes of the natives. I couldn't even get low-paying mundane jobs at gas stations or convenience stores, and was giving up hope, with just a few bucks left to my name, and having to steal food more often.

I went to the motor vehicle agency to get an Oklahoma driver's license, hoping it would help me appear more of a local, and not a transient worker. Focusing on my military logistics training, I stopped wasting time with the penny-ante jobs and went for shipping and receiving opportunities. There was a lot of trucking in the area. Finally, I landed an interview at a large hospital, medical center, and university complex just out of town. I told Barry and Jean about it, excited about how well I fit the job description and how great the initial phone interview had gone after I'd let them know about my adept forklift skills.

Barry and Jean both looked at each other, laughing. "You never heard of Eugene Walters, dumbass?" Jean asked.

"Um, some TV guy, right?" I slightly recalled the name.

"Big-time TV preacher, evangelist," Barry chimed in. "That complex is the Village of Prayer. You'll fit in there as well as you did in the gay club the other night. Except I won't be there to protect you," he said with a prideful look.

"Hey, I did alright in there," I said.

"They're not as loving and accepting as my gay friends, despite all Jesus said about that stuff."

I borrowed Jean's dusty, unused Bible to brush up over the next few days. Barry had a pair of khakis, decent shoes, and a button-up shirt that an old boyfriend had left behind. After determining they'd fit, he laundered and pressed them for me. I thought about getting a decent haircut. The job paid OK, but nowhere near enough to get me to sell out to that degree. They could take me or leave me. *Strong words for a broke guy.*

Interview day came and nothing better had come up, so off I went. Jean actually wished me luck. She had changed her tact and was decent to me. Maybe it was a ploy to talk me into reuniting with her sister. She saw I wasn't a bum, I worked hard, and paid my share.

Barry gave me a ride. We drove out of downtown and into the flat plains surrounding the city. The Village of Prayer was visible a long way off. Golden high-rise buildings shimmered in the Tulsa sun like a forbidden oasis. A man-made river flowed through the property, leading up to and underneath a massive bronze sculpture of two hands pushed together in prayer. Barry said it was all meant to symbolize the unifying power of faith and medicine. The university sprawled out over the adjoining tracts of land.

"When you go in there for an appointment," he explained, "you don't get to see a doctor first. You meet with a prayer partner, who will place hands on your afflicted area and pray for healing. If that doesn't work, off you go to the doc."

"I'm guessing which one of those two people makes less money."

"Yup, it's the prayer partners. It's very cost-effective medicine if that part works. They bill the insurance company full price."

He pointed out Eugene Walters' mansion up on the hill. "I've seen pictures of that place," he said. "Circular driveways lined with Bentleys."

"The preaching business is mighty good, it seems."

He parked and settled in, turning on his radio as I got out of the car. I walked along the river and stopped at the enormous sculpture of the hands, gazing up in wonder. A family with Arkansas plates on their junker had parked nearby and piled out to kneel and pray loudly at the base of the sculpture. Someone they loved was sick. They were all shabbily dressed and looked tired.

As I walked by, the elder of the group stopped me. "Do you know where we can give our donation to brother Eugene?" he asked.

I felt horrible at the idea of it, the blatant hypocrisy. It was the same thing that had always offended me about the Catholic church and their immeasurable wealth—all those priceless works of art and prime real estate all over the world, much of it spent to cover for pedophile priests and other offenses to what they allegedly stood for. Yet, every Sunday that basket got passed around, people on their last measure giving money they couldn't afford, sacrificing the quality of their lives and their kids', all for a hope and a dream. The church, like this one, could solve almost all these folks' problems easily, but kept taking from them. I wondered what

Jesus would think of it. The thought of working in a place like this, around people like this, repulsed me. *You have to start somewhere. You have to eat.*

The interview went well. It wasn't as cult-like as I had expected, and they were nice. I got pressed as to whether I was a "believer," to which I gave my religious history and talked about my favorite part of the Bible, the Sermon on the Mount in Matthew 5. Since I had invoked that passage during the interview, the words wouldn't leave me. I couldn't escape them. They ran through my head in a loop, like one of those songs you can't get out of your mind for days after you hear it on the radio.

Blest are they who show mercy; mercy shall be theirs.

Blest too are the peacemakers; they shall be called the sons of God

Given the opportunity, I had done none of that. *If you had, you'd be dead, or raped.* I fought back by recalling other Beatitudes, the ones I most believed in.

How blessed are the poor in spirit; the reign of God is theirs.

Blest too are the sorrowing; they shall be consoled.

Blest are the lowly; they shall inherit the land.

Those, I felt, were the actual words of Jesus, before much of the biblical text became polluted with the words of man, to serve man's agenda and natural tendency toward greed and control of others.

As I left the complex and walked toward Barry's car, I looked up the hill at the mansion, which seemed to stand in opposition to those principals. *Hypocrites.*

"How'd it go?" he asked, excited, as I got in. "Were they psychos? Did they pray on you or speak in tongues?"

"No, none of that. They were pretty nice. We started with a prayer, which they had me lead. That was the first test. Then they finished with a prayer and said they'd pray on the decision and let me know."

"Damn. That's a lot of praying. Well, I hope the Lord hires you."

"Me too. Wouldn't that be something? Although I'm not entirely sure he's in the chain of command in there."

THEY HIRED ME, AND I showed up early for work on my first day. My new supervisor, John, started the day with a group prayer with our team all holding hands. A guy my age with dark, curly hair grabbed mine and gave me a smirk. "Welcome aboard," he said. The nameplate on his shirt said 'Kirk,' and he didn't introduce himself. I detected the faint smell of booze on his breath, and his hand was cold and sweaty at the same time.

John then gave me a tour of the facility. It was new, shiny, and modern. Everything was a huge upgrade from the environment I had worked in at the military base. It excited me to try out the big yellow forklifts.

After the tour, we sat at his desk in the middle of the vast, open medical supply warehouse floor. As we went through some on-boarding paperwork, I noticed John's hands twitching. Suddenly, in the middle of handing me a form, he jumped up, began strutting in circles, shouting random phrases, and flinging his arms above his head. "Yeah! That's right! Hey, Levi! It's OK!"

I stood up, not sure what to do. Kirk rolled up on a forklift and laughed. "Go, John, go man!" he shouted. A woman ran out of the administrative office, surveyed the situation, and ran back inside. She came back seconds later with a guy in a suit and tie and another woman in a gold dress.

They ran to John and then guided him back to his chair. The woman in the gold dress moved behind him, holding him down by pushing on his shoulders with both hands, and she prayed loudly as the others bowed their heads and placed their hands on John's head as he struggled to get up.

"Heavenly Father, please give our brother John peace and free him from this affliction, give him rest to do your work here and for brother Eugene..."

This continued for a while, with Kirk watching in amusement. The gold-dress woman became louder and more forceful, switching to babbling in tongues, until the seizure eventually subsided. John slumped back in his chair, exhausted and breathing hard.

"It took much longer for me to heal you, and chase the evil away this time," the gold-dress woman said to him. "Are you sure you're still strong in the faith, brother John?"

"I am..." he stammered. "The kids... work... I have had little time for services, but I'm going to the chapel today at lunch. You can count on that."

"Please do," she admonished. "The spirit must be strong for me to work through the Lord."

Everyone went back to their tasks and John and I finished the paperwork. He seemed embarrassed and didn't talk about what had happened.

On break, I sat outside on the loading dock, enjoying the sun and clean air. Kirk came out, leaned against the wall next to me, and lit a cigarette.

"It's Tourette's," he said. "Always a fucking clown show when that goes down, but fun to watch."

His southern accent was thick, and he spoke slowly. I nodded but didn't engage him, already getting a bad vibe. *You need this job, avoid the troublemakers.*

"You're faking it, like me," he said. "I can tell a mile away. You ain't no Christian."

"I'm just trying to get on my feet," I said. "I got no problem with it."

He pulled a flask from his hip pocket, unscrewed the cap, and took a hit. "Have some," he demanded more than asked, shoving it at me.

"No thanks, Kirk. I'm gonna try to keep this job. I'm good."

"Right on. Fuck ya, then," he said, stabbing out the cigarette and heading back inside.

7 Mary

The days and weeks drifted by and I fell into a rhythm, doing well at the job, keeping Kirk at arm's length. I spent as little money as possible, scrimped where I could, and eventually had a few hundred bucks to buy the most minimal functioning vehicle possible—a $300 dual purpose on-off-road dirt bike.

I took a side job at a local donut shop, working the late shift on the bad side of Tulsa. The shop catered to cops. The manager told me rule one is that any cop that comes in gets white-glove treatment, and free coffee and donuts. It kept them around, which meant fewer robberies.

She asked me if I was OK with getting robbed, said it would happen, and told me to just hand over the cash in the drawer. The other rule was to make frequent drops in the back-office safe to keep the loss to a minimum. There were bullet holes in the windows.

One night, around midnight, a bum came in as I was making a fresh batch of donuts. He fumbled with shaky hands to count out enough change for a coffee, and looked like he weighed less than a hundred pounds beneath his sagging, raggedy clothes.

He had enough for a medium, but I gave him an extra-large. I took the time to talk to him and he told me about the tragedies of his life, how he'd lost a young child and couldn't cope after that, and how it had cost him his marriage and his job. The entire time we talked, he eyed the well-lit display case of colorful donuts with spittle in the corner of his mouth. I sensed he had too much pride to beg.

"Look," I said. "It's almost shift change. In about an hour, I have to throw out the old donuts and replace them with this new batch I'm cooking up. I'll put them in a clean plastic bag and set them on top of the dumpster out back." He smiled happily, did a little dance, rubbed his stomach, and thanked me on his way out the door.

A few nights later, I showed up for my shift just after dark. The manager was there, which was unusual. The girl I was coming in for smiled at me and wagged her finger as she picked up her purse and clocked out.

"Come here," the manager said. "Come with me."

I followed her out the back door. Bums surrounded the dumpster, smoking cigarettes and eagerly awaiting the night drop of stale donuts. The one I had met pointed me out, and they all cheered.

"We ain't putting them out," the manager yelled to them. "Might as well leave, afore I call the cops."

There was an angry burst of murmuring among the crowd, but they all shuffled off in different directions. I didn't want to imagine what their interactions with the Tulsa cops were like. The ones I'd met in the shop were real hard-asses. Compassion seemed to be a disqualifying trait for the job. It was a tough town.

"You understand now why we can't do that?" she asked when we were inside. Without giving me a chance to answer, she continued. "The place fills up with bums. People pull in and get intimidated, drive off without ordering. It becomes a shit-show. We don't make money, and we have to lay off the help. Including you."

I nodded and apologized, telling her it wouldn't happen again.

JEAN'S BIRTHDAY ARRIVED, and we had a little party for her, as Buck was away for training. Barry and I made her dinner and bought a small cake with some party hats. We drank screwdrivers and played her favorite music without complaint.

After we'd cleaned up, she announced she wanted to go to her favorite place, a small, run-down country dive bar not too far away.

"Sure, give me a minute to get cleaned up. You in, Levi?," Barry asked excitedly.

"No," she said right away. "I wasn't talking about you two. I just need a ride."

Barry became angry, his mood deflated. "Well, I'm not driving you. One more DUI and I lose my license for a year this time. What, we're not good enough for you Jean? After everything we've been through?"

He had hit a nerve, and she appeared to reconsider.

"How about we go to the gay club?" he countered. "We'll have the best time ever."

"Oh, fuck that," she said, retreating to her tough facade. She looked at us and I saw rare compassion in her expression.

"OK," she finally relented. "Come with me, but keep a low profile. They're not exactly fans of gays and long-hairs in this place."

It was settled, and after she gave us a short amount of time to clean up, we headed out in Barry's car. I agreed to drive to settle that argument.

"Remember, keep a low profile, both of you," she warned as we made our way across the parking lot. We followed behind her, mocking her silently.

It was quiet for a Friday night. A few of her friends embraced her as we entered. She was quick to introduce us, declare us as her friends and off-limits to any mean-spirited prejudices. She cashed some bills and set up a long country music playlist on the jukebox, and the party began.

We didn't pay for much, as her friends bought round after round of shots. People danced, and Barry and I engaged in deep, drunken conversations with rugged oilmen and cattlemen with flat-top haircuts and western shirts. We covered our lifestyles and views without condemning each other.

Jean went off to another place with friends, and the bar got more crowded as it became late. Barry and I quit while we were ahead, our shield gone, and went back to the parking lot.

"I'm not driving, and you shouldn't either," he said as we stood looking at the car.

"Let's just walk. It's not that far."

He looked at me like I was crazy. "Are you kidding? It's over a mile to home. I have a morning shift at the hospital. I need my car. These animals might trash it."

"Jesus, Barry. Stop being difficult." A solution came to my compromised mind. "Get in and put it in neutral. I'll push it home. Thank God Oklahoma is flat."

He laughed at the idea, but got in the car and we started down the road. He put it in accessory mode and played the radio. We sang along to the songs as we went down the road, two fools, as more daring drunks drove past us and honked their horns.

About half-way home, I was tiring and about to ask for a break. Suddenly, a kaleidoscope of lights flashed all around us. "Hit the brakes," I yelled and stood up from my position behind the vehicle. A city cop pulled up behind us and got out of his car.

"Don't say a word," I yelled to Barry. "Let me do the talking."

"Well, what have we here?" the policeman asked with a bemused expression.

I looked him over. He was young, no decorations on his uniform, probably a rookie on the force, stuck on the graveyard shift and bored. Young cops were often overzealous and by-the-book.

"We're just trying to be safe, officer," I said. "To be honest, we've been out celebrating a birthday and didn't want to drive home since we were drinking. Barry here needs his car for work in the morning."

Barry had gotten out and stood by the side of the car. "So," the cop said. "You figure it's safe for two drunks to be pushing this huge vehicle down my city streets? I don't consider that safe."

Barry started to say something, and I glared to silence him. The cop stepped over to Barry.

"Sir, you're operating a vehicle while under the influence. I'm going to have to take you in."

"The car wasn't running, I was pushing it," I objected.

"Doesn't matter," he said. "Under the law, he's behind the wheel, key in the ignition, directing it, and he's the driver." He grabbed Barry by the arm and turned him toward the car to handcuff him. Barry sobbed.

"Wait," I said. "Please. Don't do this to him. He works at the hospital as a nurse's aide and he has a shift in the morning. You're in there a lot. You see how compassionate and hardworking they are. Please, just let us walk the rest of the way home." I wondered if it would cross his mind to give us a ride, but didn't dare ask.

"Somebody is going to jail tonight, son," the cop said firmly.

I thought about how Barry had forgiven me and taken me in when I had nowhere to go. "Then I guess it has to be me."

"Fair enough," he said, as he turned away from Barry and cuffed me instead.

I talked him into dropping Barry off at the house. Barry promised to wake his neighbor and come to the jail to bail me out. I asked him to please try to do it quickly.

The cop administered a breathalyzer at the station, took my belongings, mug shot and fingerprints, then put me in the drunk tank, a large cell filled with other men of different sizes, races, and ages. Some slept, and some ranted, angrily pacing and peering through the bars like animals in the zoo. *Barry would have never survived this.*

I found a spot in the corner and sat there, protecting my back. A big black dude stormed over. "That's my seat. Get the fuck up," he demanded.

"It was empty. I don't want any trouble."

He reached down and grabbed me by the front of my shirt to pull me up. I got to my feet and struck him in the chest with both palms, causing him to stagger backward across the cell. He tripped over someone and fell, then struggled to get back to his feet.

"Here we go, show time," one cop sitting at a desk nearby called to his peers. A few filed in and leaned on the desks to watch. The rest of the drunk tank came to life, some of them cheering, some jeering.

"Fight, fight, nigger and a white!" a cowboy yelled, clapping his hands.

The black dude stood, unsteady, then bull-rushed me. I had foolishly stayed in the corner and didn't have anywhere to escape to. He swung and missed, then slammed the weight of himself against me, grabbing my long hair and swinging me around. I flew to the cement floor, this time in the center of the cell, with room, as everyone had shifted to the perimeter.

He came at me again and I spun away, glimpsing the smiling cops as I turned. Nobody was interested in helping me, they were only there for the show. My adversary came at me again, fortunately drunker than I was. He grabbed my arm as I tried to side-step and hit me with a punch to the side of my head. Tiny dots of light swirled throughout my field of vision as I fell back against a wall.

The blind rage that had gotten me in trouble so many times before welled up. I imagined ramming his head into the bars until his skull split open, then imagined the consequences with a squad of cops looking on. I took a knee and tried the only advantage I had over him. "Take your spot. I don't want to fight you. Let's not prostitute ourselves for the enjoyment of these cops."

He stood above me, breathing hard, considering what I'd said, then went to the corner and sagged against the wall, slid to the floor, and closed his eyes. I tried to stay on my feet, watching the rest of them, avoiding the agitated ones. Some were bailed out, but more came as hours went by. I wondered what had happened to Barry.

Eventually, I yielded to exhaustion and sat. I fell asleep leaning against the bars and awoke some time later. My adversary was being called out as an officer held the cell door open.

"Sorry about that shit," he said, shaking my hand on the way out.

"Good luck," I said. "That's a good right hand you have."

It was six in the morning when they finally called my name and opened the door for me. They led me out to where Barry stood in his scrubs, with Jean by his side.

"What the fuck?" I asked, pointing to the clock.

"Sorry," he said sheepishly. "The neighbor didn't answer the door. I waited for Jean and fell asleep. I had to wait until I was sober. But we both chipped in and paid your bail." Jean just smiled and shook her head.

"Well, happy birthday to you and thanks," I said.

We drove home in silence. I panicked about possibly losing my license to suspension, before remembering I'd kept my New Jersey license. I dug it out of my backpack and put it in my wallet for safekeeping.

DESPITE THE SETBACK, I fell in a groove, and before long, I had enough saved up for a deposit and the first month's rent somewhere. Barry let me know the people on the other side of his duplex were moving out, and he'd speak to his landlord about me. I wanted to get away from Jean and the constant menace of Buck, who continued to taunt me with vague threats, but thought it would be good to have friends so close. We had formed a bit of a community.

I settled the deal shortly thereafter. After moving in, I scrounged for basic furniture, using Barry's big boat of a car to visit yard sales for the basics. I only needed something to sleep on, a sparse desk to write at, and a table to eat at. I didn't worry about accommodations for visitors, because I didn't have any friends.

I used my GI Bill benefits to enroll at an associate degree program at the junior college—just one class to start out. I was interested in computers, and I was still interested in Mary. It was thrilling to be back in a classroom and learning. I had finally made it to college. *A start, anyway.*

When I received my first programming assignment, I wrote the simple program in a hurry and brought my stack of punch-cards to the window for processing.

And there she was, Mary, looking beautiful. "Well hey there, stranger," she said with a smile.

"Hi, Mary. Here I am, Mr. Computer Guy." I handed her my rubber-banded deck.

"How's it going for you?" she asked, taking the cards.

"I'm getting on my feet. Got a vehicle a few weeks ago, and just this week got a place. I'm on fire."

"Sounds like it, Levi. Good for you."

I got real nervous, working up the courage to ask her out. The line behind me was growing, and students were making me aware they were losing patience.

"So, do you want to grab a bite sometime?" she asked, saving me the trouble.

"I was just about to ask you. You beat me to the punch," I laughed.

"Great. I like Dino's right down the street. Let's make it easy. Just meet me there after my shift, around seven."

"Tonight?" I asked incredulously.

"Yes, if that's OK. Now let me get to those people behind you before one of them hits you."

I smiled again and moved on, feeling full, forgetting Tennessee and the Beatitudes for a while.

The rest of the day was a blur. I picked up my output listing and saw that she had circled my syntax errors and chided me with some comments. I revised and resubmitted, careful this time in knowing she was watching, and it ran successfully. She drew a gold star on my results.

I considered myself fortunate that I didn't have to pick her up. I hadn't told her my 'vehicle' had two wheels, and wasn't sure how she'd react. Some girls liked that, and it terrified some. I checked my bike on the way to the restaurant, and felt bad to leave it there alone, locked to a light pole in the darkened parking lot.

She was sitting in a booth when I entered Dino's. I sat across from her and could tell by her face that I'd already screwed something up. I just wasn't sure what.

"Come sit next to me, silly," she said. I slid out and joined her on her side. She gave me a quick kiss, and I wished it had lasted. She smelled like the fresh air on the first warm day of spring after a long winter. I enjoyed being next to her, our bare legs pressed against each other under the table.

We ordered and ate slowly, drinking more than we probably should have on a weeknight. The topics we covered revealed many similarities in our viewpoints, plans, and outlook on life. Neither of us came from money, and we were making it on our own, with little help. We had been laughing so much that after a while I realized we were annoying those at the nearby tables, and I didn't care. Time passed without notice, and we kept going long after they had cleared the table in front of us. The drinks kept coming.

We were both stuffed, but ordered dessert anyway, deciding to share an ice cream sundae. When it arrived, she scooped whipped cream with her finger and planted it on my nose. I returned the favor, and we giggled and fell into an embrace and kiss that lasted until a jealous guy shouted for us to get a room.

"Let's go to my place," she said. "It's not far. Is your car nearby?" she asked.

"Um, I have a confession to make," I said, lowering my head, hoping the news wouldn't upset her.

She waited patiently.

"My ride is a dual-purpose dirt bike. It's not safe to ride after this many drinks, and I wouldn't put you at risk by doing that. I'll pay for a cab."

She laughed. "Oh, man. Well, you're right. But when we're sober, I'll show you how to ride that thing in some dunes on the reservation. OK, we'll take my car, but you're driving, buddy."

I felt relieved that she'd taken it in stride, and it impressed me she could handle a dirt bike.

We made it to her neighborhood, and she guided me down the streets. On almost every corner, someone leaned against a building, or staggered aimlessly. "This is the state your people have left us in," she said. "They conquered and destroyed a great, prideful people."

"I know the history, and I'm sorry, Mary. I read *Bury My Heart at Wounded Knee*. It was incredibly sad."

"A story repeated many times over the history of humanity," she said. "We're a brutal species."

We pulled into a long dirt driveway that led back to her small ranch rental. "I have a roommate," she said. "We'll have to be quiet. You don't want to wake him, I promise."

I wondered if it was the brother who picked her up at the bus stop, but why wouldn't she refer to him that way? Perhaps it was some other dude. I worried about a confrontation and got jealous. *Why the warning?*

She took my hand and led me into the house, stealthily opening doors to muffle their worn creaks and squeaks. The place reeked of skunk. We made it to her bedroom, and she pushed the door closed behind us. "I'm sorry about the smell," she whispered. "It got under the floorboards and sprayed before I could flush it out."

She moved to me and kissed me. I pulled her light cotton shirt up over her head and embraced her. Her skin felt smooth, and the moonlight shone off her hair through the open bedroom window. I released the clasp on her bra, threw it to the side, and she removed my shirt. We embraced and kissed again, bare chests against each other, each now sweating.

"I haven't rewarded you for your chivalry at the bus stop," she said.

"I don't want a reward, Mary. I want the start of something amazing."

She took my hand again and led me to her bed, and we fell upon it, methodically removing the rest of our clothes. We took our time, taking turns reminding each other to be quiet, sometimes cupping a hand over each other's mouth to muffle the sounds we made. It had been a long time since I'd made love to anyone, and I didn't want to make love to anyone else ever again.

We lay on our backs, side by side, catching our breath, holding hands. I looked over the length of her, perfect, shining with sweat in the night, her breasts and toned stomach rising and falling slowly with each breath. For the first time in a long time, my troubles weren't present in my mind, and I could only think of a future with her. Maybe getting my degree, a good job, settling down, having a kid or two. *Maybe it's time to stop the road nonsense before it kills you.*

We both dozed off. A thump sounded from somewhere down the hall, followed by a loud wail. She sat up immediately. "Oh, no," she said.

I looked toward the door, wondering if I'd need to protect her, to protect myself. I reached to the floor for my underwear and pants, not wanting to fight naked, if it came to that.

"And now *I* have a confession to make," she said, taking my hand. "It's my son. He's three and his father's in jail. We're not married. He's a drunk, and he's trouble, but my boy misses him terribly. I don't want to confuse him. You have to leave."

"He was here by himself last night?" I asked as I got dressed. The boy cried louder, calling for his mother.

"No, my sister sleeps in the room with him when she babysits. It's complicated. Please go out and wait in the car. I'll quiet him and get him back to sleep. He just needs to know I'm here, and he always goes right back to sleep."

I waited in her driver's seat until she finally came out and got in the car. We traveled in silence, back toward the school.

"Does it matter?" she finally asked.

"It does," I answered honestly. "You should have told me before we took this step."

I pulled up next to my bike. It was standing alone next to the light pole like a trusted steed.

"It's disqualifying that it matters at all," she said. "Maybe we're not good for each other. He's the most important thing in my life."

I got out without answering, and she slid over to the driver's side. I knelt down to unlock the chains on my bike while I watched her taillights move slowly toward the street.

The bike was stubborn, but finally came to life after I had jumped on the kick-starter until I was out of energy. I rode off, exhausted. *Just like Sarah, another one who wants me to raise a kid that's not mine*, I thought, navigating my conflicting emotions along with the grid of Tulsa neighborhoods. *All they want to do is pin me down, take away my freedom.*

I realized she was right, loved her son very much, and I was being selfish. Sometimes, people run around with this impression of themselves as virtuous and good, when really they're just like everyone else, or worse. I was having one of those moments and trying to be honest with myself.

Pulling up at a stoplight, I had a feeling I was being watched. The car that had been behind me for the last few miles pulled up alongside. It was a cop car, and he looked at me, trying to assess my condition, likely assuming I was trashed at this hour. I forced a smile and waved, and he nodded and drove past. I let out a long breath and pulled away slowly behind him.

I couldn't wait to get home to bed. There were only a few hours left until I had to be at work, and I knew I'd be heartsick, exhausted, and hung over all day. I already was all of those things.

8 Holidays

I woke the next morning with a stiff and sore neck, unable to turn my head. It almost caused an accident on the way to work, as I failed to notice someone running a red light to my left. The squeal of her brakes and the sound of rubber sliding against asphalt jacked my heart. It hammered along with my throbbing head.

Kirk arrived at about the same time, gunning the engine of his brand-new pickup truck to make sure I noticed it. I knew I was late, because Kirk always was. He got out and gave a long whistle, admiring my bike.

"Damn, boy, that's a nice bike you got there." He inspected it while I ran the long chain around a light pole and moved the tumblers to release, then close and secure the padlock.

We walked in together as John gave us a disapproving look from his desk. Later that morning, as I was checking in the contents of a delivery, he came over.

"Where's Kirk?" he asked.

"He said he had to make a phone call. He'll be right back." I looked over at his abandoned forklift.

"Listen, Levi. You're a good kid. I sense the Lord is with you. We picked that guy up as somewhat of a project. He was just out of jail and rehab, and we like to give folks a chance. It's the Christian thing to do."

"Don't worry, John. I'm not a fan of Kirk. I just tolerate him."

"What's wrong with your neck, Levi?"

I turned my body to face him. "I slept wrong, I guess. Do we have any aspirin?"

He said he might have some in his desk and went back to look. I continued my work, and noticed John coming back empty-handed, but followed by the gold-dress woman and a few others.

"Brother Levi," John began, "just set still in that chair and let the Lord do his work." He nodded to the woman. "It's his neck."

She spoke from behind me. "Brother Levi, I'm Christine, a prayer partner here in the Village of Prayer, and a pastoral grad student over at Eugene Walters University. Be strong in your faith. Minor troubles such as this can often be solved by asking for the Lord's help."

I had little choice, as she was already behind me. The rest of them spread out in a circle. Kirk returned and climbed up on his forklift, smiling.

She repeated her earlier performance almost verbatim. I noticed she was massaging my neck as she prayed and chanted. Her hands were powerful, and it felt professional, like she had some experience she was leveraging to bring the desired result. I moved my hand up and pressed the Saint Christopher medallion, my talisman, to my heart. I believed in it, and I didn't believe in whatever it was she was doing. After some time, she relaxed her grip.

"Well," John asked excitedly, "how does it feel, brother Levi?"

It was as bad as ever, but I didn't want to let on. I tried to turn my head toward him as much as I could, but the pain was intense. I had to half turn my body to look at him and answer. "Much better. I think I'm good. Praise the Lord. Thank you, Christine."

It was obvious my neck was no better. She must have felt I was making her look bad. She seized my head and neck, this time in a tighter grip, as if to warn me to go along with her con. Launching into the babble of tongues, she raised her voice and commanded healing. When she stopped, the same verification repeated, with the same result.

"He's not a believer," she said as she walked away. The others dispersed, and John looked at me and shook his head before following behind them. I felt bad about disappointing him. Kirk drove off, laughing and shaking his head.

I worked late, picking up some overtime and checking in a ton of medical supplies, enjoying the chance to work alone as the warehouse had emptied. Long after it had turned dark through the few windows we had, I realized I was starving and punched out.

I made my way out of the building, wanting to get home and crash early to recover from the previous night. I was still down about how things had left off with Mary.

Out in the parking lot, I walked toward the usual light pole, head down and lost in thought. As I approached it, I stopped. My bike wasn't tethered. I immediately thought I had gone the wrong way in the massive parking lot surrounding the complex. I scanned all the poles within the visual field. None of them had a bike attached. I checked my bearings and verified I was in the right place.

Rushing up to the pole, I noticed the long steel chain laying curled at the base like a dead snake. Next to it was the padlock, the hatch sprung open. I ran back into the facility, taking the hospital entrance. It was the tallest of the three buildings and faced the lot. I made my way up the elevator and got off on a familiar floor. Each day I replaced and replenished the medical supply carts for the staff in the units there.

A nurse I was familiar with was working at her station near the windows. I'd pointed out the bike to her during some of our conversations and she had admired it. I asked her if she'd seen anything during the day.

"Yeah," she said. "A pickup showed up late afternoon, when I first came on shift. I saw two guys get out and put it in the back. I thought maybe it had broken down, and you were getting it fixed."

I wanted to shout at her for not alerting me. She was sweet, but not the brightest. I realized it wasn't her fault and thanked her for the information. On the long walk home with my thumb out, I retraced the events of the day. Kirk had admired the bike. He had leaned in as I unlocked, then locked the bike to the pole, stupidly exposing the combination. He had stepped away for a long while earlier in the day to make a phone call.

Fucking Kirk, that dirtbag hillbilly.

I vowed to put him on my enemy list, and someday extract retribution, along with the others who had done horrible things to me. I thought about filing a police report, but was nervous about being on their radar, given what happened in New Jersey and Tennessee. Cops made me paranoid each time I saw one, always waiting for Buck to show up and arrest me for something. The motorcycle had cost a few hundred dollars. I vowed to work more overtime and make it back. I loved that bike. It made me feel like I was making progress for a while. It was getting colder, and I was back to hitching. *Somehow, I always end up hitching.*

I learned to time my route around when I knew John was on his way to work, resulting in a 'coincidence' every day where he'd see me with my thumb out. He'd pick me up and take me the rest of the way. After a few days of that, he asked where my bike was.

"Got stolen two weeks ago," I told him. "Right out of the Village of Prayer parking lot, imagine that."

"Oh, Lord, Levi. I assumed it was in the shop. I'm so sorry. Well, don't be down about it. It's all part of the Lord's plan for you."

I knew he was sincere and trying to be helpful, but I wanted to roll down the window and vomit. I wanted to argue, "What if I decide my dog is god and insist that everything that happens henceforth is because she had willed it?" It was insanity, and I was working in a lunatic asylum.

On Friday that week, John called me over as I was preparing to clock out. We were the only two left, Kirk having left presumably to make it to happy hour on time at some redneck bar. John had a serious look on his face, and I thought maybe I was getting fired.

"Levi, I have something to tell you," he started. "My wife and I have been speaking to the Lord and praying on this, and we feel what I'm about to do is what the Lord wants."

"OK," I said, wondering what it could be. *I'm fired.*

He slid open a drawer and pulled out an envelope. "We want you to have this, and buy yourself another motorcycle."

The envelope looked fat and inviting, but I felt bad at once. "Oh, John, thank you so much, but I can't take that. I really appreciate—"

He jumped to his feet in a rage, his face red and twisted. "Son, you do *not* question the will of the Lord!" he shouted. "How dare you question the will of the Lord? He came to us, spoke to us in our home, and guided us in this decision!" He twitched and went into another Tourettes seizure, and there was no one nearby to help. I picked the envelope up from where he had dropped it on the floor.

"I'm sorry, John," I said, following him as he walked in circles, ranting and raving. "I didn't think. Of course, it's the Lord's will. Certainly. I was just being dumb for a minute. Long day, long week, I'm exhausted, John. I'm so sorry. Please calm down."

I guided him back to his desk and got him into the chair as the seizure passed, leaving him out of breath, and slumped back.

"Whew," he said. "Thanks, Levi. That was a bad one. Want a ride home?" It was as if the whole thing hadn't happened.

Relieved, I hastily agreed. On the way, we talked about what type of bike I might get, and where. It made him feel much better.

After he dropped me off, I rushed inside, pulled the envelope from my pocket, and opened it. Five hundred bucks, more than what I had paid for the first bike, and a lot of money.

I went out that weekend and found a small-engine Japanese street bike that would do just fine. On the test drive I was so excited to be riding again I cornered hard around a turn, hit a patch of gravel, and laid it down. Since I was going pretty slow and it had crash guards, it was only minor damage to the bike, a ripped pants leg and bloody knee on my end.

I hoped the seller hadn't seen or heard it happen, since it was just around the corner from his place, and tried to hide the damage to the bike and myself. "I think I'll take it, if you can drop the price a bit," I told him.

"Damn right you will, since you just crashed it," he answered. "The price is firm."

I had lost my leverage, but the price was fair, and I rode off to get it registered.

THANKSGIVING WEEK CAME, and Shayne and Tim arrived, as promised. They rolled up on their big Harley Davidson bikes, upsetting Jean and Buck with the noise. They came out to glare from the front porch as we all hugged and embraced. Shayne was loud by nature, and neither Jean nor Buck liked that, other than when it was in some dive bar. Done enjoying Buck's discomfort and not wanting to upset him further, I moved the guys inside my new place.

We spent some time catching up. After they had warmed up and caught their breath, they went on a booze run, and came back well stocked with food and drink. We gorged on sandwiches and drank well into the night. It was Wednesday, and thankfully there would be no work until Monday because of the holiday.

They teased me relentlessly about my 'rice burner.' I told them what had happened with my dirt bike, and the reaction was immediately to find out where Kirk lived and go raid the place, kick his ass, and get my bike back. I nixed the idea due to needing my job and not wanting to go to jail. *Kicking Kirk's ass would have been great, though.*

The next day was Thanksgiving day, and we realized we had no turkey to eat. Shayne and Tim wanted to hit a local diner or restaurant, but I didn't want to spend the money. I went next door to check in with Barry and Jean. They were already drinking and in the same predicament. Thankfully, Buck was with his family for the holiday, and preparing for hunting season to begin. I wondered if it was a deer or me he had his sights set on.

We rode to the convenience store in formation. We found a pile of frozen turkey TV dinners and bought them all, along with more beer and bags of assorted chips and pretzels. Back at the house we invited Barry and Jean over and we all spent the day drinking, watching football on the color TV they lugged over, and feasting on those TV dinners, with the bright red cranberries all bled into the cardboard-tasting mashed potatoes. It was delicious, and one of the best Thanksgivings I've ever had. When you're poor, good company and laughter make for just as good a holiday as any mansion and gourmet dinner. *It's the people that count the most.*

The next day, Shayne pulled me aside. "Look, man. Tim's got a problem. He screwed some slut at the campground we stayed at in Virginia, and thinks he has the clap, and it's getting worse. He's kind of embarrassed, so keep it on the down low. Don't you work at some hospital?"

I laughed and told him about the Village of Prayer and how it worked. "They'll treat you, even if you don't have money or insurance," I said. He thanked me and said he'd talk to Tim about it. A while later, I saw Tim leave on his bike.

It was a sunny, warm day, so we all assembled on the porch on our side of the duplex, given the steep slant on Barry and Jean's side. Some neighborhood kids threw a football around on the street, so we joined them for a fun game of touch, then listened to music and chatted casually. Barry and Jean inquired a few times about where Tim was, and we lied about it.

A few hours later, he came roaring up, bouncing over the tiny front lawn in front of us. He cut the engine, threw the kickstand down, flipped his half-shell helmet to the ground, and stomped half-way up the steps to the porch.

"Uh-oh," Shayne said.

"What the *fuck*?" Tim demanded. "What the *fuck* kind of whacked-out place did you send me to? Some dude in a gold coat made me pray with him while he put his hands on my dick before they'd give me a shot of penicillin."

Barry launched into a giggle-fit and we all laughed hard, imagining the scene. After the uproar died down, Jean said she might head over to the Village of Prayer for some of that crotch action, and it all started again.

The weekend passed by too fast and my friends headed back to New Jersey. I became wistful watching them go down the road on their bikes, wearing backpacks, sleeping bags tied under the handlebars, off to the road ahead. Even though I spent far more time hitching, I preferred to travel on a motorcycle. It felt like real freedom going down a highway with the wind in your hair, with no worries of cops or predators. I was getting the itch to get back on the road. It always happened after a while.

SOON AFTER CAME THE news that John Lennon had died. It made me sad, because of all the good he stood for. We were in a dangerous, scary cold war with Russia—the very reason for the underground missile silos I'd worked in on the desolate areas of the military base we called the bomb dump. Humanity was quickly getting to where one rogue maniac could end it all for our species.

We went into the Christmas season, which intensified as every day went past. It meant far more religiosity at the Village of Prayer, making each day harder. I noted families with small children out shopping for Christmas trees, kids excitedly pointing out their preferred toys in the stores and sitting on Santa's lap. Parents my age and Carla's age smiled and beamed with pride. The holiday music was on a loop in the donut shop, so I had no escape from it.

The semester ended, my occasional visits and chats with Mary along with it. We hadn't really connected after what happened, but we talked often as friends. Everything changes when a kid comes into the picture. It's an enormous commitment, and I didn't feel up to it. But I had fallen in love with her, making it difficult to be around her, and more so when I saw other guys chatting her up and hitting on her. I poured my time into working and saving my money for whatever would come next.

It was a joyful time of year, but everything became intolerable. I had a phone line installed, so Sarah called once in a while, and sent pictures of the baby on Santa's lap. I wondered how Carla was doing, and spent my little spare time on the front porch alone, writing and thinking about what I wanted out of life. Mom called too, and we talked about that together.

On one night off, I found myself under the dim, flickering porch light flipping through the few pictures I carried. I stopped on one of me and Carla, smiling on the beach when we had ditched school the day after prom and gone down to the shore with a few friends. It was a carefree time in life, when all things were still possible.

I thought back to the first time we connected. She had come over to me as I ate my lunch alone, a pathetic figure in the corner of the high school cafeteria at the start of junior year. I hadn't hit my growth spurt yet and always ate fast, always nervous someone would come over. It never ended well when they did. I pulled off my thick, bandaged glasses and looked down at my plate, letting my long bangs hang cover my face.

"Look up," she said.

I kept eating, hoping she'd give up and go away, and waited to hear the students laughing at her stunt. I was sure she was there to get credibility by goofing on me, as others did.

"Look up," she said.

I usually never let my food touch, but I scraped the peas into the mashed potatoes in a hurry, trying to finish. The song *Please Go All the Way* was playing on the cafeteria juke box. I always wished I could sing it to some girl while we were making out in the car I didn't have yet.

"Levi, look up," she persisted. It kind of sounded authentic, so I did what she asked.

"What?" I asked, trying to not show my braces or blush. Out of all the non-clique girls in the school, she was the prettiest. I could never figure out why she didn't hang out with the hotshots. "Are you going to rank on me to make the cool kids laugh?"

She pushed my bangs aside and looked at me like a math problem she was trying to solve. "No, I need a project. And you need contacts."

So that's how it started. She fixed me up; I got the contacts; the braces came off a few months later, and we started going out. Love took me like a huge python, slow and steady. It was more than I ever dreamed it would be. We made a lot of promises to each other back then, and we were inseparable for two years. We learned to be intimate with each other, and we learned to be careful.

I graduated and went into the military. Carla promised to wait for me, and we planned to go to college together after I got out. She started her senior year, and it wasn't long before I got a letter that she was going to the homecoming formal dance with some goober on the football team.

I put the picture away and went inside to get ready for bed.

THE DAY BEFORE CHRISTMAS, I got a huge package from home. Rather than open it immediately, I used rare restraint and placed it under the scrawny tree I had bought. It was the only present there. I considered not immediately opening the gift box an achievement, hopefully a sign I was growing up. I had always been a Christmas-gift bloodhound, sniffing them out early, in secret, no matter where my mom would hide them. My younger sisters paid me bounties to find and disclose theirs. The holidays were always a time of great anticipation, excitement, and bonding with family and friends. I missed it, so far away and alone.

I woke early on Christmas day and made coffee, eying my treasure beneath the tree. I put on the local radio station, and it was playing all the great holiday songs. Eventually, I gave in and settled on the cold wooden floor in front of the package. Dad was a shipping man as well, so he had carefully taped it together and wrote the address label in his neat print. I missed him and thought we could get along better if I ever went back.

Inside the shipping box were gifts wrapped in bright holiday paper. They wrapped a few in Sunday comic strips, the one day they were in color. Those were from Dad. It was a thing we always did, our thing. After I'd turned eighteen and was legal to buy booze, we always gave each other a case of fancy beer we wouldn't otherwise buy, wrapped in those comics, and we always enjoyed it together during our holiday cease-fire.

The more sloppily wrapped gifts were from my sisters, who had always insisted on wrapping their own presents, no matter how bad it went. I savored each one as I unwrapped them to the symphony of music we'd always all enjoyed on this day, and tears came steadily.

There were clothes I needed, all my favorite candies, wonderful cards with hand-written, sincere messages of love scrawled on them. *They wrote 'we miss you' on each.* The last present I opened was from Dad. It was a large fold-out buck knife. He knew I liked them, but he had no way of knowing how much I needed a replacement for the lost bayonet, since I felt naked without it. *Parental instinct.*

I felt sad and angry about my situation, and wondered if this mission I was on about freedom was worth giving all that up. I went to the kitchen and poured a tall glass of eggnog with an ample dose of rum.

After relaxing on the couch, staring up at my water-stained ceiling for a while, the phone rang. I talked to the family, with the same holiday music playing in the background back at home. The house likely smelled of fresh-baked cookies, Mom's huge Christmas breakfast of sizzling bacon, sausages, and eggs, and kiddie perfumes my sisters had received. I could hear them still opening gifts, shouting excitedly at each one. After they had worked their way through the stack, my conversations with them were the most heartbreaking. *Some big brother you are.*

My thoughts shifted to the man in Tennessee, and I wondered if his family somewhere were hoping he'd come through the door in a Christmas surprise, maybe having found Christ. Because of what I'd done, I realized it was quite possible that I'd have to stay on the road forever, running to stay one step ahead of the law and life in prison. I realized that in my pursuit of freedom, as in a Shakespearean tragedy, I might never be able to go home again. *Be careful what you wish for.*

I spent the rest of the day with Barry and Jean, drinking and watching holiday movies on his TV. It was our own little Yankee expatriate clan. I sensed the sadness and longing in them as well, and we all eventually got around to talking about it as evening fell. They were missing home, too.

I told them about Thomas Wolfe's novel *You Can't Go Home Again*, and how the main character was a writer who wrote a book about his hometown. When he returned, having missed it, they treated him with hatred due to how he had portrayed it in his book, and forced him to leave.

"Well, that's a buzz kill," Jean said. "Whatever the fuck you're always writing in those notebooks, keep me the hell out of it."

"Me too," Barry said, giggling through the exhale of a joint. "I'm in the closet."

"You're in the closet like I'm Marilyn fucking Monroe," Jean said.

We all laughed at the comment, Barry the hardest.

We repeated our Thanksgiving feast of foil-wrapped turkey TV dinners, but it was a whole different vibe than the one a month ago. Shayne wasn't around to keep everyone laughing. I was no good at it, and not in the mood. None of us were, and the food tasted especially bad.

Jean crashed early, leaving Barry and I to sit and talk, the music muted and low by then. I brought up something that had been worrying me.

"I heard about some new disease that's killing gay men," I said.

"Yeah, AIDS. It's been happening here, because of the large gay community. We had a few patients at the hospital already."

"Aren't you worried?"

"Scared shitless, Levi. Wouldn't you be? Are you worried about being around me?"

I took his hand over the tabletop. "Fuck that, Barry. You know me better by now. Just be careful, please. Be safe until they find some kind of preventative or cure. We have some damn smart doctors and scientists."

He sighed. "Yeah, we sure do. But nobody gives a shit. It's just us gay people. A lot more people will be happy to be rid of us. They say it's God's will."

"You'll be OK, Barry. Just be careful." He cried, and I stood up to hold him before we each went off to bed, the night and our Christmas ending in sadness.

THE MOROSE CONTINUED, and I went on a bender in that sagging week between Christmas and New Year's Day. It culminated on the big night, New Year's Eve, which was a Wednesday. I had work the next day, but went out to the gay clubs with Barry and his crew.

We got in at three in the morning, and I woke up late after having hit my snooze alarm several times without even remembering it. I scrambled up, splashed icy cold water on my face, put on my work shirt with my name embroidered on my chest.

Work was fortunately slow, as the key staff were off for the holiday. I had volunteered to cover, having nowhere to go, and preferring to get paid instead.

I refilled the medical supply carts slowly, exhausted and my head throbbing. I hadn't shaved in a few days and was trying to keep out of sight. The booze that still reeked on my breath was making me sick, and wouldn't go away no matter how many sodas I coaxed from the machine with my loose change. I even pulled some small bottles of mouthwash from the supply carts and tried those, to no avail.

The last task I had to accomplish was to get the full carts to the nursing floors high above. I made a few trips up the golden elevators, hiding behind them while wheeling them to their position on the floors and bringing the empty ones back down. With the light traffic, my trips were express, nobody getting on and off on various floors like they usually did.

On the last trip up, the elevator began whizzing through its chute; the acceleration making me nauseous. Then it slowed, and I checked the panel. The button was lit for floor seven. *Oh, shit.* As it slowed to a stop, I pulled the tall medical cart to the side and hid behind it in the corner. The seventh floor comprised the executive offices—the suits, the bigwigs.

I heard a few men and women enter, chatting about the facility as if giving a tour to someone important. They described the new MRI equipment they were about to show off on an upper floor. My heart felt as if it had stopped when they called him brother Eugene. I suppressed a belch, shifting uncomfortably behind the cart. As the doors closed and the elevator lifted off again, they ran out of things to say.

A moment later, one of them said, "Who's back there? Come on out and meet someone special."

I pushed the cart forward a touch to make some room and emerged in my rumpled clothes. There stood the man, the myth, the legend. I didn't know what to say, and therefore, I remained silent. He seemed to glow with some faint aura, as celebrities always did in person. I knew it was a psychological effect, our tendency to elevate and revere such people, even though in almost all cases they weren't worthy of it and were, in fact, worse people than us normal folk. *Pay no attention to that man behind the curtain.*

His hosts looked at one another disapprovingly, and I knew they could smell the booze on me. They could certainly see that I was unshaven, and my clothes rumpled. The place had a strict dress code, as it was new, and everything shone with that newness.

"Well," he said, leaning forward to read my nameplate. "Levi. Do you know the Biblical significance of that name, son?" he asked. I knew it was a test, and I knew the answer, but it wouldn't come to my booze-addled brain.

"I do, sir, but it escapes me at the moment," I confessed.

"Levi," he said, elevating his voice, displeased. "Son of Jacob and Leah. Book of Genesis, and Moses' great-grandfather. Time to get back to your studies, Levi," he further admonished.

They reached their floor, and the group stepped off. As the tour leader began pointing out features to brother Eugene, the other suits looked back at my nameplate once more, shaking their heads at me. I knew at that moment my time in Tulsa was coming to a close.

I called in sick the next day, and spent the weekend drinking, sulking, and wondering what was ahead. Barry and Jean were already making plans to head back north for the spring. Despite my bravado about freedom and individualism, I couldn't imagine being there alone without them to talk to.

As soon as I clocked in on Monday, John called me over to his desk. "I heard you ran into brother Eugene," he said. He looked at me with grim but sad eyes, as if I were a son that had let him down by being gay or committing some horrible crime. "How could that happen, Levi?"

I told him I had no excuse, and that I was going through a bad time. I saw Kirk lurking a row behind him on his forklift, eavesdropping with pleasure. "Well, Levi, the facility manager wants to see you in the office." He sighed and gestured toward the administrative area.

I got up without a word and began my walk of shame. Just before I reached the entrance, Kirk pulled up. "Damn boy, you sure fucked up, didn't ya?"

"Fuck you, Kirk. You took my bike, and someday, motherfucker, I'm coming for you, when you least expect it." I hadn't wanted to tip him off; I rarely did that for anyone on my list of retribution.

I went in and reported to the general manager's secretary. She made me sit and wait until his meeting was over. It reminded me of a similar scene, when I had sat outside the base commander's office, awaiting a similar fate. The word was out and everyone stared at me and whispered as I sat there, waiting to be fired. *So much for all that forgiveness that Jesus had talked about.*

The conversation was brief, and frankly, I've forgotten what he said. It's not important, and all I recall is that it was what I had expected. On the way out, I exchanged a heartfelt hug with John, and flipped Kirk the bird.

9 Katie

I picked up extra shifts at the donut shop, but it only paid half of what I was making at the Village of Prayer. I gave the landlord thirty days' notice and planned my next move.

Since my phone would be disconnected soon, I took full advantage of it, making calls to everyone I thought could help me. I rang up Diego Takata, my old military friend and roommate, who was out as well and living back home in San Antonio.

"Levi, man," he answered in his long Tex-Mex drawl. "How you doing, bro?" It was good to hear his voice again. Along with Damon, the other member of our informal group, we had raised some hell during the three years we'd been together. One white, one Mexican, one African-American, and nobody else liked us much, unless we were selling them strong weed, pills, or hallucinogens. Diego was instrumental in that endeavor, often ferrying product to us when he made trips to see family in Acapulco.

I described the entire ordeal to him in summary and told him I was looking for a place to live and work for a while.

"Ah, shit, brother. You know, well, Lucille and I are getting married soon and shit. We're gonna have a kid, man, and we're working a lot. Besides, she really doesn't put up with any crap. She's a *tough* lady. I don't drink hardly at all. We're still here at my parents' place, but we'll be buying a home soon. We all have to grow up sometime, right, brother?"

I got the message loud and clear. We reminisced for a while, relived some old war stories, Diego speaking in a whisper about those events. I pictured him hiding in a closet, out of earshot of his nemesis. We ended the call cordially, a mutual understanding between us. He had moved on, and I accepted it because I loved him like a brother, and wanted the best for him. *And none of the misery I was experiencing.*

I sat at my sparse kitchen table and wrote notes about the call. It was the only chair within reach of the long coiled cord from the phone handset to the wall mount. I thought about Diego, the wild man, now settled down, cradling a baby, going to work every day, worrying about bills. He's be doing that for the rest of his life, pretty much. His tone with me felt condescending, and I felt bad about it for a while.

The phone rang as I was eating lunch at the table. I reached back, tipping the chair to its limits, and pulled the handset off the wall. Before I could get a word in, a stream of loud dialog flew out of it.

"Yo, Levi, man! Damon Q Green reporting in here, Airman Green, you know, right? Diego called and said you need help. I'm doing my thing here in Charlottesville, old Virginny. I'm out of Ohio, man, I left. Back on *tour*, brother. Black dude can't make it there, too many white-trash redneck muhfuckers, and it's *cold*, Levi. Shit. C-Ville's where it's at, Levi. Big college town, so plenty of work and great drugs. Plenty of poon-tang. You know what I'm sayin', Levi? Educated people, too. I'm staying with my friend Carl and his old lady. They're law students and they're *cool*, Levi. Cool as hell. They got a basement place. I call it the submarine, Levi. Cool as hell. Come out, Levi! Hello, C-Ville calling! Ronnie Raygun won, he's going to be busting unions, he's a white supremacist racist mofo." He took a breath, finally, then added, "How you doing, Levi?"

I had missed his enthusiasm. As a fellow Gemini, he was usually very up or very down. I'd seen the guy weather all sorts of brutal treatment and discrimination, just because of his skin color. After growing up in the white suburbs, it woke me up to the reality of racism—something we had always dismissed as 'complaining' from our lofty stature as the entitled suburban demographic.

I gave him the same status update as I had given Diego, but Damon marveled and reveled at each of the events that had transpired. I didn't tell him about Tennessee, and I hadn't told Diego. They were my best friends in the world, brothers, along with Shayne, but I knew I wouldn't ever tell anyone. Not for a long time, anyway. Maybe, someday, I'd put it in a murder story or something, just to get it out of my system. That kind of thing is a heavy burden to carry, and the longer you do, the heavier it gets. Like a slow-feeding cancer, it changes someone. I finally understood the hollowness and emptiness that I'd seen in the Viet Nam vets I served with in the military. I knew if I confessed to him, Damon was one person who would understand.

When we were in the military, he began growing weed in the apartment he shared with his girlfriend. Diego and I got a place a block away, finally moving out of the barracks and off-base, a monumental achievement for a low-rank enlisted man. Damon was proud of one of his plants and potted it to ride over on his bicycle to show us. He never made it, as he had the misfortune to pass a traffic policeman. The local cop turned him in to the base military police and he did a stint at Leavenworth for something so small. I had always thought that if it were me, a clean-cut white military guy, the cop probably would have laughed it off and sent me on my way. At worse, he'd have taken the weed for himself.

Damon told me he had talked to his roommates, and I'd be welcome any time. Then he got to the catch. He was a hustler, always looking for an angle. It wasn't a bad thing; it was a survival instinct, and I was no different. When everything is harder because of who you are and how you look, you have to try harder to get where you want to go. "So listen, Levi. I don't know if you're going through St. Louis, but my ex-old lady Katie is there, and she wants to come out too, but she's been out of work. She has a car, so you could drive the rest of the way. I've been trying to get her out here. Maybe this is it, right? That would be cool, Levi. Can you help a brother out?"

I ended the call by telling him I had some thinking to do, and I'd let him know. In reality, I had already decided. Like Shayne, his enthusiasm was infectious and what I needed at that point. I needed a change. The four of us always helped each other, and I owed them all for the many times they'd helped me.

Charlottesville had seemed inviting as I passed through on the way to Tulsa. I remembered thinking about the university there, and dreaming about what a college town would be like. I wouldn't be a student. A place like that would deplete my GI benefits in a hurry, but I could at least be in the environment and soak it up. *Maybe take one writing class.* I'd be closer to home and have a good friend to confide in and hang out with—something I never had in Tulsa.

I grabbed my long-neglected road atlas from the drawer of my little writing desk and traced routes. The same southern route I had come out on made sense—it would be warmer. The thought of Tennessee again made no sense, though. I could very well be a wanted man there, and through reporting, to the neighboring states. *For murder.* It still tempted me to go through Memphis and Nashville, and take some time to explore them and listen to great music, but was going to have to wait (again) for another time. *After the statute of limitations expires.*

Tracing the northern route up I-44 with my finger, I became convinced it was the way to go. I had never been through St. Louis, and wanted to see the great silver Gateway Arch. Kentucky and West Virginia scared me for the same reasons Tennessee did, but by then we'd be in Katie's car and breeze through those danger zones. I wondered what she looked like. With Damon, you never knew what to expect. Diego as well. One of our favorite forms of entertainment was to get up early on Sunday mornings to see what form of beast might emerge from Diego's room, confused and wondering where she was, greeted by us sitting there in amazement hitting from a bong and eating my world-famous French toast.

The plan formed day by day, and it rejuvenated me. My small bike was no good for the highway and long stretches in the saddle. I sold it, along with the furniture, piece by piece, until it was just me and the mattress on the floor for my last days in Tulsa, Oklahoma. I used the money to buy warm clothes for the trip, and build up a nice bankroll to hide in my pack.

The night before I left, Jean was at work, so Barry and I drank a case of beer together. Around two in the morning, I resolved to satisfy my one piece of unfinished business there. I had him drive me to the convenience store, where I bought a few gallons of bleach. We then went out into the boonies, where I had him stop a half-mile from Kirk's house. I had stolen the address from Joe's desk before I had left. I walked down the dirt driveway and saw his beloved new pickup truck sitting in the dark. After unscrewing the gas cap, I deposited the full containers of bleach and replaced it. We drove back in silence, and I told Barry to never mention it to anyone.

The following morning, I made sure the duplex was spotless, and looked over it one more time before picking up my backpack and locking the door behind me. Barry gave me a lift to the entrance ramp to I-44. Jean even got up early, a rare thing for a Saturday, and came along. We said a tearful goodbye, and I thanked them profusely for their help and getting me started there. Jean even asked if I might stay a little longer.

After I watched them pull away, I took a moment to wonder what I'd accomplished, exactly, during my time In Tulsa. *Not much. It was life; an experience. It was freedom.*

I put my thumb out, now cautious to stay on the on-ramps after the encounter with the Tennessee State Trooper. It seems counter-intuitive to hitchhike in the cold, but in fact, it was easier. Folks were much more likely to be sympathetic about some poor wretch out in the elements, looking for a ride somewhere. When they stopped, getting into the warm vehicles was an incredible feeling, the warmth of it and their generosity.

I pulled trucker rides up through Cherokee nation, across the Missouri border into Joplin, and up to Springfield. The weather had been nice, considering it was winter. It was one of those trips where it felt like someone had greased the rails for me and I was making good progress. The trucks weren't always tractor-trailers. Sometimes it was big box delivery trucks, the drivers bored and wanting companionship, to learn and dream about having freedom for themselves someday.

Every so often, after a truck-stop meal, I'd check in with Damon and then call Katie, to give them status updates. I passed through the northern end of the majestic Mark Twain National Forest and replayed his novels and characters in my head as I took in the beautiful scenery. I wondered if someday I'd be able to touch people's lives the way he had with his words, and I felt a long way from that.

An African-American salesman said he was going to Sullivan, Missouri, just off the highway. I consulted my atlas and found it was just below St. Louis. I was confident about making it to Katie's by nightfall and was starving, as it was well past lunchtime. He would deliver me into the town, hoping to splurge and celebrate my progress with an enormous meal.

As we took the exit, I noticed a sign by the roadside. *Whites only within city limits after dark*, it proclaimed. "What the fuck is that about?" I asked him, incredulous.

"You're still in the south, white boy," he said, laughing. "It's called a *sundown town* and there's still a lot of them. These motherfuckers are still fighting the war over slavery. Check it out—you'll see more confederate flags than US flags." I thanked him when he dropped me off and found a great BBQ rib joint for lunch.

As I ate the delicious food, I looked around the dining room. Everyone was white and way overweight except myself and the young waitress behind the counter. I imagined the stares if the black salesman had walked in to eat. It was amazing, given all that had happened in the 1960s for civil rights, and people like Reverend Martin Luther King who had died, that it was still this way.

I called Katie to let her know I was close. She advised me to stand by and said she'd come and get me. We agreed on a time to meet outside the restaurant. She said she was a little more than an hour away, but had to get dressed first, so make it two hours. *Who takes an hour to get dressed?* I again wondered what I was in for. I didn't enjoy traveling companions, but a ride was a ride and her car would make the rest of the trip easy.

I left the restaurant and looked for a place to have a beer. After walking into two taverns on the same street and receiving dirty looks and comments about my hair, I spotted a place with a few black folks loitering outside.

"You think I could get a beer in there?" I asked them, motioning to the entrance. "Rednecks won't have me in the white places."

They looked at each other and laughed. "Welcome to our world, white hippie boy. Can't guarantee your safety in there. Depends on how you handle yourself pretty much. I'd be polite, tip well, and keep your head down. Might go OK. Might not."

I went inside to the stares I had imagined the salesman might get in the rib place. It was quiet, with just a few patrons scattered at the bar and tables nearby. I picked an empty spot at the bar, dropped my pack, and slid onto a stool. The young black woman tending bar looked my way, did a double take, then continued washing out mugs.

I waited her out, and after she realized I wasn't going away, she came over. "Well, look at you. New in town?"

"Yeah," I answered. "I didn't quite fit in when I went to the other places on the block."

"You ain't fitting in here either. We try to keep a low profile, and you, being in here, would draw the law. Anything out of place draws the law."

"I don't fit in too many places. I'd just like a cold draft, if that's OK."

She nodded and brought it, demanding payment immediately. I fished double the price from my wallet and told her to keep it. She smiled and said, "Now you fitting in just fine, white boy." She kept the drinks coming and gave me a free shot of bourbon.

I wandered to the silent jukebox and found it full of the great electric blues that Damon had taught me about. I dropped a few quarters in and set up a playlist of Buddy Guy and Junior Wells, Little Walter, Muddy Waters, and Sonny Boy Williamson I and II.

By the time I had made my selections and made it back to my seat, a few patrons were coming to life. "That's right, that's the stuff, whitey!" they yelled, dancing alone on the open floor. "Turn that shit up, Belle," one demanded of the bartender, and she complied with excess.

Another shot waited for me at the bar, and I threw it down. The girl came out from behind the bar and grabbed my hand, yanking me up to dance with her. I bought a round for the place and felt like an instant celebrity. It was spontaneous joy, everyone forgetting their problems for a while.

The party continued, getting louder, drawing more people, until I looked at the clock above the bar. *Oh, shit.* I left my change and ran outside as the sun was setting, looking up and down the street for Katie. She hadn't described herself, but I told her what I was wearing and looked like.

I stood there outside the bar, my new friends egging me on to come back inside, tempted, wondering if I'd blown the ride with her, when a car pulled up to the curb. A guy was driving, and a girl sat looking out the passenger window. She motioned me into the back seat.

"Levi, are you fucking crazy, hanging out in that nigger place?" she asked. "You know you're in Missouri, not New Jersey, right?"

"Hello to you too, Katie. It's the only place that would accept me," I said as I boarded the vehicle. The comment was surprising, given she was going to be with Damon. Her driver glared at me from the rearview mirror. We weren't off to a good start at all.

She introduced him as Mac, "a friend." It was apparent that he was or wanted to be more than just a friend. He never said a word to me, just cast dirty looks, and dropped us off at her parents' nice, upper-middle class place in the St. Louis suburbs. *Rebellious rich girl.*

"They're off on vacation somewhere, again," she said, showing me in. "Real entitled assholes. I can't wait to get out of here."

We sat in the comfortable living room. I sank into a plush sofa that seemed to embrace me. The earlier buzz was wearing off, and I wanted to crash. She went into the kitchen and came back with two cold beers and some snacks. I guessed she was about nineteen, not long out of high school. She looked and spoke roughly, despite her youth. I guessed she had run with a tough crowd in school and I knew she wouldn't stay that slim and pretty for long.

"So where do you know Damon from?" I opened as she sat next to me and placed the snacks on the coffee table in front of us. She created a dramatic pause and took time to fish a pack of cigarettes from her purse and light up. *Great, Damon didn't tell me about this.*

"Met him in a club in St. Louis. He was visiting family there just after he got out of the military with you. He's different from most black dudes, so he caught my attention."

"That's for sure," I added.

"He's told me a lot about you, Levi. He read a bunch of your letters to me, great stuff. I read all Kerouac's books."

"Yeah, he was an amazing writer." *Great, another Kerouac wannabe.* He was a literary hero of mine, and I'd read everything he'd written. But the people that set out to *be* him were often just posers, and not cut out for it. I felt I was doing a completely distinct thing, although in search of the same goal: freedom. In many ways, he wasn't someone to idolize. It was the same with so many influential writers, athletes, entertainers, politicians, and other would-be heroes.

She kept bringing beer, and I was getting drunk again. I lit a joint to take the edge off, and we shared it. Each time she passed it back to me, she edged closer on the sofa, until she was placing her hand on my knee each time she emphatically made a point.

Finally, she made a big act out of pretending to fall over and put her hand on my crotch to catch herself, and left it there, squeezing softly. "Oh, excuse me," she said, leaning in for a kiss.

"I can't," I responded, lifting her hand, but holding it. "He's one of my best friends. We've been through a lot. We fought for each other constantly. You're pretty, but I can't."

She yanked her hand back. "Oh, fuck. Goody two-shoes here. Jesus fuck, Levi. You'll change your mind. They always do. Unless you're gay."

"I assure you I'm not, Katie. It's just a matter of principle. I've done enough damage in my life. I have enough to feel bad about."

"That's your problem, hon. Feeling bad. You only get one life. Isn't that what you say in your letters all the time?"

"Yeah, and I'd rather not live it with any more regret and guilt. It's a buzz kill." I changed the subject. "So, how about I check your car over for the trip tomorrow?" I offered. "I'll go through the fluids, check the tire pressure, and go fill the tank."

"Car?" she said, laughing. "Damon didn't tell you? I wrecked that fucker recently. DUI. That's why they're kicking me out of the house. But I'm damn excited to be out hitching with a pro like you. You'll be Sal Paradise and I'll be Neal Cassady with tits."

Fucking Damon. I immediately began scheming for a way out. In no way did I want to be hitching with someone else, let alone this inexperienced lunatic. I hated pretentious people, the ones who always acted like they were the star of some TV show or movie. I figured I'd get some sleep and sneak out before she got up in the morning.

"Well, it's gonna be a long day tomorrow, and damn cold, too. I'm going to crash, if it's OK. You should too."

She agreed, yawning. After showing me where the bathroom and guest room were, she went upstairs to her own bedroom. It was still pretty early, and even though I was tired, I couldn't resist the huge, gleaming bathtub. I filled it with hot, soapy water and settled in with my book.

The door opened, and she came in with a white towel around her. She dropped it ceremoniously and slipped into the other side of the tub, facing me. "I don't like this," I said immediately.

She sighed. "Yes, you do. We're just cleaning up for tomorrow. I thought you were a fucking hippie, Levi? Didn't you watch *Woodstock*? Hippies bathe together. It's no big deal. Calm down. Don't be a prude. Did those religious wackos you were working for damage your brain?"

The overhead lights shone off her wet body. She stimulated me, and thankfully I'd added lots of soap. She ran her foot up between my legs playfully, teasing, tormenting, as she yammered on about her life. We made small talk until she got bored and stepped out, making a show of her body. I didn't look away. She looked amazing, perfectly toned and not hiding a thing.

When sleep took me, not wanting to drown and die there, I drained the tub, toweled off, and got into the comfortable bed naked. It felt like heaven and I passed out immediately.

In the night, I heard a noise and before I could react, she was under the covers with me, wearing only a lacy bottom. She crawled onto me, her breasts pressed against my chest, her mouth against me, and her hand on me. I was already hard, from a dream, I guessed; probably about her or Carla. For any man, this was the point of no return, and it was for me. *The spirit is willing, but the flesh is weak.*

She tried to mount me. "No. I told you no." I pushed her off.

"Fine," she said, her hand still on me, massaging, stroking. I didn't push it away, and she knew what that meant. She went down on me and I let her, to my shame. When it was done, I rolled over, disgusted with myself, to face the wall.

"I knew you'd give in," she said with a laugh. "You gonna tell Damon?"

"Probably," I said. "It shouldn't have happened."

"I'm not married to him, Levi. We're not even dating. I just need a place to stay, and he invited me out. There's no commitment." I noted her response, and I'd be sure to fill him in.

"It's more than that, Katie. It's an implicit commitment. You know it."

"Stop with the big words, Einstein. Stop trying to be Jesus. Damon and I have different rules."

"And I know him far better than you do. This will hurt him." She was already asleep, having succeeded.

I woke again before daylight, and she nuzzled against me. She was pulling me in. I felt myself wanting badly to make love to her. To save myself, I wondered how I'd feel if I'd found that Damon had made love to Carla, or Sarah, or Mary. The thought made me sick, and I eased out of the bed, ready to escape alone.

I was almost at the door when I heard her call, "Hold up!" I had to wait while she dressed and grabbed the pack she had prepared. She locked up behind us as we set out on the road together.

10 Submarine

The rides were slow, as they always were when hitching in tandem, even with a pretty girl. Despite our warm gear, we were cold, and she was getting frustrated. We had crossed the mighty Mississippi River at the start of the trip, and I had seen the beautiful Gateway Arch. It took us until early afternoon to get across the border into Evansville, Indiana. If we'd been driving, as we should have been, it would only have taken a couple of hours. I cursed her deception again. The rides were pedestrian and choppy, an exit or two at a time.

To make things worse, she was annoying everyone that picked us up, talking non-stop and putting on an act. It led to early drop-offs with feigned excuses from our rides. She saw a town called Santa Claus and wouldn't shut up about it, launching into exaggerated story after story about her childhood.

We got dropped off near Leavenworth, in the Hoosier National Forest, just short of Louisville, Kentucky. We took a break and sat off I-64 under hemlock trees to eat supplies we'd taken from her parents' pantry.

"This is where Damon was," she said. "He told me about it."

"No," I corrected her. "The military prison is in Leavenworth, Kansas." She always took it personally when I corrected her. I took pleasure in it, as I did when I corrected the snotty BMW driver about Roanoke. In just twenty-four hours, we had gotten past the sex and honeymoon period and were bickering like an old married couple. The road sped up everything.

"You know, Levi, you're a real fucking narcissist. Just full of yourself, aren't you?"

I thought about it for a moment and grudgingly agreed. "Sure. Guilty as charged. But there's a reason for it—survival. I spent my entire childhood being told I was weak, stupid, and not good enough. I believed it. Why not, right? Everyone around me seemed to send that message implicitly or explicitly. Then someone came along and saved me; showed me that if I didn't believe in myself, I'd spend my entire life like that, a self-pitying wretch. If someone says you're shit, you can either believe them or believe in yourself."

She got angry and stood up. "Fuck this, Levi. I'm cold. It's taking too long to get there."

I became hopeful she was going to bail out, maybe cross the highway and start back toward St. Louis on the other side. I thought about offering her bus fare and escorting her to the station in town. It surprised me. I thought she was tough enough to endure. She certainly acted like it.

She took her pack and walked behind the trees. I waited, hearing rustling, cursing, and she eventually emerged. She had changed into cowboy boots, a miniskirt, and tube top under a high-cut denim jacket that exposed her small waist.

"Stay here, stay back," she said, advancing back to the shoulder of the highway. *What the fuck...* I positioned my backpack behind my head as a pillow and lay back to enjoy the show. I wasn't out of sight, but not exactly visible, either. She was out there, next to the highway, one smooth leg extended with her thumb out toward the road.

Sure enough, the first truck that went by screeched past and wound down to a stop, retarders rattling and brake lights flaring like the nostrils of an excited bull. I picked up my pack and ran, worried she'd get inside and tell the driver to leave me behind.

I beat her to the cab. "Hold up," I said. "I need to make sure it's safe." I climbed up and opened the side door. "Two of us, that OK?" I asked the driver. He was a middle-age black dude, clearly disappointed.

He motioned to the sleeper cab behind him. "Sure, you can grab the back. Let the girl set up here with me."

I crawled in, and she followed me up, taking the passenger seat. She filled him in on where we were heading and demanded he turn the heat full blast. I heard him say he could get us to Charleston, West Virginia, about halfway to Charlottesville. *Great, hitching in hillbilly country again, with a woman this time.* I laid back in the sleeper as she went to work talking his ear off. I learned to grab sleep when I could while hitching, because you never knew how long and hard the night was going to be.

The truck swerved, rousing me from my nap. I peeked into the cab and saw her leaning across, her head in the driver's lap, bobbing up and down. She was doing her thing, and it disgusted me. I laid back again and used his pillow to cover the sound.

Unable to get back to sleep, I heard them talking after a while, signaling it was over. I slid open the curtain that separated the sleeper from the cab.

"Good evening, sunshine," the trucker said. He had changed his tone dramatically.

I noted our location. It was early evening, and we'd run clear through Kentucky, thankfully, and crossed into West Virginia. I began seeing signs for Charleston, our halfway point.

"Guess what, Levi? He's going to take us *all* the way to Charlottesville!" she proudly announced. "I talked him into it!" *Sure you did.*

Truckers were smart. They knew the road life, and how dangerous it could be. They always started by saying they could take you a short distance, making some excuse, and would only agree later to extend if they were comfortable with you. She had made him very comfortable.

We had made several pit stops at truck stops, where he would take her in and show her off to his peers. I went by myself, used the bathroom, and occasionally stole something to eat. I was careful to monitor them, so they wouldn't leave me. Katie had changed back into layers of comfortable clothes. I still wasn't sure what she was capable of. Back in the truck and on the road, it was getting dark, and I heard him telling her we'd have to pull over and bunk up for the night.

"Ol' Levi can sleep up here, and you and I can sleep in the back," he told her. It was clear what he was angling for. She was ambivalent, probably stringing him along to squeeze more miles out of it, but I let them know I wasn't down with the plan.

"We've only got a few hours to Charlottesville. If you're going to do that, I'm out. I'll hitch the rest of the way and get there tonight."

"I'm out of duty hours," he said. "Cain't drive more than a certain amount each day. Cain't do it, Levi," he lied. He had told us he was just starting out for the day when he first picked us up and I had seen him take his breaks. No trucker would stop just a few hours short of their destination if they could continue and finish. It was how they were measured, how they were paid, and they usually went to great lengths to complete the trip as fast as possible.

I gently made my case. He took umbrage at being called a liar and got upset.

"Come on Levi," Katie urged. "Don't get him mad. He's been good to us."

You've been good to him, I thought. "I already said you can do what you want. I'm not forcing anything on anyone."

The trucker's demeanor changed. He stated DC was his destination and was doing us a favor by diverting to Charlottesville. If we wouldn't let him 'rest', he would have to let us off in Staunton, VA and drive north on his intended route, rather than divert west to Charlottesville as a favor. I knew he would use her during the night, and then continue his itinerary.

"Fuck that, it's cold out," Katie said. "I'm not hitching again. And I'm tired. I want to sleep and get there fresh in the morning."

"That's my girl!" the trucker said, grabbing her knee.

"So be it," I gave in.

We pulled into a truck stop, and I grabbed her while he went to take a piss. "Listen, Katie. This is dangerous. These fuckers drug women and pass them around like a bottle of cheap wine at these truck stops. They traffic them. You might wake up tomorrow somewhere halfway across the country. Or worse, on a ship. Don't do this."

"I can handle myself," she responded angrily. I had a feeling she was transposing her parents onto me and acting defiant rather than rational. She had to be scared, at least a little.

"So, you're going to fuck this guy, then show up tomorrow at Damon's?"

"No. He's not getting anything. He just doesn't know it yet. I don't want any diseases."

"Yeah, Katie. We'll see how that works out. Add 'in a ditch' to the places you may wake up tomorrow, or maybe not wake up at all, ever."

I had brought her close to tears and felt bad for her. She stuck to her guns and wiped her face as he emerged from the men's room.

"I'll see you tomorrow. Be careful," I said, kissing her on the cheek. "Take good care of her. I have your license plate," I warned the trucker. He smiled at me in triumph and gave me a sarcastic thumbs-up and wink.

They walked off toward his rig in the overnight area, and I found myself alone again. The thought of going out to the highway in the dark was nauseating. It brought back the vivid memory of what had happened that night in Tennessee.

I began working the truck stop, offering drivers coffee, a few joints, or some cash to take me through to Charlottesville. Most of them had parked for the night, so I focused on the gas pumps and found success after a while.

A trucker took me all the way to the highway exit at the edge of Charlottesville. I thanked him and found the nearest pay phone. Damon and his roommate, Carl, showed up a while later.

I expected his enthusiastic rap to greet me, but he looked alarmed and disappointed immediately. "Where the fuck is Katie, Levi? You kill her or some shit?"

I wasn't sure of his relationship with Carl, who seemed to be a buttoned-down straight-laced college guy, so I decided not to go into the details right then in the car. "Long story, dude. I'll fill you in back at your place. Don't worry though, she should be here in the morning."

He relaxed a little and began a long stream-of-consciousness spiel about all we would do and experience during this time together. Carl drove without speaking, smiling and offering an occasional chuckle. I was sure he knew Damon by now and was enjoying his bright light.

Back at their place, the 'submarine,' we settled in. It was late on a Thursday night, and they all had school and work the next day, so I didn't want to keep them. Carl and his fiancée, Diane, seemed nice and were welcoming. *Let's see how long that lasts.* They excused themselves and went off to bed, leaving Damon and me alone.

"Listen, dude, Katie's no good, she's trouble," I started out. "She tried to get over on me from the minute we met, and blew the trucker that gave us a ride. She's staying with him in the truck tonight, a few hours down the road. He's a brother."

"What the fuck?" he said, lowering his head. "So, what did you do?"

"I begged her not to stay with him tonight, and keep going with me. She was tired..."

"No," he cut me off. "What did *you do*, Levi?"

I understood the question, finally, and felt sick to tell him. "I pushed her away all night at her parent's place. But she crawled into my bed in the middle of the night and went down on me. I was exhausted, and it was too late before I realized what was going on. I didn't fuck her, man, I swear. We're brothers, and I couldn't."

"You pretty much did," he said, looking me in the eye.

"No, it's not the same, you know that. It shouldn't have happened, and I'm sorry and pissed off at myself that it did. I wanted to come alone, Damon. She's no good. She's fucking crazy."

"Well, that's never been disqualifying for any of us before," he said, and the tension broke as we shared a laugh. "Bitch thinks she's Jacqueline Kerouac or some shit, always talking smack."

"Yeah, it gets old fast. We got kicked out of some cars because of it."

"Well, I'll take care of it. She's not bringing her sloppy-ass pussy in here. Probably got the fucking herpes by now."

I laughed. "Are we good?"

"Yeah, man, you know blood is thicker than water. Let's get some sleep. I gotta get to work early. She's gonna call me when she gets into town. I've got some other potential strange around here, anyway. I'm an X-Man, Levi. You know that. I've always got some X-missions up my sleeve."

I cleaned the place up and lay down on the couch, enjoying the end of the trip and the peace that came with it, already dreading Katie's arrival the next day.

The morning was a buzz of activity. Diane was up early and making pancakes. She introduced herself as she bustled at the stove.

"Thanks for taking me in," I said.

"You come well recommended, Levi. We need the money, but we're careful about things like that. Well, I am, anyway. I don't want this place turning into party central. Carl is predisposed to such things, and he doesn't handle drinking or drugs well. We're working on our future here, and I don't need him going back into frat-boy mode."

She turned away from the stove and faced me. "Do we have an understanding, Levi?"

"Sure do," I said firmly.

Damon and Carl emerged from their respective bedrooms. Damon headed immediately to the turntable to play a soft Marvin Gaye album, explaining the meaning of the lyrics to no one in particular, dancing a shuffle around the room.

"Diane, this is Levi," Carl began.

"Don't bother," she cut him off. "We already met. He cleaned the whole place last night. You guys bring in some messy strays, but I like this one," she laughed, turning her head and winking at me.

She was preppy too, and they made a good pair. Both were in grad school at UVA, working to become lawyers. *That could come in handy,* I mused. After we all ate, I offered to clean up, and they gladly accepted. Diane and Carl headed to early classes, and Damon left with them for his maintenance job on campus.

Happy to have the place to myself, I cleaned it and set off as I had on my first days in Tulsa. It was a longer walk to the store, but I found everything I needed. As I had spotted a library nearby, I skipped buying the paper and instead settled in there at a table to read their copies.

I pored through want ads, unable to circle or cut them out, as the paper wasn't mine, and it hurt me to deface any kind of written material. Instead, I took copious notes and sweet-talked the woman at the reference desk into letting me use a nearby desk phone for local calls.

I lined up a few interviews that day and visited the places that had only addresses in their ad. It was easy hitching around the town, as the locals just figured you were a harmless college student. Students with cars were also eager to help.

A few of the campus jobs were intriguing, but paid little. I would have loved to be in the environment, but I had to eat. I kept moving throughout the day, avoiding the submarine and Katie. Toward the end of the day, I stopped by an art and framing shop for the final interview I had scheduled.

It was an old rustic two-story building in an idyllic setting at the foot of a hill covered in pine trees. I got there early and found a comfortable place in the fallen pine needles to read a little while I waited.

After I entered, filled out an application, and sat down with the manager, she asked me what I had been reading outside. "Steinbeck," I said. "Travels with Charley."

She reviewed my application and put it down. "Lonesome traveler, huh?" she asked, probably testing me to see if I'd catch the Kerouac reference. She was a little older than me, wore a long cotton flower-print peasant dress, and smelled of exotic herbs. *Most definitely at least a former, actual hippie.*

"Something like that, and I liked that novel too," I said.

She gave me a tour, and explained they were looking for someone with shipping and receiving experience, to package and send out prints folks had ordered. The job also involved helping frame the prints, plus receive and stock the new blank ones.

"The prints are all hand-colored," she said, leading me toward the back. We entered an area where there were rows of women sitting at desk easels painting the prints. They were young and beautiful, some with flowers in their hair.

We made our way back to her desk, and she offered me the job at a surprising hourly rate. "They'll keep you jumping," she warned. "You don't want to slow them down by not having the prints they need ready. They get paid a piece rate."

I took the job and thanked her.

"I'm an old hippie, Levi," she said. "You had me at Steinbeck."

As I was leaving, she added, "And no flirting with those girls!"

I checked my local map and made my way back to the submarine, eager to tell everyone. Damon was putting an album on the stereo as I entered, and Carl and Diane were at the dining room table studying.

"Did Katie make it?" I asked, looking around for her.

Damon looked at me and smiled. "Talk to the boss," he said.

I turned toward the dining room.

"I bought her a bus ticket and took her ass to the station," Diane said firmly. "As I said, we're careful about the strays we take in here in our little college commune. As much as we need help with the rent, we don't like people who present problems for us."

"Sorry, man," I said to Damon. I imagined the scene she must have made, and how angry she must be at me. *Add her to the list.* I hated to know I'd made anyone angry, but seemed to have a knack for it.

"No worries, brother. You did me a favor and saved me a lot of trouble."

"Any time," I answered, relieved he wasn't mad.

"Just don't be vetting any more of my old ladies that way."

"Promise."

AS I HAD IN TULSA, I settled into a routine of work, writing, and trying to save money. The art studio job kept me so busy the days always flew by. I took my lunch out into the pines to read on the soft floor every day, as the weather was warming.

I developed schoolboy crushes on several of the girls, particularly Abby, who had natural platinum hair and Norwegian features. She was a student of philosophy and often joined me outside to read. We took breaks to talk about logic, truth, and life, often blowing through lunch hour, requiring the manager to yell for us through the window and scold us when we entered.

One day we got deep into it, juxtaposing history with current events. We'd been talking about how Reagan was already changing things to help the wealthy and hurt working people.

"Karl Marx and Friedrich Engels said this is what would break capitalism," she said. "Greed, inequality. Working people aren't getting raises coming out of the recession, but profits are up and executive compensation is through the roof. They'll eliminate the middle class, and with it, democracy, eventually."

"China always said that too," I added. "So what's the solution, socialism?"

She scoffed. "In this country, they paint socialism in light of the failed autocratic socialist countries. But it was because of the autocratic part, not the socialist part. It was socialism from above, not democratic socialism, which has thrived for eons in places like Scandinavian countries where my people come from. They're the happiest people in the world, Levi! They have excellent health care, schools, education—even college. It comes from the taxes they pay. It works. That's *why* we pay taxes, after all."

"Those are smaller countries. It's easier."

"Bullshit! It's harder in smaller countries. This is the USA. We have immense wealth and resources. America is the richest country in the world. We did the New Deal, and it was amazing. We won two world wars! You could even add countries like Canada and Australia, our allies and friends. They're not exactly small. They've done it."

"Face it, Abby, we're a Machiavellian country. The people in power now believe that power at any cost, even oppression, is good. They believe it's better to be feared than loved. Anyone that is in the way of your goals is the enemy, and you must step on their necks, trample over them, to succeed."

"Well, we need to change that, Levi. Our generation. The hippies were idealists and gave it a good try. We need to continue the effort, or we're screwed. We'll eventually elect someone who wants to be a real dictator, and they'll take power for good."

A yell came from the window. We scrambled to our feet, laughing, and rushed toward the building entrance. I stopped her just short and tried to kiss her. For a brief, beautiful moment, our lips touched, her white hair grazing my face, but she pulled away.

"I can't, Levi. Sorry." She looked sympathetic. I was disappointed. Some of the girls were gay and didn't hide it. I didn't know if Abby was. It could have been a million things. I realized I was using an age-old misogynist's justification for being shot down and laughed at myself.

11 Carl Day

Carl got a good behavior hall pass from Diane one Saturday night and took us to a party at his fraternity on the university campus. After we parked, I wandered the campus alone, awestruck by the enormity and beauty of it. There were old stone ivy-covered buildings whose only purpose was to enlighten and educate. I could only imagine what it would be like to spend four years in a place like that, not having to work, just soaking in knowledge and honing the craft I yearned to practice the rest of my life.

I made my way back to the frat house. It was a huge old Victorian house with a sign above the door.

TKE

Tau Kappa Epsilon Fraternity
Better Men for a Better World

Inside was a stumbling mess of wasted frat boys and giggling coeds. They were well-dressed, despite an intentional hint of sloppiness. Guys led girls up the stairs to where I presumed the bedrooms were. I could hear a band playing somewhere, competing with shouts, yelling, loud laughter, and the occasional sound of things breaking.

I made my way to the basement and found the band there, crammed into a corner and slamming out punk rock, gyrating wildly and throwing their hair around. It was all

161

concrete and exposed wood beams, plumbing, and wiring above. The walls had been spray painted with rough murals and slogans in garish colors. Everyone held red plastic cups filled from the beer from kegs that lined the wall or trash cans full of grain alcohol, juice, and various types of floating fruit.

Damon and I had some fun by telling girls we were grad students, assistant professors of philosophy, and confusing them with pointed questions about their lives, parents, and childhood. Some of the guys took exception to the attention we were getting, caught on, and exposed our deception.

No sparks caught, and I suspected Damon felt as I did—that we were out of place and didn't fit in. We wandered back outside and sat on benches to talk for a while and enjoy the beauty of the place, before going back in to herd Carl back home before anything bad happened. We wanted more hall passes for him.

DAMON AND I GOT IN the habit of going out on Saturday nights to a roadhouse called the Coal Mine. It was a place for the local working-class kids, not the college crowd, and featured great rock bands, and sometimes even blues legends. We'd go out, have a ball, then sneak back in so we didn't wake Diane and Carl. Sometimes Carl waited up for us, sneaking cigarettes outside with a bottle of scotch, and wanted to hear what had happened that night. I felt sorry for him. He desperately wanted to join us. Damon hinted at something bad that had happened in the past with him and drinking, as had Diane that first morning. They were getting closer to setting a date for their wedding. I got the feeling he was realizing his freedom was slipping away forever, and he wasn't ready for that.

I got to know a shy country girl named Jolene, after asking her to dance a few times at the Coal Mine. She had a crooked but pretty smile, so I liked to make her laugh just to see it, and chastised her when she tried to hide it with her hand. Often wearing overalls and flannel, she put her hair in pigtails and it looked just right for her. She had a modest but sincere way about her, self-conscious about having dropped out of high school and her lack of education.

I was cautious after the sting of Abby's rejection, but eventually asked Jolene if she'd like company when we were saying goodnight after the bar had closed. To my delight, she invited me back to her place.

When we arrived, there was a teen-age sitter asleep with the TV on. After waking her and paying her, Jolene explained she had a five-year son old whose father had left her when the baby was just a year old. "He wasn't cut out for it," she said, looking at a picture of the three of them on the wall. "I sure wish he'd have thought about that before he knocked me up."

We talked for a while on her couch, and I got angry at him for abandoning them, as Mary's boyfriend had abandoned her and her son. I wondered how anyone could do that, especially to a child, and then I wondered if that was exactly what I was doing with Sarah and Leah. The pictures and letters kept coming, and they were on my mind more and more. *Was some dude listening to Sarah's story and feeling the same way about me?*

I sensed Jolene was worried about it happening again, and I didn't want to hurt her. I thought about leaving, but I liked her very much, and was comfortable there. She hadn't tried to hide it from me until setting the hook, as I felt Mary had.

We ran out of things to say, both tired in the early morning, and kissed. "I can't promise you anything, Jolene," I said as we broke off to catch a breath.

"I know it," she said. "That's why I don't want you to meet him, not yet. I don't want him getting attached to someone else who's going to go away, leaving him to ask me why."

I told her I understood. "I've been called a farawayer," I said. "That's what I am, I guess. I thought you should know."

"What's that?" she asked.

"Someone who always seems to want to be far away. From responsibility, maybe. I don't think it will always be that way, though."

She seemed to think about that, and I hoped I hadn't given her false hope. "Well, I have needs too, farawayer," she said as she stood up and took me by the hand to lead me to her bedroom.

We made love in a slow and tender way, not the typical first-time raucous passion. I felt we were very much alike, two lost and lonely people. We kept it casual, only seeing each other when we agreed we both needed that human connection, and it worked well for us.

DIANE LEFT ON A THURSDAY, taking a long weekend to go home to eastern Virginia to plan the wedding with her mom and bridesmaids. Carl went to the Coal Mine with us that Friday night, where he proceeded to get drunk and try to fight everyone in the bar. Eventually, he succeeded and got knocked down by a hard punch to the face.

We pulled him up and escorted him out the door. I drove his car home, as he was in no shape. Damon wiped the blood off his face, exposing a huge shiner. We got him to his bed and retreated into the living room. It was still early, so we put on some music, not having to worry about waking either of our hosts.

"There'll be hell to pay when Diane gets home," Damon said.

"Yeah, old Carl is in for it." We both laughed, thankful we weren't in his place.

We shared a joint, and both noted we were starving. Damon began scrounging for something to cook up. Diane had left just before our monthly community food shop, so there wasn't much. He pulled a stepladder from the closet and widened his search, opening a cabinet high above the stove hood.

"Dear Lord Jesus!" I heard him yell. "What the hell is this? Buried treasure!"

I saw what the commotion was about. There were about a dozen bottles laying on their side in the small space and he was pulling them out one by one, handing them to me. He called each one out in turn.

"All top shelf!" he exclaimed. "Johnny Walker...Black! Grey Goose! Crown Royal, my favorite! Bacardi 151! Cuervo! Call Diego. Tell him to get his ass out here!"

We assembled the bottles on the counter. "Whose is it?" I wondered. "Maybe Carl's secret stash? Diane doesn't really drink."

"Nah," he said. "It wouldn't be unopened and he would have told me. Besides, check it out, they're all dusty. This is ancient bounty from the sands of time, Levi!"

We decided the only viable theory was that the previous occupants of the submarine had left it behind, hidden and forgotten. Putting caution first, we agreed to only crack open the Johnny Walker and enjoy a shot of good scotch before crashing. We'd run it by Carl in the morning.

I woke to the clinking of glass against glass. The sun was up; I had slept late. Walking into the kitchen, I saw that Carl, in his bathrobe with a huge puffed-out black eye, had been sampling the treasure. Each bottle now had a shot glass in front of it, and he stood grinning to the side of them, gesturing broadly like a disheveled alcoholic game show host.

"What the fuck did you guys do, rob a liquor store last night?" he asked.

I filled him in as Damon appeared in his underwear, scratching his crotch and yawning.

Carl poured a shot of the Crown and held it up high. "I hereby declare this my bachelor party! Today is Carl Day! Gentlemen, let's have breakfast. There's a long day ahead of us."

Damon and I found ourselves in child care mode, trying to get Carl to pump the brakes until early afternoon, when we gave up. It was a joyous day, and we were all thrilled to do as we pleased. Albums scattered the floor. We took turns playing DJ for each other, shouting and dancing around the place half-naked. At some point, we went to the Piggly Wiggly grocery and bought bags of snacks and huge steaks. Carl ran around the store with a News York strip pressed on the puffed-out eye, alarming the other shoppers and staff.

After dinner, he demanded that we return to the Coal Mine. He struggled to walk or talk by then, and we tried to keep him in the submarine.

"It's my goddamn bachelor party!" he bellowed, becoming angry. "I'll bust this place up!"

Damon and I conferred during Carl's frequent trips to the bathroom. We hoped he'd fall asleep on the toilet, but had no such luck. After agreeing to keep a close eye on him, we gave in. We didn't need him doing damage to the home with Diane due back the following afternoon. He was overweight and could become a raging bull if drunk enough and provoked.

Things went well at the bar. He announced to everyone he encountered it was Carl Day and his bachelor party. Someone fetched him a leftover paper New Year's Eve party hat, and he ran around all night with it on, asking the prettiest girls in the place to dance. Damon worked the crowd as he always did, also finding much success.

"Where have you been keeping that animal locked up?" Jolene asked, pointing at Carl. "I've never seen him before."

"He's a kept man," I said, laughing. "And you'll probably never see him again after his fiancée comes back tomorrow."

The band was spectacular as the night roared on. I emerged from the men's room and saw Damon coming off the dance floor. "Where's Carl?" I asked. "I thought you were keeping him close."

"Did you see who I was dancing with?" he responded. "I ain't babysitting when someone who looks like that asks *me* to dance!"

We searched the place and found him playing foosball, shouting and taunting his opponent. He spotted us approaching. "Tie game, boys! Game ball, last one, here we go! Twenny bucks! Winner take all!" He dropped the ball into the chute and his opponent quickly slammed it into Carl's goal and raised his arms in victory.

"Fuck that!" Carl shouted. He lifted the handles and flipped the heavy table over, the crowd stepping back and his paper hat landing on his face, making it look like a big clownish nose.

The bouncers were on him quick and dragged him out as we followed. They tossed him from the door and he landed on his back in the parking lot. We expected that he'd try to bull rush back in and grabbed him.

"Come on, man. You want to go to jail?" I asked, grabbing him by the shirt. "You want Diane to have to come and bail you out tomorrow?"

The thought seemed to scare him, and he settled down.

"Look, boys. We had a great day," I said. "Let's end it well. We have a gigantic mess to clean up in the morning before Diane gets back. Let's get some rest, so we're not sick all day."

None of us could drive. But Jolene was always careful with her drinking, so I asked them to wait while I went inside to talk to her. She agreed to give us a lift.

When we pulled up and the boys got out of the car, Jolene put her hand on my knee and quietly asked if I'd come back to her place. I smiled at her and got out to let them know.

"Just get to bed," I warned them both. "Please. We've done enough damage. I'll be back early and we'll get the place spotless for Diane. We need to find a good excuse for that eye of yours, Carl. Maybe we'll say it was a game of tackle football."

They agreed and went inside.

12 Homeless

I woke next to Jolene the next morning. We snuggled, spooned and were at peace together. I wanted to stay, and wondered what that would be like, making a life with her and her kid. She was a strong and good person—a rare thing.

She stirred and said I had to go before her son got up. I acknowledged, remembering the task ahead at the submarine. She kept the place blacked out with heavy drapes to help her and the boy sleep. When she raised them, brilliant sunshine filled the room, blinding me.

"Damn," I said. "What time is it?"

"Oh dear Lord," I heard her say. "It's after nine! He's going to be up any minute. We have to go. I'll get my downstairs neighbor to come up for a few minutes while I take you home."

I scrambled out of her bed, anxious about the morning ahead. I didn't want her son to find me there, upset her, and ruin things between us. "Sorry, Jolene. I can walk or hitch back. Stay here."

Good as she was, she refused to allow it. She kissed me on the cheek and said it wouldn't take long. I was happy that she was OK. She put a church station on the radio for the drive back and said she took her boy to services every Sunday. "Maybe someday you can join us," she said.

As we came down the road toward Carl's place, I saw Diane's car in the driveway. *Oh no,* I thought, as fear struck my heart about what scene I'd find inside. Jolene pulled up at the curb. We talked for a few minutes and kissed goodbye. "This will not go well," I said as I got out of her car.

She pulled away, and I approached the front door. Damon met me there on his way out. He carried my backpack and an enormous duffel bag of his own. "Don't go in," he said. "It's not good. She doesn't want to see either of us. We're kicked out. She bought that booze on sale for their wedding reception and was hiding it from us."

I realized we were both now homeless. Damon made little money at his campus job and lived paycheck to paycheck. We'd paid very little in rent, compared to the rates usually charged, as it was a college town. I'd been sloppy and partying with my money, not saving as usual, not expecting this turn of events. We didn't have enough between us for utility deposits, let alone first and last month's rent and a security deposit. *Stupid.*

He said he knew a place where we could crash, and we headed off walking and hitching. He took us away from the college area, and block by block, the landscape changed, becoming more decrepit. I put my thumb out a few times, but nobody in that area was picking up a long-haired white dude and a black guy with a big afro haircut, both carrying bags.

We were in the poorer section of town, the black section, as the whites called it. Funny how it always worked out that way. Families were making their way out of shabby homes and getting into their old cars, dressed in their Sunday best for church. A few sat on porches, welcoming the morning. They all stared at us, and the children pointed.

A pickup came toward us and slowed down as the driver and passenger windows rolled down. A huge confederate flag adorned the hood. Two fat, short-bearded rednecks leered out the windows at us, wearing T-shirts with the sleeves cut off. "Nigger, nigger, nigger!" they shouted. "A nigger and a nigger-lover! Get a job, freaks!"

I snapped in my exhaustion and state of despair, and dropped my pack, running after the truck. "Let's go then, you fat fucks. Man up!" I shouted. The truck slid to a stop and the one working white backup light blinked on, like an ogre suddenly waking. Damon ran up beside me and threw his bag to the curb.

"Damn, Levi. Get ready for Ali mode. Better hope these white boys fight like Jerry Quarry. You still undefeated?"

"I'll let you know in a few minutes, brother." We had both been on the base boxing team a few years back. "You know the drill," I said. "Same as always. They're out of shape. Make them move and wear them down."

"Rope-a-dope again," he said as the two fat men flung the truck doors open and ran toward us. Damon took his stance and called out to them as they approached with their fists up. "Just like Muhammad Ali. I'm gonna sting you like a bee, son."

We spread apart and put our backs to each other for protection. The first one reached me and I dodged to the side and circled. "You're a big gay fella, aren't you," I taunted, trying to enrage him into making mistakes. "Is that your boyfriend? Your butt buddy?"

I heard Damon talking shit as well, using the same tactic. "This nigger's gonna whoop your white racist ass, fat boy," he said in a menacing tone.

The ploy worked. Each of the rednecks swung wildly and tried to bull rush us to knock us to the ground, where they'd have the advantage. We both danced and spun away, conserving energy.

Master Sergeant Taylor was a tall, black, grizzled special forces man who had done several tours in Viet Nam. In exchange for the excellent weed I had kept him supplied with, he taught me martial arts at the base gym—specifically Bruce Lee's Jeet Kune Do method. I fell back into the stance and put my mind into a calm state. *Be like water.*

The concept was to strike when your opponent was about to strike, using speed and a straight lead punch. But Taylor had taught me to be vicious, because in hand-to-hand combat in the jungle you had to, or else die. *Always take the eyes first. They can't hit what they can't see.*

My adversary lunged in and swung hard. Rather than move backward, I stepped in and forked my fingers, spreading them rigidly and thrust them into his eyes, then stepped back into my stance again.

He turned away and bent over, rubbing his eyes and cursing me. "You dirty motherfucker..." I could have finished him then, but I waited. Primal instinct had taken over, and I wanted to hurt him again and again.

He straightened, angry as a bull, and came at me in a rage. *Never lose control of your emotions.*

I moved up again. Using John Barrack's signature move, I faked the left. As he put his hands up to block on that side and ducked down a little, I stepped in and slammed my right fist into the center of his forehead as hard as I could. His knees buckled, and he staggered. I closed again and threw a roundhouse kick against his jaw. The big man fell backward, rapping his head on the street with a hollow thud, and remained still. *Nose and mouth for blood, forehead for the knockout.*

I turned to Damon. He and the other redneck were on the ground, struggling. Damon had torn up the bigger man's face—he was bleeding, but was on top with leverage. Primal instinct welled up again. I wanted to strike hard enough and in just the right place with my square-toed boot to break his neck. But this time, thankfully, I check my swing, taking four quick strides and planting my boot hard in his ribs. It caused enough pain to make him stop, likely breaking one or two. I was ready and willing to counter if he did not. Damon pushed him off and jumped to his feet.

I pulled the fold-out buck knife my father had sent for Christmas and snapped it open, hopefully signaling to them it was over.

"Let's get the fuck out of here," Damon said.

"Want to take the truck?" I asked as it idled just ahead of us, smoke leaking from the exhaust.

"You fucking crazy?" he said, laughing and out of breath.

We heard clapping and turned to see an old black man watching from his porch, wearing a red hat with the yellow United States Marine eagle, globe, and anchor insignia. "That's right, that's right!" he exclaimed in joy. "That's how you do it!"

Damon's opponent had roused and was making his way over to his buddy. He got up and went to the truck, then produced a pistol, pointing it at us as he walked closer. We froze.

"Hold on now, it was a fair fight. You don't want to go to prison for this," I said.

"Now we're gonna die on this street together, Levi. Don't bring a damn knife to a gunfight," I heard Damon whisper in despair.

"Git back in the truck, take your friend, and go," we heard someone shout. The vet was now on his porch steps, aiming a double-barreled, sawed-off shotgun at the redneck. He lowered the pistol and moved back toward his friend, who was now sitting up in the street.

"Good old Virginia," Damon said. "Everybody packing heat," he laughed as I snapped my blade shut.

We grabbed our stuff and ran, zig-zagging through the neighborhoods Damon knew well. An old white dude in a barely running car stopped to pick us up a few blocks later. The muffler was shot, and the engine rattled and knocked, desperately trying to stall. "Sit up front," Damon said as we approached it. "I need to be in the back, or he'll get spooked." It hurt me to realize he was right, so I complied.

The man looked homeless, and he was nice, offering us the remains of his bag lunch. "You're both vets, aren't you? I noticed your surplus gear," he said.

"Yes, sir," I replied. He said that he was as well, and had landed at Normandy on D-Day. We thanked each other for our service.

"Everyone should have to serve," he said.

Damon had been quiet, but suddenly spoke out. "People say everyone should spend a year in the service; I say everyone should also spend a few days as a black person. That would fix this racist shit in a hurry."

"I live just down the street," the man replied. "We're all black in the ghetto, so I hear you, brother." He pulled into the dirt driveway of his shack and let us out to continue our journey.

Passing an empty lot littered with trash, Damon pointed at a broken-down two-story house. The roof was coming off—patches of missing shingles and a hole decorated it. Most of the windows were broken. A sign on the front door said *Condemned*.

"Are you serious?" I asked. "What's this?"

"I stayed here before I met Carl on campus. It's temporary. You got a better idea?" he asked, raising his voice.

We had no home and no car between us. I realized I'd allowed myself to become dependent on others, and this was the result, again. We had no way to get around, other than on foot. The situation wasn't looking good.

"Where are we going to shower?" I asked him.

"The rec center at the college," he said. "I'll get you in. This is temporary. Let's go inside and figure things out, Levi." His expression didn't match his words. He was down and didn't seem to have much hope it would work out.

We went inside and rested in an empty upstairs room, leaning against a wall, the floor littered with mouse droppings. We talked about all we'd been through and made plans to save up and get a place. Maybe each get a second job.

The problem was that school was almost out for the summer, and the town was about to dry up for a few months. We made the best of it, day after day, only going back to the shack to sleep and spending our time in libraries and coffee shops after work. They were exhausting days with lots of walking. The nights were chilly and desolate, and my body ached each morning after sleeping on the floor wearing layers of clothing, with the remaining items balled up for a pillow. We had no drugs to use as an escape from the stark reality of our situation.

The framing shop got slow, and then shut down one day, making things worse. Damon got laid off as the spring semester wound to a close. We blanketed the town looking for better work, and an obvious pattern emerged. I always got called for interviews, having checked that Caucasian ethnicity box on the applications, and Damon never did. Other than that one box, our resumes were essentially identical. We were both veterans, the same age, both having served our country. I got offers; he got none, and we both knew exactly why.

"The college is the only place in this redneck-ass place to give a brother a chance," he said, exasperated. "Maybe I need to get back to my people in Oxford."

It made me sick, and more and more I wanted to be out of the south. I thought about the coming summer and the sparkling lake back home. I thought about my home, my family, my friends at the Bivouac tavern, and I thought a lot about Carla. Maybe she was ready to try again. With each phone call there, I missed my mom, and even my dad, more and more. No matter where you are, home and family always pull at you like a loving magnet, calling toward its embrace and safety.

In the silence and darkness of each chilly night, I held the medallion, whispered whatever prayer I could remember, and asked for help. We made sure to never waste a single thing; every tiny crumb of any food got consumed, anything we discovered along the road or in trash cans found a purpose. It shaped me for life, and I'd never be comfortable with waste in any form again.

I spent some nights with Jolene, always careful to leave at dawn, but leaving Damon in that cold abandoned building nagged at my conscience. She told me one night after we made love that I could stay there, but not without a commitment. I struggled with it. I really cared for her.

I landed a job cleaning a department store before opening each day, working from three in the morning until nine. It was minimum pay, barely nothing, but enough to buy a little food. We were living on two dollars a day, and I was back to stealing food. I warned Damon not to do it, as I'd get a slap on the wrist, but he'd get hard time if caught. I talked the manager at my new job into hiring Damon, and we walked there and back together every frosty morning.

Once inside the vast store, we raised the heat to warm the place, and went to work vacuuming, cleaning glass, emptying trash, and making the place spotless. We took time during our breaks to marvel at the expensive jewelery under the blinding lights in the glass cases. "Damn," he said. "I'd sure like to give my mother something like that. She spent her whole life cleaning up for white folks and ain't never had shit."

When it was time to clean the sporting goods department, we'd break out a badminton set and play a game on our break, slamming the shuttlecock around the store, running after it to keep it from hitting the floor.

We made a habit of cranking up the local rock station on the store's sound system, and modeled some of the expensive clothes for each other, laughing at the ridiculousness of it. We'd often grab the sexy, scantily dressed female mannequins and dance with them, waltzing them around the floor. Since we had no TV or radio, it was our only form of entertainment.

Once I heard him talking to someone and snuck around the corner to see what he was doing. He stood facing a male mannequin that was dressed in khakis and a plum golf shirt with an alligator logo and the collar upturned, as was the preppie fashion then. A female mannequin stood next to it, and they held hands.

"Why you all want to hate on black people?" he asked. "We just want a chance to be successful and happy, to be like you, even if it is so much harder for us."

Shaking his head at their lack of response, he turned the male's collar down and turned to walk away, spotting me. "Fucking preppies," he said, switching his vacuum back on and singing a slave chant under its droning noise.

THE DAYS ONLY GOT HARDER. When life's energy seems to drive you in a certain direction, resistance is futile. If you fight it, things only get worse, and it never goes well. That's when you know it's time for a change.

On a Sunday, when we were out walking, we saw people streaming into a neighborhood Baptist church. "Let's go," I said on a whim.

We entered and found a place toward the front, as most of the pews were full. We were directly in front of the full band, with electric guitars and a big worn-out drum set. The musicians counted in and began playing fast and beautiful religious songs as sweat rolled down their faces. The crowd jumped to their feet and danced and hugged one another, arms raised above their heads, growing into a fervor. It was nothing like I'd seen at the Village of Prayer. It wasn't fake or devotional to one living man. Instead, it was a joyous celebration of life, and of Jesus. The preacher danced to the center of the altar and motioned the band to slow, then began a passionate sermon about loving one another, helping one another. He mentioned John 4:20.

"Whoever claims to love God yet hates a brother or sister is a liar. For whoever does not love their brother and sister, whom they have seen, cannot love God, whom they have not seen."

There was no begging for money, or Old Testament threats and admonishment. It was pure and real. It was pure love of God and neighbor. During the praying times of the service, I bowed my head and asked for answers, asked for guidance. The second sermon focused on family and the proverbs he quoted seemed to answer my questions.

"Honor your father and mother, so that you may live long in the land the Lord your God is giving you."

"The one who troubles his family will inherit nothing, and the fool will be a servant to the wise person."

I left the service feeling that it had given me my answer. That night, Damon and I both seemed to come to the inevitable conclusion at once. He told me he was going back home to Oxford, Ohio the next morning. It was near Cincinnati, at the intersection of the Indiana and Kentucky borders. His cousin had a job waiting for him, and I could tell he was excited about it. I told him it was OK; I was going home as well.

"This tour is over," he said, before immediately resuming his upbeat and optimistic nature. "But let's regroup, save up some dough, and go somewhere nice next year. Maybe go see Diego in Texas and then go west to California for a while."

As I broke my backpack down and then reassembled it, I found two old twenty-dollar traveler checks I thought I had lost and had reported stolen long ago. Despite knowing it was a federal offense to cash them, I did. It was an incredible bounty for us and we celebrated with beer and burgers. *And now you'll have to worry about going to jail someday for that, too.*

We spent his last night sitting in the condemned house, celebrating our new start in life with a gallon jug of cheap port wine. We even ordered a pizza delivery from a nearby pay phone and had to run out of the house to catch the driver as she pulled up and pulled away, thinking it was a prank.

The following morning, we said goodbye to the dump together, and he boarded a taxi to the bus station. Jolene picked me up a while later to spend my last night with her. She had left her son with family for the day and night, so we spent it relaxing at her place and later went to a restaurant for dinner together.

After retiring early that night, we talked in bed until we fell asleep in each other's arms. In the morning, we made love one last time and cried together, making promises we knew we couldn't keep, as she dropped me off by the highway to hitch back home.

"Bye now, farawayer," were her last words to me. I said goodbye and closed the car door.

I hoped someday to find her again, or someone just like her.

13 Home Again

I avoided the more direct route up through Washington, Baltimore, Philly, the heart of NJ, and skirting New York City. I didn't enjoy hitching near the big cities. There were too many cops, too many nut jobs, too much pollution, and too little scenery.

Instead, I retraced the route I had taken down, now almost safely out of the south. My first ride took me a short way on I-64 West to I-81 near Staunton, VA. It was the place that the trucker had threatened to drop Katie and me off if he couldn't have his way. I wondered where she was, how she was doing, and hoped she was OK.

A trucker took me up along the West Virginia border once again, then into the state, and dropped me off in Martinsburg. Normally, I'd be in a hurry to get through the area because of my redneck-phobia, but I tempted fate and went into town for lunch.

The people there were warm to me. I ate in a greasy burger joint, a fabulous double-decker cheeseburger slathered in cheese and bacon and accompanied by the best onion rings I'd ever had. It was all washed down with ice-cold root-beer and the waitress kept bringing me refills as fast as I could drink it.

A good old boy took an interest in me and after we talked about life and politics for a while, he said he was retired and bored and he'd take me up to Hagerstown, Maryland, since his brother lived there. Another patron then paid for my meal, and I left what I would have paid as a tip for the waitress. She waved to me with a cheerful smile as she picked up her stack of bills.

On the road in the man's old pickup truck, I thought about how I'd pre-judged everyone in the south, and how it wasn't different from the people that were prejudiced against someone for the color of their skin, the language they spoke, or what god they worshiped. I'd been a hypocrite, and no different from them. There were certainly nasty people up north. I'd served with some very lazy white guys in the military. Would I be right to classify all white people as lazy, as some did with blacks and Mexicans?

I thought about all the good folks I'd met in the south, those who had helped me. Old John at the Village of Prayer came to mind, and I smiled at the thought of him. I remembered Diane, who had helped me and whom I had let down, and I felt bad about that again. I reminisced about Mary Jefferson and Jolene and my heart sagged to think that I had hurt them and disappointed them in the end.

Finally, I thought about Sarah and Leah. The usual pangs of doubt and guilt returned. *What if I'm wrong there too, and Leah is my child?* I wondered if I were heading home for good, and this would be my last trip as a free person. Maybe the relentless tentacles of life would pull me in, and these times would soon be nothing more than a dream and a faded memory.

A college kid on his way home for the summer picked me up in Hagerstown and said he could drop me off in Harrisburg, Pennsylvania. During the drive, we talked about our lives to date, and how they were a contrast in society. We were about the same age, and ironically, each had always dreamed about doing exactly what the other was doing. *The grass is always greener...*

"I'll take a break after college," he said. "Yeah, just take a break and travel like you before settling down."

"That sounds good," I told him. "It's a good idea, but what will probably happen is you'll meet someone and fall in love by the time you graduate. You'll start making plans to get married and start a family as soon as you've locked up your first cushy corporate jobs, and you'll start looking for a house and some nice cars. Then you'll find yourself in enormous debt and unable to quit the jobs you now hate, and the kids will drive you nuts."

He shifted in his seat and turned the radio up. I was on a roll, so I spoke a little louder. "But don't worry, if things work out OK, you'll be able to retire in about forty-five years, when you're around sixty-five. Just when you're getting sick and have lots of medical problems. And by then, you'll be taking care of your parents and your kids will borrow money from you left and right."

I felt bad about bursting his bubble, and it killed the mood. Fortunately, we were just arriving in Harrisburg. *Maybe he'll be happy. Happier than me.* I realized I was just jealous because he'd gotten to go to college right off, and I hadn't.

He dropped me next to a bridge over the Susquehanna River, on the west shore in a little town called Lemoyne. I took some time to sit on the hill by the riverbank and enjoy some snacks I had packed. Boaters and fishermen enjoyed the water, and Harrisburg's capitol complex loomed above on the other side of the river. It was a pretty place. I vaguely remembered Kerouac having some trouble there in *On the Road* at the beginning of his journey. I was at the end of mine—for this trip, anyway. Maybe forever.

I wondered if I were giving up, giving in, by going back home. The more hopeful, idealistic me, before I had embarked on this trip, would scream to keep going, go west, and see what's there. I was road-weary though and thought maybe I'd do that next time. I had to regroup. *You have a whole life of freedom ahead to enjoy, after all. Unlike Carl, and unlike that poor kid who just dropped you off.*

The weather was glorious, so I took the time to walk across the iron Market Street Bridge, stopping to look down at the water. It reminded me of the metal bridge over Lake Sussex at home, only much bigger. I wandered around City Island in the middle of the river. An old-timer told me Babe Ruth had played in an exhibition game there, and it had been a Union military camp, set up in case the Confederacy overran the north in the Battle of Gettysburg in the Civil War.

On reaching the other side of the river, even though I had intended to hitch toward the highway, I stopped again and sat on the hill above the riverbank. I looked across to where I had sat earlier on the west shore and envisioned myself there. *Who is that lost soul sitting there alone? What does he want from his life?*

Guitar music caught my ear. A lone black man sat on a bench playing acoustic blues. I wandered over to listen, and he introduced himself as Rocky Johnson, a member of the local blues society. We talked about our favorites while he played, then I just sat and listened. After a while, he said he had to work second shift, and gave me a ride up Front Street to the I-81 ramp. I liked the little capital city on the river.

School buses were dropping kids off along the row homes on our route. I looked into those house windows and thought maybe there's a ten-year-old kid in there counting his baseball cards in the comfort and secrecy of his bedroom, reading under the blankets at night and dreaming of being a writer, like I did not too long ago. Maybe there's a kid in there in his senior year of high school flirting with his girlfriend on the phone, dreaming about finishing high school, going to college, becoming a great, happy, famous writer and living with her happily forever.

The home is a nurturing petri dish, a warm protective cocoon, like an egg we live within until we finally chip away at its shell, ready to leave and join the world, to create an egg for our own chicks. I wondered where I'd be in ten years, and whether I'd be happy and in love.

Just two rides took me the last few hours toward home. We rolled back through Pennsylvania's Lehigh Valley on State Route 22, past its three cities in quick succession—Allentown, then Bethlehem, finally Easton, and then across yet another river (the Delaware this time), another metal bridge and into Phillipsburg, New Jersey. I was back in the Garden State. Back home again. *Almost.*

My final ride dropped me off back at the edge of town. I stopped in at the bar my old high school football coach owned, wanting a beer to celebrate and take the edge off. It was early evening on a workday, so it was pretty empty. After ordering, I asked the bartender where Mr. Fancy was.

"Dead," he answered. "Heart attack. Place is under a new owner."

I looked down the bar and recognized a kid from my class. It was Mike Keeler, who was a big guy, a lineman on the football team; a bully who had tormented kids like me. He was wasted, falling asleep in his beer, and had gotten extremely obese. Despite the hell he'd put me through, I felt bad for him. *This is what happens when you don't move on in your life.*

I had purposely avoided the Bivouac, which was closer to home. I didn't want to start my return by brawling with John Barrack, and worried the cops might still be looking for me for siphoning gas at the service station. Another summer had passed, a new one was imminent, and those times kept them busy with drunken tourists raising hell.

And then the same enormous bubble of fear welled up in me again, as I realized my actual concern should be whether the guy in Tennessee had died, and who he had left behind. Maybe there was an interstate warrant out for me. I thought about how ironic it would be for someone who ranted about freedom as much as I did, who went to such great lengths to be *free*, to end up in prison for the rest of his life, or death row. *What a great novel that would make; a Shakespearean tragedy.*

The old metal bridge was no longer there when I reached the place where it connected the two sides of the lake. A newer, modern, much prettier painted concrete one had replaced it. *Another thing gone,* I thought, stopping half-way across to look down into the water, searching for trout I might catch that summer.

It was almost dark when I made it home. Mom, Dad, and my sisters were there, waiting for me as I'd phoned ahead the day before. There was even a cake ready for after dinner, and presents, as my birthday had just passed unnoticed and quietly a few days earlier. I hadn't bothered to let Damon know, because he'd have bought me something, and I knew he didn't have the money. I missed him already.

Dad went out of his way to greet me, and I sensed a change in him. Outwardly, his hair was longer, a genuine surprise. After we'd all shared hugs and kisses, I excused myself to clean up. I went downstairs to my basement bedroom. It was like entering a time-warp and memories came flooding back. All my stuff was there, preserved like a museum and kept clean by Mom. I took time to review my crude kindergarten drawings, Neil Young and Led Zeppelin posters, and a picture of Carla and I together on a scenic overlook nearby on the day we'd had a spontaneous picnic there. After rummaging in my dresser drawers, I found a small stash of pot I'd left behind.

It felt good to be home, but I felt I had outgrown that room. I was a man now, and shouldn't be living with my parents. I vowed to change it as soon as possible, although I wasn't sure how long I'd be able to stay in that one place, or any one place, for long.

Mom made her special stuffed peppers, and we feasted as a family for the first time in a long time. I teased my sisters, incredulous at how much they'd grown in the relatively short time I was gone. They looked at me admiringly and I wondered what kind of example I was setting for them. I certainly didn't want them living the type of life I was and didn't want them turning out like Katie. I wanted good things for them, and for them to have happy and easy lives and good fathers for their children.

Dad gave me the traditional case of beer, wrapped in the Sunday comics. We sat on the back deck drinking a few while mom cleaned up and the girls went to their homework assignments. He told me he was sorry for being distant, and I apologized for being a pain in the ass. He said he had a new coworker, a black dude, and it had opened his eyes.

"We spend our lives afraid of people who are different because we don't know them," he said. "And when we do, we find out they're not any different from us."

He sounded like me, and I was proud of him for saying it, for finally realizing it.

I dared to ask if he'd tried pot, and he verified he did. "Nice and mellow. No hangover, and the music sounds better."

We laughed, and I reminded him he used to say we should put people in jail for life for smoking it, and that it turned them into heroin addicts. I fired one up, and we shared it, until Mom flung open the kitchen window above us, stared, and said "Oh, good Lord. Put that out, the girls will smell it!"

Realizing she was right, we went to the Bivouac for a beer to end the night. Joe the barkeep welcomed me back with a free round and told me that John Barrack had hurt someone bad in a fight and was in the county jail for a year. I felt bad about it. The guy had his demons, but I was happy I wouldn't have to deal with him.

Dad and I played a few rounds of pool against a few of the locals. While we were talking about job ideas for me, one of our opponents said his place was hiring forklift drivers. His name was Jesse, and he was a few years older than me. I remembered him as a quirky druggie in high school.

"Show up tomorrow at lunchtime. I'll fix you up with an application and interview," he said.

Dad and I stayed longer than we'd planned, and drove back home over the new bridge high from the pot and beer, laughing together for the first time that I could remember.

It was good to be home. *Maybe you can go home again.*

14 Concrete and Blacktop

As I did in Tulsa, and then Charlottesville, I got right to work the next day looking for work. I checked the newspaper and put in some applications while driving around in Mom's car.

At lunchtime, I drove out to the plant where Jesse worked. He was outside in the parking lot with some other rough-looking guys, standing around their motorcycles smoking and discretely passing around a bottle wrapped in a paper bag. I walked up, and he introduced me to them. One offered me the bottle, but I passed, saying I didn't want to go inside smelling like booze for a job interview.

"Don't be a pussy," he said. "We don't work with pussies."

I stared him down. "If I get the job, I'll show you who the pussy is. And if I don't get the job, I'll still show you who the pussy is." They all broke out laughing and he clapped me on the shoulder and wished me luck.

It was a plant where huge rooftop silos of concrete mix and blacktop fed into the building, where workers bagged them, sewed the tops closed, and stacked them on pallets. The pallets had to be picked up immediately by the forklift drivers and stacked to the ceiling or loaded on waiting trucks. Everything worked in sync, and it all had to go like clockwork, or the line would stop and everyone got pissed off, since they got paid by their production and their time. They were cogs in the wheel, by design, just like the girls at the print shop in Charlottesville, but not as pretty.

After my interview, I watched in amazement as the guys came back from lunch and took their positions. It was like a symphony in both sound and movement. They were all very good at what they were doing. At one point, a machine jammed and there was a lot of cursing and scrambling to get the band back in sync and the money flowing.

The foreman came up behind me and put his hand on my shoulder. "You feel up to it?" he asked.

"I think it's pretty amazing," I said. "Sure do. I helped load bombs under fighter plane wings with a forklift, so I can handle this."

He asked me to start the next day, and quoted a rate that was good, but a little disappointing. "Don't worry," he said. "It's a trial rate. If you pass muster, you'll make a lot more. It's hard to find good lift drivers, and we don't enjoy losing them."

AND SO BEGAN THOSE days of driving the forklift and living at home. It was rough at first—the workers were unforgiving at my initial inefficiency while I learned the ropes. A few times, when attempting to stack the massive pallets up high, I would miss by an inch and rip a bag, the concrete mix pouring to the floor. It incurred the wrath of the foreman, who would then dock my pay without mercy. I was like a new ranch hand, learning the ropes, the big forklift my bucking bronco.

I took occasional shifts on the line, slinging the heavy bags. It was brutal, back-breaking work. I grew a beard and wore overalls, getting into the industrial spirit of my new life, and to help gain acceptance with the other guys, who were mostly bikers, some patched in with the Pagans and Warlocks.

Eventually, it all came together. I became quick friends with the other guys, accepted into their circle. They were all tough blue-collar young men, all fallouts in one form or another of America's promise. They weren't the best influence on me, as we often drank and did drugs on the job. I felt that more and more I was trying to bury things deep inside me, push them deeper where they'd no longer well up. I tried not to think about my promise to be free and travel, the night in the woods, and Sarah and Leah. Conflicts, guilt, and regret all swirled in my mind, and I tried to quiet it with substances.

After I'd received a few paychecks, I started looking for a cheap ride and place to stay. Jesse invited me to rent the spare room at his place, so I started there. He still lived in town, at an address a block away from the Bivouac. I went over on a Saturday morning to check it out.

The place was an old summer rental cottage from way back in the day when Babe Ruth had frequented the lake resort. The outside was white, but filthy with time. Wide, wooden old fashioned siding hung from the front and sides of the shack diagonally, waiting for gravity to free them from it.

I walked through a tiny front yard with more weeds than grass, on a concrete walk that was a mosaic of broken geometric fragments, and knocked on the door. He answered in a ratty bathrobe, blinking his eyes in the light, and rather than invite me in, he came out and motioned to a small, rusted wire patio table and two chairs in the yard.

"Whew," he said, exhaling stale booze breath at me. "Wild night in the Bivouac. Where were you?"

"Eh. I took a night off. I was shot."

He laughed. "You're getting old, Levi. Our job does that to people."

I felt like I was getting old. "I'll be there tonight, saved up my energy," I vowed.

"Well, let's take a tour of my mansion."

We went inside and it was surprisingly neat. I wondered how much of that was him preparing for company, and what it normally looked like. The place was tiny, with a small kitchen just big enough to stand in and cook. Everything seemed just a little better than dollhouse-sized.

"I guess people were smaller back in the twenties," I joked.

"Good thing we're skinny fuckers."

The second bedroom was more like a closet, just big enough to hold the rudimentary single bed and a small dresser.

"It ain't much," he said. "But I'll only charge you a hundred bucks a month."

I wondered if that was all he was paying, but it solved one of my problems, for now. I agreed, and we walked over to the Bivouac for a beer to seal the deal.

I SOLVED MY OTHER PROBLEM by buying a bike from a guy at work. Except, it was a 'basket case,' an old '69 Triumph chopper that came in boxes. It was a rehab project that had proved too much for him to reassemble, given he had a disapproving wife and two kids already.

The front of our shack had an overhang, so I set the bike up under it, and used a tarp to provide more cover from rain as I worked to put it together on days when I had time and energy. It had an extended front end, ape-hanger handlebars, and a metallic-green teardrop gas tank adorned with flames.

I completed the job a few weekends later. Jesse came out to inspect the finished product. I hopped on and jumped hard on the kick-starter to fire it up. The engine burbled and purred in that Triumph way, and I was damn proud.

"Nice," he said. "But it still ain't a Harley."

"Fuck that," I said. "Prices on those are through the roof and they're using Japanese parts now. The Brits who make these Triumphs are our allies."

"Looks like those bikes on *Easy Rider*," he said. "Pretty sweet."

He suggested we celebrate for the rest of the day.

"What do you have in mind?" I asked.

He pulled a small white notepad from his back pocket and tossed it to me. "I've been using these, but they're on to me at the pharmacy. Nobody knows you there, though."

It was a prescription pad. "Where the hell did you get this?" I asked him.

"Lifted it from the doc's office back when I hurt myself at work."

He took it back and went inside with it. A few minutes later, he handed me a single slip of paper from the pad. It was a prescription made out to me, barely legible.

"What's this for?" I asked.

"Robo. Prescription-strength. Codeine. That stuff will put us in dreamland, a buzz like you're floating on a cloud, nice and mellow."

I didn't like to get outside of booze and pot much, other than an occasional psychedelic. We had nothing planned for the day. I was looking for any excuse to get on the finished bike, so I jumped on it and took a ride to the pharmacy by the lake. By the time I returned, Jesse had gone to the nearby mini-mart and bought a large bottle of Pepsi and a bag of ice.

It was a beautiful day, late in the morning, when we settled in at the little garden table in the yard, and put on some music. I hadn't tried codeine before, and wasn't sure what to expect. Jesse was mixing the drinks, so I was subject to his mercy and expertise in the matter.

Lunchtime passed, but we didn't eat. The effects came over me like a slow-moving storm you watch over the horizon, never seeing it move, but knowing it was coming, inch by inch. We shared a few hits from his bong, and before long, we were sitting there smiling at each other.

He was right. It felt like I was sleeping, but awake. I got up to piss, and it seemed to take forever. My body moved in slow motion. Our speech came as a slow drawl whenever we tried to communicate. It felt like I was going into a catatonic state, and I didn't like it. I wished I'd just stayed sober and gone for an enjoyable ride on the bike up into the woods in the state park.

We sat there, wasting the gift of a day, two fools laughing at each other. To my horror, I saw Dad's car come up the road and pull up in front of us. My sisters piled out excitedly, Mom and Dad approaching cautiously. Mom always had accurate radar for trouble, and I could tell it was going off in five-alarm style the moment she looked at us, sitting there slouched in the broken chairs. We didn't even have a place for them to sit.

The girls had run inside. "It's so cute!" I heard one of them exclaim.

"We thought we'd stop by and see your new place," Mom said.

We tried to make small talk, but it was futile. I felt helpless as she grew more sad by the moment. Dad had gone inside to round up the girls. I thought about the sink full of dishes and table full of empty beer bottles I'd neglected, as Jesse wasn't as particular as I was about keeping things neat and clean.

Dad came out with my sisters by the hand and guided them toward the car.

"I don't think this is a good time, is it Levi?" Mom said more than asked. "We would have called first, but you guys don't have a phone installed."

"No," I slurred, struggling for some way to make it better. I couldn't even get up to hug her goodbye.

She started toward the car, then charged back at me, now angry. "What's wrong with you?" she demanded. "Why do you want to live like this? You have so much potential, Levi. What are you punishing yourself for?"

I didn't answer, I couldn't even if I'd had a suitable response and could get the words out.

"Well, that didn't go well," Jesse said. "I'm gonna head over to the Bivouac."

"I'm gonna go inside and go to sleep," I said.

I COOLED IT FOR A WHILE after that, focusing on work, and spending more time with my parents and my sisters. They begged me to come home, but I couldn't take that step backward. I told them I was saving, and would get a better place and a better job soon, and maybe start college on my GI Bill.

On a Saturday not long after that, I rode the Triumph toward their house and spotted one of the neighbor girls, Doris, that hung out with us as kids. She was sitting on her parents' front steps, and Carla sat next to her. They were engrossed in conversation, laughing at something. The sound of the bike approaching caused them to look up, but they didn't seem to recognize me.

I pulled over, put the kickstand down, and walked over to talk to them. Carla looked beautiful, her teenage girlish look now morphed into a striking young woman. She was well dressed and minimally made up. I saw shock and surprise on their faces the moment they recognized me. Carla seemed a different version of herself; one I didn't know, one that matured and grown past me.

"Hey," I said. "How's it going?"

They looked at each other, not sure what to say. It wasn't the greeting that I had expected. I took a moment to put myself in their place and figured it would surprise me too at what I looked like. I had spent much of my recent time in the dregs, and fit in well there, but now perceived the shock of the difference between myself and normal people my age. People who were doing something with their lives. *Normal people.*

"Oh, hey Levi," Doris said. "We hardly recognized you!"

I tried to engage them, particularly Carla, but it was uncomfortable and the small talk never bloomed into an actual conversation, no matter how hard I tried. They seemed disappointed in me, and eager for me to leave so they could discuss what I'd become. Carla motioned with her hand when saying something to Doris, and I noticed a sparkling engagement ring on her finger. I broke it off awkwardly, making an excuse and heading back to the bike.

As I pulled away, I realized I had blown the opportunity I had been dreaming about—finally, another chance to talk to her and maybe get back together. I thought about how stupid I looked and gunned the bike through town. She had always polished me, taught me to dress well, and I had allowed myself to decay. For a moment, I wished I'd studied business with my GI Bill, got some cushy job and drove up in fine clothes, a sharp haircut, and in an expensive car to impress them. Then I felt sick and wished I'd stayed in Tulsa and never come home. Nothing was the same. Nothing was the way I'd imagined it would be, and I realized it probably never would be. *Time waits for no one.*

I vowed to put Carla out of my mind for good. It gave me closure. She was gone to me. She belonged to someone else. I realized she was just a metaphor for the past, my past, and we'd never be teenagers again. Pining for her represented more shackles. It was one less thing to trouble me, but at the moment, my heart ached with the finality of that dream. It felt like when my grandfather died, and I had to accept I would never see him again.

I KEPT GOING, LOST in thought, and on a whim got on the highway toward Shayne's. He was my oldest and best friend, and he understood me in a way nobody else did. That evening we ate dinner at his parents' place, a great Italian meal made by his wonderful mom. I was angry, and wanted to blow off steam, so he took me to a rock club near where he lived. He had a nice new bike, so we rode in tandem, after reminding each other to take it easy on the drinking.

We sat at the bar; me ordering beer with chasers and him drinking his usual Jack and Coke. A band set up and started their first set as the tables and dance floor filled. I took notice of a pretty girl with blond hair down to her waist and a thin leather headband across her forehead. Her smile never left her face, and she danced like someone without a care in the world, the epitome of tranquil hippie essence. She wore faded, patched jeans, a flowered cotton shirt, and a sleeveless brown suede vest embroidered with peace signs and flowers. *I want to be carefree like that.*

"Why are you still living with your parents?" I asked Shayne.

"I've been saving. I'm ready to book out. Bought a new bike, and I'm heading to Florida right after New Year's Eve.

I'm not freezing my ass off up here for another winter. I'm still landscaping, so they'll be laying me off for the season."

"Damn. Finally getting back on the road, huh?"

"Why don't you come with me?" he said. "We've always talked about taking a trip together, but the timing is always off. We always go without each other."

It tempted me, but I thought about the progress I'd been making, and getting a decent place, a better job, and starting school. "Pass, bro. I'm still trying to recover from my last trip."

"You have a few months, Levi. Keep it in mind. Things change."

They sure do. I was still watching the girl, and pretty drunk by then. The booze having kicked in, our conversations done, we got off our asses and mingled. He knew many people there. Some he had gone to school with, others just because he was so outgoing; he met and befriended people effortlessly.

"Get me an introduction to her," I asked him, nodding toward the hippie.

He engaged a dude at her table over a fresh tattoo the guy had, then motioned me over to admire it. I grabbed the empty seat between Shayne and the blonde, who was talking to her girlfriend on the other side.

After spending minimal time on the tattoo, I turned to her and asked her name.

"Starr," she said with that same broad, white smile. The band had started a slow song. "You want to dance?" she asked, taking my hand and leading me to the dance floor.

"Seems we're birds of a feather, ponytail boy," she said as we turned slowly on the dance floor, pressed against each other.

"Yeah, I'm thinking about chopping it though, and losing the beard," I said. We got to know each other as we danced and talked, and continued our conversation back at the table. She was from that area, but had spent the last few years living in California at some kind of commune. She had recently left it, and was now living with her sister nearby. We found we liked the same literature and talked about philosophy.

Her sister pulled her away to dance, and I moved back to the bar. Shayne was busy working on the other girls in the place, and one in particular. After a while, he grabbed me and pulled me aside. "Listen, bro. That girl over there invited me back to her place. My bike's fine here, so is yours. Don't ride back. Just grab a taxi back to my parents' place and crash. I'll see you in the morning."

She was a beauty, and I felt jealous, and alone again after he left. I did a shot, then another, trying not to think about what had happened earlier with Carla. Starr came over and pulled me back to the dance floor. I had avoided her as it had gone well earlier, and I didn't want to ruin it now that I was too drunk. I didn't want to blow it and embarrass myself.

I asked her to go outside for some air and took her hand. I showed her my bike and kissed her. She kissed me back, but broke it off, examining me for a moment.

"Do you always drink this much?" she asked.

"No, it just got away from me a little tonight. Let's go back to my place," I suggested, trying not to slur my words.

"I'm not getting on that thing with someone who's been drinking as much as you have, and neither should you."

I didn't want her to think I was stupid and apologized. "You're right. Let's take a taxi."

"Back to Lake Sussex? That'll cost a ton! I can't though, got to go back with my sister. I'm the designated driver tonight, and they're all past the limit. Not as much as you are, though."

Maybe it was paranoia about my condition, but her comment sounded condescending and I felt like a fool. Her sister came out and asked to leave.

She borrowed a piece of paper and pen from her sister's purse, and scribbled her phone number on it. "Promise me you'll take a taxi over to your friend's house," she said, holding it out of arm's reach until I agreed.

"I will," I lied, taking the paper.

Music and laughter still flowed from the bar, so I thought about going back in. I sat on the bike for a while, thinking about the shitty situation I was in, eying the pay phone on the outside wall of the building. *Just call a cab.*

Maybe it was because I'd already had a bike stolen from me in Tulsa. Maybe it was just my irrational, self-destructive side kicking in. Or, maybe it was my frugality, not wanting to spend a lot of money on a taxi, but I decided I just wanted to be home and in my crappy little bed in my crappy little shack. *If I can just get home, everything will be OK tomorrow.*

I unlocked my bike, got on, and fired it up, pulling away and leaving Shayne's sitting there alone, as he had left me. It was about a half-hour ride back. Not long after I left, it started to rain, and my headlight went out. Something must have allowed water to get in the casing and short it. I put on my flashers and cut my speed.

I made it to the highway off-ramp, almost home. Those ramps are excellent fun for cornering—perfectly curved and smooth blacktop. I could never resist, and I didn't resist this time. I twisted the throttle and cornered hard, scraping my foot peg, delighting in the sparks shooting up in my side-view mirror.

The other thing about highway ramps is that they often have leaked oil from big trucks. That's what I must have hit, because I felt the rear tire slide out, heard the crunch of the bike hitting the road, and felt my body slam against the tarmac.

15 Bad to Worse

The rain on my face woke me. I remained still, staring up at the drops coming from the black sky like a million relentless tiny bullets attacking without mercy. Blood filled my mouth, and I put my tongue against my teeth, immediately recoiling in sharp pain. Half a front tooth was missing, leaving behind a dangling, exposed nerve.

An attempt to sit up revealed that my left arm was unusable. I lifted it and tried to look in the dim light. It hung from my leather jacket at an unnatural angle half-way down my forearm. Everything else hurt as I struggled up the embankment I'd rolled down. Trash and loose, wet, early fall leaves covered it. I slid and fell several times, screaming in excruciating pain. I had learned to fight pain by embracing it. It was the only non-narcotic thing that worked. You had to welcome it, embrace it, take away its power over you. After that, it wasn't bad.

When I reached the top, I saw the bike had slid off the shoulder and onto the grass. The lights had gone out, so it wasn't visible enough for anyone to see and stop to help me. I was thankful for that, not wanting another drunk driving charge. My half-shell helmet lay on the edge of the road, a shattered mess.

I was about to leave everything there and start walking the rest of the way home when I heard a siren in the distance. *Fuck, someone must have called it in.*

I saw the police car through the trees, down on a side road. It would take him a few minutes to get onto the highway at the next entrance, double back, and come up on this side. I knew I only had a few minutes, and he'd find the bike with his searchlight.

Moving to the left side of the bike, I hooked my right arm under the handlebar, pulled it up, and guided it toward the embankment. After taking one last look at the treasure I had nurtured and polished, I shoved it. The foot peg snagged my pants leg and dragged me down again, smacking my broken left arm against the ground. It was as if the bike didn't want me to leave it. *What parent abandons their child?*

I scrambled back up and limped down the exit ramp, hoping to find somewhere warm and dry to hide until the cops came. Hopefully, they'd decide whomever had crashed had ridden off, and would give up the search. The next day I'd confess to being the rider, blame it on the wet weather, and avoid a drunk driving charge.

They made good time, and I saw the ominous blue and red flickering lights up on the highway, about to take the exit. I ducked down toward the end of the exit ramp, sliding down the embankment again on my butt, and lay still, trying to cover myself with leaves. My head throbbed slow and deep, like a nuclear reactor about to blow. Now that I could rest, I switched to a meditative technique to calm myself, still my breathing, and tried to block out the pain.

The tree canopy became a kaleidoscope of light, a natural disco ballroom, as the cop pulled up with his bar flashing full strength, and then another cop car, and then a third. I saw their searchlights scanning the area up the ramp where I'd crashed and heard their conversations.

"Maybe he rode off."

"Nope. Here's where it went down. Check out this gouge in the road. I don't think anyone rode away from this. Bike's got to be a mess, let alone the rider."

"Where the fuck is it, then? Where's he? I'm getting wet. Find the sumbitch."

A few moments of silence, the swooping, searching lights then found their prize.

"Yup, Here's the bike. Damn, it's trashed."

"Here's the hat, smashed like a watermelon. This fucker's layin' out here dead somewhere. Call an ambulance just in case, and the coroner. My shift's almost over. It's Saturday night—they'll take a while."

Coroner. I reached into my shirt to clutch the medallion and imagined myself lying there dead, and what that would do to my family. *For what? Help me out here, Saint Christopher, and I'll change, I swear it.*

They fanned out in a search pattern, some going further up the ramp, some heading down my way. The lucky winner shone his light directly on me and announced his triumph.

"The motherfucker is right here, fellas, he's awake."

The rest of the cops hurried down the ramp, excited to see the mess I was in. They then ran down the embankment, kicking sticks and debris in my face. The first one there eagerly grabbed me under my left armpit and tried to yank me up. I screamed in agony. "Easy! It's fucking broke!"

"Tough shit. That's what you get for trying to hide, boy," he said.

They took me by both sides and pulled me up the slope to the road.

"Cuff him, he looks shady. We don't know what kind of nut he is or what he's on," one said.

Another cop strode up with authority. I noticed he had three stripes. "I'm a vet, sergeant. My left arm's broke. Maybe some other stuff. I'm sorry. I didn't mean any trouble for you or your team tonight."

It was all I had to say. He let me know he was a fellow vet, also Vietnam-era, but he was older and had gone over to fight. He made sure they treated me well from that point and helped ease me into the back of the warm cop car until the ambulance arrived.

The medics arrived and treated me with compassion, sliding me onto a gurney and then loading me into the warm, dry bus to work on me. "You did a number here," one angel said.

"I always seem to do a number," I remember replying.

I must have passed out from exhaustion, the pain, maybe the booze. Or maybe they shot me up with something, or the trauma was so bad I just blacked it out. The body complains immensely when it's abused to such a degree, and the mind joins it in concert and remedy if the host refuses to be rational.

I woke up in a hospital bed the next morning. It was well lit, and everything was dry and soft. My arm was in a cast and they had bandaged every appendage plus my head. My leather jacket had saved my trunk, I guessed. It hung from the back of a nearby chair, which held my folded up ripped and bloody clothes.

A nurse came in. "Well, look who's awake," she said cheerily. "Rough night, huh?"

"I guess you could say that. One I'll regret, for sure. What's the damage assessment?"

She consulted a clipboard attached to my bunk. "Let's see here, Mr. Terra. The obvious to start with—clean break in your left radius and ulna. They did emergency surgery last night and you now have a steel plate screwed into them to keep everything in place until it heals. You broke off a tooth, and they cauterized the nerve. You'll need a crown or something on that, unless you want to let it ride. Other than that, just a concussion, cracked ribs, and a long list of contusions and skin rashes. It seems like you slid along the road and it ripped your pants leg off almost completely, so some deep skin loss there."

I listened to the summary patiently, all the while asking the same question my mother had asked. *What's wrong with you?*

"What about the cops?" I asked.

She put the clipboard down and gently put her hand on my leg. "It's not my area, so I shouldn't comment, but I care about you. They took blood and wrote you up for DWI. The citations are with your things. You were well over the limit, and shouldn't have been on that bike. We see the results all the time in here, and it's always sad."

"I know. I've had a rough patch lately. Poor decisions. I guess it's live and learn."

"You're awfully lucky to be in that category. Think about it."

My mother and sisters came rushing in, and the nurse excused herself. I wished I'd had time to tell her to refuse visitors and shut the door, but it was too late. The hurt I felt just by the look on their faces was far worse than the physical pain.

"Thank God you're not dead," Mom said, breaking down in tears and moving to the window, looking into the sky as if for help. I could see the stress on my little sisters' faces and feel their disappointment in me as well.

Mom turned back to me. "Your father is parking the car. He'll be right up."

"Great," I said. "Just when things were going well with us."

My sisters went about inspecting the various medical gadgets in the room, then found the television remote control tethered to my bed.

"When will it end?" Mom asked. "Isn't this enough? When will you wake up?"

"Look, Mom. I have a plan. I'm saving money to go to school."

"Every time you tell me that, no matter what state you're in, you suddenly upend everything and then have to spend all the money you've saved to go to school."

"Not on purpose, Mom. Every time it was circumstances beyond my control."

"No," she said, squeezing my leg and causing pain this time. "Because of choices you've made. Like getting drunk last night, and getting on that bike. Now you don't have a job."

I realized she was right. Perhaps it was all subconsciously self-destructive, punishing myself for something, maybe losing Carla, or not being with Sarah and Leah. *Or for killing someone.*

"I'll do better, Mom. You'll see. I'll make you proud someday."

"I hope so, son." Tears welled up again in her eyes, and it broke my heart. "Have you thought about Sarah and the baby?"

"Sure," I said. I hadn't, because I'd been pushing it away. But after she brought it up, I wondered if maybe it would be nice to be like Diego, have a family and nice things. *Life would be easier, and far less painful.*

Dad entered the room, looked at me, and shook his head. "You did a number on yourself this time," he said. "Nice work."

They hung out until someone wheeled my lunch in on a cart. Mom and the girls left first. Dad said he'd meet them down in the lobby and sat on a chair next to my bed. I turned the TV off.

"Listen," he started. "We spent years not getting along, barely talking. But someday you'll find out for yourself that there's no greater love than that of a parent for a child."

He paused and looked at me in a way I'd never experienced before.

"Levi, you know how brutal your grandfather, my father, was. It was rough for me, physically and mentally. I haven't been Father of the Year, but I know I've done better than him. And I hope you'll be far better than me. You have that in you."

"Yes, thank you, Dad."

"I dropped out of high school, went into the Army, got out, married your mom. You came along while I was in Germany and I couldn't be there. I didn't get an education. Hell, back then, all I wanted was to own a Corvette someday. That changed when we had you kids. I work hard, but I don't make much. Parents always try to shield their kids from the reality of that. But I know you've seen your mother crying at the kitchen table when she's doing the bills. I know you've heard our fights over money. I'm a proud man, but I need to tell you my silence and distance from you has been out of embarrassment, a failure to provide, not out of a lack of love for you."

I choked up. "Dad, you've done great. We've had a great life, thanks to you guys."

"I couldn't help you with college, Levi. You don't know how much that hurts, to have to say no to your kid for something they want so much, something that would give them a future. You had to enter the military, give up years of your life, and I know you didn't want to. That's my fault."

"I wanted to serve, like you did, and Grandpa."

"But it wasn't your first choice. Look, Levi. You're different—damn smart. You could have a brilliant future and break the generational cycle of our family having to bust their asses to get by. Nothing would make your mom and I happier before we have to go. Set an example for your sisters. You have it in you."

Tears rolled down my face as his words sank in. He stood and leaned over to hug me gently. I hadn't remembered him ever doing that before.

"I love you, son," he said on his way out, and I hadn't remembered him saying that either, at least not since I was a little kid.

Alone again in the room, I picked at the cold, tasteless food. I kept the TV off to rest and think. I realized I'd lose my job and have to move back to the house. *One step forward, two steps back.*

Later that afternoon, Shayne bounced into the room. "Oh, my God!" he said in his loud, exuberant way, scaring the nurse that was taking my blood pressure with her back to him. "What the hell happened? You were supposed to take a taxi to my parents' place."

"Didn't work out that way, obviously," I said. "I really don't want to rehash the whole thing. I fucked up, I know that."

"OK. I called the cops, and they said your bike was still in the woods. Tim and I used his buddy's pickup and went and grabbed it. We took it to your parents' place. It's not as bad as you might think."

The thought of getting back on it, as much as I loved that bike, repulsed me at the moment. My entire lifestyle did. "Thanks, bro."

"So, what now?" he asked.

"I don't know. I'm pretty fucking down right now. It's difficult to think. Too much pain. I'll figure it out."

"You're going to be laid up for a while. File your unemployment ASAP. Take that trip to Florida with me this winter. We'll have a blast. There's plenty of work down there. We'll hit the beach every day. You love the beach."

It sounded good, the beach part anyway, but the thought of another trip made me sick. *Freedom is the ability to choose, not always just taking off to prove you have it. Maybe I choose to stay.*

His attention turned to another nurse that had come in. "Give this man some drugs!" he implored her. "He's in pain! In fact, so am I! I need drugs, woman! We *both* need drugs, and lots of them!" He got up and limped around the room, stooped over like an old man, one hand on his spine. The nurse laughed and flirted back as I laid there, taking it all in. *He'll probably be dating her by the time I'm out of here.*

He left, and I asked the nurse when I could get out.

"It'll be a few days," she said. "No promises, we just need to make sure you're healing up OK. Stay put for now, and we'll check you out in the morning, get you up and moving around."

When I was alone, I slid the covers down and looked at my legs. Everything was a mess, bandaged in gauze with dried blood and white tape. I slid my legs over the edge of the bed and pain shot through me as my knees buckled.

I carefully put one foot on the floor, then another. Grabbing the handrail on the bed, I tried to stand. After a while, I could. My whole body throbbed in pain, one giant pulse after another. A wave of dizziness almost took me down, so I sat again, and reversed my actions and pulled the sheets and blanket back over me, defeated.

That night Sarah called, surprising me. I could hear the baby in the background, and I knew it wasn't intentional on her part. She was better than that. She was a good person and never played games.

"How are you?" she asked. "Your mom called me. She thought I should know."

"I'm OK. She shouldn't have, though. You have enough on your plate without worrying about me, Sarah."

"I still care about you, very much. No matter what happens. I know you, Levi. I know you're lost, but you'll find your way. Underneath it all, you're a good person."

"Well, how are you doing?" I asked, eager to change the subject.

"I'm alright, I guess, trying to get it together too. I'm studying for my GED and working at Lilla's bar."

I remembered the place; it was a dump downtown where the alcoholics went to drink after they'd received their welfare checks. "You can do better than that, Sarah."

"I know. Things are tough here. But it's a start. It's some money, for now. I get food stamps for me and Leah."

The thought of them living like that hurt me deep in my soul. I felt it was my fault, felt guilty again, and that it was more lives that I'd affected. *Some freedom.*

Neither one of us said anything for a long moment. I sensed she was trying to get something out.

"I'm um, I'm seeing someone, anyway," she finally revealed. "It's not serious. Just some bowling and stuff. He works at the dairy, and he's on the men's softball team."

It made me angry and jealous. *What right do you have? You left her.* I quickly course-corrected and admonished myself. "Well, that's good, I guess. I'm happy for you, Sarah. I want you to be happy, and I'm trying to be happy."

"It doesn't seem like it, Levi. But I still care about you, remember that. I still love you."

I told her I cared about her, and we said goodnight.

16 Healing

They tested and prodded me over the following days, changed bandages, and finally wheeled me to the door in a wheelchair with a new pair of wood crutches to use at home. Dad came to get me, and it surprised me to see him in good spirits.

"I got a promotion at work, floor manager now," he said with pride.

"Wow, congrats! You earned it, way overdue."

"They said they might hold my old spot open until you're healed up a little," he said. "I think you could manage it with one arm for a while, with some help. What do you think?"

I thought about how he'd described the years of struggle and toil in that job, trying to get by, just making it, foregoing things other people had, like nice vacations and cars. He would be my boss, which wasn't a good thing. I didn't want to crush his hope or his mood, or undo the progress we'd made. "Yeah, Pop. Maybe that's something to look at, after I'm ready."

We were quiet the rest of the way, enjoying the crisp fall breeze with open windows. The leaves turning color and whirling in symphony with each rush of wind. I remembered gathering them as a child, and pressing them between sheets of wax paper to preserve their beauty forever. I wondered where those sheets were now. *Nothing lasts forever. There is no preservation; only memories and either fond ones or regret, depending on the decisions you've made.*

When we arrived back home, they settled me into my old room. I was back again to that place that kept pulling me there, or maybe I was pushing myself to. It was my safe space, a place where, as a child, I didn't have to worry about anything except getting my homework done. Everything else was being taken care of in other areas of the house and life. I took down the picture of Carla and myself and put it away in a desk drawer.

I laid on the bed for a while, my feet touching the wagon wheel foot board. I had outgrown it, and felt silly, as if I were a grown man in a crib. Reconsidering my father's offer, I became offended at the idea. *Another trap. I don't want to be a cog in a wheel. I want to write a great novel someday, that people will cherish and enjoy, and be free to travel and write for the rest of my life.*

Exhausted from the day and the sheer effort of any kind of bodily movement, I dozed off.

THE PERIOD OF HEALING began. I started receiving unemployment checks, and spent my days working on the bike, reading, writing, and often going to the Bivouac for a few beers, but not drinking to excess. Court appointments came and went, and I lost my license for a while after paying my fines and bail money that I shamefully had to borrow from my parents.

I called Starr, and she got mad at me for being so stupid, but came to the house to see me after she'd cooled off. We worked together on the bike in the garage, often ending up covered in grease. She did what I couldn't do, essentially being down to one functioning arm. I could tell that Mom liked her, but preferred I focus on Sarah. Starr got along well with my father, who fashioned himself now as some sort of hippie cowboy type.

Dad's birthday came, and we all celebrated it. Besides our traditional case of beer, I got him a huge Corvette model car kit. He went right to work on it, and finished it within a few days, as excited as if it were sitting outside and drivable. He made an acrylic display case for it at work and proudly sat it in our living room, to my mom's dismay.

"I finally got my Corvette," he'd say to his friends when they visited.

I told him I'd buy him a real one someday, after my first novel made it big. He didn't have the heart to tell me it would probably never happen, but I could see it on his face. The model car made him happy for a while, and that's all that mattered as far as I was concerned.

One day when we were working on the bike, I asked Starr what she thought about going to Florida for the winter, just after New Year's Eve. I was hopeful she'd go, as I liked her and thought we might have a future.

"Nah," she said. "I enrolled at the county college. I'm going to take some classes and get my degree."

The disappointment of it stung, and I felt again that everyone was moving forward in their lives except me. We launched into a discussion of destiny and metaphysics as we turned wrenches and bolted junk-yard replacement parts back on. She was spiritual that way, even mystical, and read a lot of interesting stuff, like Oswald Spengler and Edgar Cayce. She had just finished *Zen and the Art of Motorcycle Maintenance* and gave it to me to begin.

"I think you're out of line with your true core self, Levi. We all have a design built into us, woven into our fabric. That new DNA stuff, right? I believe that if we go in a direction that's at odds with that, going against that grain, we can't be happy. It's unnatural, and things don't go well. I think you're going against your grain, Levi."

It correlated with much of what I'd been feeling. The problem was, I wasn't sure what my path should be, or how I was truly wired in the sense she described. What she said was what I needed to hear.

Since I wasn't doing as much drinking, I spent a lot of my time at the Bivouac playing pool. I had watched old Jimmy the house hustler for years, learning his tricks. I was just never as good as he was at the game. My condition gave me an advantage though—I had filed a notch into my cast and used it as a bridge, a steady base for my shots, and it worked well. I started making side money that way.

I had been noticing a gradual change in things. The Bivouac wasn't the same. Most of the regular crowd I had known and hung out with weren't around. I asked about Bobby Russo and was told he'd married Gwen and was no longer drinking. He had a kid. Everyone was moving on, life was moving on. *You can't stop the wheel.* A new crowd was taking over, and the music was changing. The drinking age was still eighteen, and I was finding myself the older guy at the bar, like the ones I used to see when I first started going there at that age. Back then, I wondered why those guys weren't doing something more useful with their lives.

Libraries were always my safe space, my home base when I needed quiet and a place to learn or to think. Since I was a little kid, I had always marveled at the walls and shelves full of books and the sheer number of stories in them. I went more, and spent a lot of time at the microfiche machine, looking at Tennessee newspapers for any stories about bodies found in the woods off the highway. I realized that part of my problem was that I was living in fear and remorse every day because of what had happened.

We moved into holiday season in quick succession—Halloween, Thanksgiving, then Christmas. Starr and I finished the bike, and she wasn't coming around as much. Every week was about the same, and I found myself in a rut. I got my cast off and had healed up. The unemployment checks had stopped coming, and I got my driver's license back. I was out of excuses, draining my bank account, and I had to find something to ease my restless mind. Rumors circulated that John Barrack was about to be released from the county jail, and I dreaded running into him.

Ultimately, I once again chose escape. I always hated the winter, other than the chance to play ice hockey on the frozen lake as a kid. But I had outgrown that too. It was no longer part of my life, but I enjoyed standing on the bridge and watching the new generation out there playing. I envied them for all they had ahead of them in life and hoped each one would make good choices. I wanted to stop their games and tell them, because the small bad choices always grew like cancer in your life.

The Triumph only held terrible memories for me and wasn't suitable for a long road trip, so I sold it and bought a big Honda 750. Shayne and I began meeting and planning for the trip. My morose had lifted, once again I felt I had purpose, I was living again, free again. It got me through the disappointment of my parents, and Sarah, after I told them I was taking the trip. I didn't understand how Sarah could think she was next in my life when she was seeing some softball-playing milkman. She didn't say it, but I heard it in her voice.

I hoped I would find my purpose on this trip. It made more sense. Warm weather, no hitching, someone to talk to. I'd be in control of things, and no longer begging others for rides. *The great American road trip, this one will go better.* Riding down from the north in winter would be a challenge. We knew we'd have to be flexible in our departure and look for our best shot with the weather. That part was exciting too, playing the game against mother nature.

We were fortunate, as it turned milder after Christmas. Much of the snow melted off the roads, and it looked good for the next week, at least. I loaded my military backpack, considering whether each item was essential. My one luxury was a small cassette player like the one Mary Jefferson had showed me. I tucked it into an accessible pocket on the side of the pack. I installed a rough cruise-control that would lock the throttle open and ease the strain on my still-sore arms, and highway pegs to stretch my legs at highway cruising speeds.

When I finished, I took the pack to the garage, where the big bike waited like a horse in its stable. I carefully strapped it onto the luggage rack with bungee cords, pushing and bouncing it to make sure it was secure. Next, I rolled up my big, warm sleeping bag with an authentic wool Mexican serape that Diego had given me. I stood them vertically on the passenger seat and strapped them to the backrest. It would allow me to lie back and relax. I had hoped that Starr would be there behind me, but she wouldn't, and I had to accept that.

On New Year's Eve Day, I woke before dawn, made a big, hearty breakfast, and checked everything over one last time. By the time I was ready to leave, Mom was up, then the girls, and finally Dad roused. They had given up trying to talk me out of it days ago, when they realized it was futile. All they had for me now was love, and hope that everything would be OK. They all put their coats on over their pajamas and followed me out to the cold, stark garage. I pulled on winter ski pants, heavy insulated work boots, and a big thermal parka. All were Christmas gifts from my parents and sisters.

"Be careful on that thing," Mom said, holding back tears.

"I want to go to Florida!" my sisters each said. "Take me!"

"Maybe someday," I told them. "Keep doing your best in school."

Mom and the girls hugged me, then Dad shook my hand and pulled me into an embrace. "Think about what I said to you in the hospital," he said. He didn't know his words had been nagging at me almost every day.

I pulled the garage door open, saddled up, pulled open the choke and depressed the starter button (a luxury none of my previous bikes had had). The engine rumbled to life, and my sisters ran around the garage with their hands over their ears. I put the earphones securely into my ears, pushed the play button on the Walkman, then carefully slid my new full-face helmet over my head to not disturb them. The road music cassette I had meticulously selected and recorded filled my head like a symphony. Everything in place, I pulled on the long, thick arctic gloves I had taken when I was in the military.

As the bike rolled down the driveway toward the road, I glanced in my mirrors to see them all waving from the mouth of the garage. For a moment, I thought about going back home to safety and security, get a good job, maybe make things right with Sarah. It would be something I could make happen, and I didn't know what lay ahead for me. It was intimidating, and I felt uneasy, another sign that I was changing.

17 New Years

The quick trip to Shayne's made for an excellent test run. I pulled into his driveway, parked, and began making some adjustments to my gear. Shayne came bursting out of the house, clapping his hands together with a big smile on his face.

"Here we go, bro! The big day has arrived!"

He said he still had a little work to do on his bike, accessories he'd just bought that needed to be installed. I pulled mine into his parents' garage, next to his. We went inside and his mom had made a big breakfast; I ate that one too. As my parents did, she also cautioned and cajoled us, attempting to talk us out of the trip.

After we ate, we spent time in his room poring over our twin road atlases—although mine was ratty and road-worn, while his was new. We debated routes to take, when to stop, where to sleep. He wanted to use I-81 to I-77, back through the Pennsylvania Lehigh Valley, down through the western half of Virginia and through Charlotte, North Carolina, to hit I-95 in South Carolina. I had just traveled a good chunk of that route twice and was eager for something different. I also wanted to stay as far from Tennessee as possible, favoring a more direct route along the coast, getting to warm weather sooner.

"We'd have to go through Philly, Baltimore, and DC," he said. "I thought you didn't like the cities?"

"When hitchhiking, sure," I argued. "On bikes, we'll get to enjoy seeing the cities from a safe distance. Let's get warm faster. Florida awaits, my good man."

He eventually conceded, after I gave in to his request to stop in Charlottesville and see Damon. He was back there working at his college job, living with some girl he'd met, and bugging me to visit. We got busy finishing up Shayne's bike for the trip. We had expected to leave that morning, but by the time we'd finished, his mom was already making us lunch.

"It's too late to leave, boys," she said. "Why not stay tonight, rest up, I'll make a wonderful dinner, and you can leave first thing in the morning, when you're fresh?"

"It is New Year's eve," Shayne said with a grin.

"Oh dear Lord," his mom exclaimed. "That's not what I was talking about."

Once he got an idea in his head, it was hard to steer him away from it. He began making calls, and soon it was settled. We'd go back to the same bar that we were at the night I had made my mistake, and celebrate the new year before leaving. *And probably hung over as hell.*

We loaded the bikes, then borrowed Shayne's parents' car and hit the bar early, vowing to leave just after the ball drop. We took a table, rather than seats at the bar, hoping for company. Tim showed up, still angry and blaming me for the treatment he had received at the hospital in Tulsa. I thanked him for pulling my bike out of the ditch. The band took the stage, and the staff passed out gaudy party favors. Starr, her sister and their friends entered after all the tables had been taken, and crowded in at ours.

As with any good time, the hours flew by. Shayne was in full Shayne mode, commanding the room, making everyone laugh with his outrageous, hilarious antics. Often, I acted like a pilot fish feeding on scraps as the women gravitated toward him, but not tonight. I wanted to spend time with Starr. We shared a chair, and she ended up on my lap. "Get a room!" Shayne shouted at us.

"We should do that," I said.

"Good luck finding one on New Year's Eve," she said. I became hopeful, since she'd even consider the idea.

"How about your place?" I asked her.

"My sister would go nuts. That's a rule with her. No overnight guests."

"And she doesn't like me very much."

"I'm her little sister, Levi. You have little sisters too. You know how it is." She rummaged in her purse and showed me a small cellophane bag. "Want some of this?"

"I'm good. Weed will just knock me out at this point."

"It's not weed. It's magic mushrooms," she said, laughing.

I put my hand out, smiling. It would allow me to enjoy the night without more booze, avoiding the feared hangover. I hated the taste of them, but loved the hallucinogenic effect. She pulled out a pinch of the plants and put them in my palm. I chewed them, gagging, and tried to wash the taste out of my mouth with beer.

"Worst part's over," I said, as she did the same.

The mushrooms took effect slowly, like drifting off to sleep but staying awake. Colors became sharper, and the hidden meaning behind everything revealed itself to me. It was another level of consciousness. Hallucinogens could expose the best or the worst in someone. They had always worked well for me, making me happier, more insightful, and able to write better.

But I'd seen them unleash demons inside of people—hidden demons that were otherwise bottled up. I could feel the greasy, lecherous, fat bastard from Tennessee lurking around the edges of my consciousness and refused to let him in. I formed a protective bubble around myself, refusing to let what he caused to happen, what he'd made me do, ruin the night.

I envisioned Sarah and Leah outside that bubble, waving and looking in sadly. I wondered what they were doing, and then shut them out of my mind, deciding I'd have plenty of time to think about them and everything else while on the road. The idea of Carla drifted by, faint on the edge of my consciousness, and I let it float by without acknowledging it.

Starr and I shared secrets and silly ideas, giggling and annoying the others. Shayne looked into my enlarged pupils and discovered the secret. "You bastard!" he said when I told him there was only a little and we'd used it all. The band started a slow song, and I led Starr to the dance floor. We embraced and kissed throughout it, holding onto each other, wordlessly touching each other's faces.

"Come join me in Florida," I asked her. "Come, be warm with me. We'll go to the beach every day after work, and all weekend."

"That sounds good," she said. "We'll see what happens when I continue to freeze my ass off. I'm used to California, remember."

I knew she never would and felt bad that this might be our last night together. Too many times, despite plans and promises, life just continued sweeping us slowly down the river on our course, and often apart from one another for good. I vowed to always live for the moment, and Starr agreed. I hadn't realized I was saying the thoughts aloud.

Suddenly, the band began the countdown, and everyone stood and joined in. "5... 4... 3... 2... 1—Happy New Year!" everyone shouted. Auld Lang Syne played, then the band kicked back in with reggae music as Shayne began leading everyone around the bar in a conga line.

"Let's get out of here," Starr whispered.

We put our coats on and left the bar, out into the clear, chilly night. She unlocked her sister's car, and we lay down together in the back seat, snuggling against each other for warmth. She pointed out the Big Dipper. Every point of light seemed impossibly bright, and a shooting star coursed its way across the sky.

"Did you make a wish?" I asked.

"I always do."

"Did you wish I'd stay?"

She looked into my eyes, hers even larger and more beautiful than ever. "I'd never wish for something I know you don't want, Levi. It would be selfish. I only wished for you to be safe and happy, farawayer."

"How did you know that name, Starr?"

"You told me, at the beginning, when you were drunk. At first I thought you were proud of it, like some kind of badge to self-validate what you were doing. But then I realized it was a cross you were bearing, and I felt you were looking for someone to take it off of you. I thought it could be me, but I guess not."

I knew she was right. "Well, I have to admit it's getting harder, and it's getting old. Maybe this is the last rodeo for me." I dreamed about being with her, going to school together, maybe getting a place. She didn't have any kids, unlike Mary and Jolene. *It would be new for both of us.*

"Maybe," she agreed. "But nobody can make that decision for you, Levi, and you should never allow yourself to make it for any reason other than it's what *you* want."

I kissed her and thanked her for understanding. Emotion caught up with me. "Starr, I've met no one like you. I feel so good around you, and we connect so well. What I'm trying to say is, I... "

She shook her head and touched my lips to stop me. "I can't do that with you going away, Levi, sorry. I'm going to have to be your serial farawayer victim this time."

We laughed at the silliness of it. I couldn't ever imagine her being a victim. She was too strong and wise from whatever things she'd been subjected to. Neither she nor her sister ever talked about their parents, and only mentioned the commune they'd lived on with them in passing, as some shared, dreadful secret between them.

"Maybe I'm tired of being a farawayer," I said. "I'm tired of leaving people I care about. It was hard and sad yesterday with my family. Now it's hard and sad with you."

"I think you're afraid to commit. Afraid you won't do well. Think about that. But understand this—I think deep down, you're a good person and you'll do just fine, if you ever get to that point, Levi. Sometimes there's no happy ending. Kerouac, Hemingway, Fitzgerald, and so many others died miserable after chasing that dream too long. Has it ever turned out well for anyone?"

We stopped talking and focused on the sky for a while. We kissed, and I tried to unsnap her jeans. She gently took my hand away and placed it over her heart instead. She kissed me on the forehead and we lay there for a long time, enjoying the silence of the winter night juxtaposed with the muffled music and commotion from inside the bar.

Eventually it disgorged its drunken, staggering revelers, some laughing and some fighting. Starr's sister and their friends banged on the fogged-up windows, ending our nestled retreat. We got out of the car and said our goodbyes until her sister honked the horn with impatience.

Our eyes teared from the cold, the drugs, and sadness as we embraced one last time and said goodbye again. Shayne was by the club door, attempting to convince an unsteady girl to join us back at his house. "Come on, we'll have a ball," he persisted.

She seemed to consider it until a girlfriend came and led her away by the arm.

He walked over. A brief look of disappointment crossed his face. It was all he ever allowed himself. Then it was always on to the next thing. "Helluva night, huh bro? Let's get the fuck out of here. Big day tomorrow."

I agreed to drive, as the micro-dose was wearing off, fading back into wherever recess of the brain it had exposed, and I hadn't had a drink in hours. By the time we reached his house, all our failed plots from the night were a distant memory. We were fully focused on the next day. Opening the garage door, we took a few minutes to admire the fully loaded and prepped machines that waited to carry us away at first light.

18 Southbound

In the morning I went up the stairs to Shayne's bedroom to tap on the door. "Let's go," I whispered. I heard him rustling inside and went back downstairs to use the bathroom before anyone else got up.

We made up enormous bowls of cereal using cooking pots and slurped them down as his parents and sister made their way to the kitchen. His mom offered to make us breakfast, but we refused, wanting to leave, as the sun was already up. She placed two aspirin and glasses of orange juice in front of each of us, and we eagerly washed them down.

Shayne flung the garage door open, and sunlight flooded the bikes, the chrome gleaming, but it was damn cold to be riding. We geared up in our winter clothes, as I had done the morning before, and the same sad goodbyes took place. After the bikes had warmed, we went down his long winding driveway side-by-side.

We headed east on I-280, and the rising sun made it tough to see. We rode with one hand, shielding our eyes at reduced speed, keeping to the slower right-hand lane. Relief came when we connected to the Garden State Parkway south. When the 95 South entrance appeared, Shayne blasted his horn ahead of me and stood on his pegs with one fist upraised. I knew he was shouting inside his helmet. I pulled alongside him and did the same. We were now on the one singular highway that would take us all the way to our destination, aside from the side trip to see Damon. Our bikes sped up onto the exit ramp, a smooth decreasing radius turn. We leaned the bikes over in tandem, reveling in the sound of scraping pegs on the roadway. We were heading south, mile by mile, degree by degree, to warmer weather.

The holiday eased New Jersey's always-clogged roadways, paving our way to make good time. There were few cops, likely because most worked the night before. The world slept, hung over, as we made our escape. After an hour and a half, the cold, not to be denied, seeped in. My fingers grew numb and the steel plate in my arm ached. I clipped on the cruise control and alternated shoving one hand after another under my coat to warm by my belly.

Families on their way home from visiting loved ones for the holidays escorted us, their kids excitedly pointing and gesturing, their enslaved parents shaking their heads and likely saying "What a pair of dumbasses," in their hidden envy. They were likely dreading their return to work and the hamster wheel of their lives.

We passed by Philly and its majestic skyscrapers, then briefly into the northern tip of Delaware, and entered the Maryland suburbs north of Baltimore. Shayne signaled, and we took the off-ramp for a service area to warm and gas up. Truckers, always outspoken, offered their opinion as we dismounted and parked the bikes.

"You're fucking crazy!"

"What a life! Keep on rollin' brothers! I wish I could join yas!"

"Hey boys, take the rig, finish my route, trade me for the bike!"

Inside, I slapped my heavy gloves on a table and bought a large, steaming hot coffee, rolling my hands around it to thaw them. Shayne was already working the room, chatting up the other travelers and truckers, asking about speed traps ahead and the weather. I watched as he made even the most grumpy-looking road warriors laugh within a few seconds of approaching them. If I'd have had that talent, my hitchhiking trips would have been effortless. *And maybe someone wouldn't have died.*

I sat at a table, wondering if I'd ever get closure over what happened. During the time I'd spent in the library, I secretly wished I'd find an article about a guy that had stumbled from the woods, wounded, and lived to go to jail forever for past offenses. It would set me free. The burden of something like that is like a cancer that never kills you to put you out of your misery. It just stays, malignant, and keeps the pain coming. *Maybe someday I'll go back and look for bones and my bayonet.*

"Why the glum face?" Shayne shouted, startling me back to the present moment.

I forced a laugh. "I didn't get any last night. What do you think?"

"Me neither! Let's go, brother. There's plenty up ahead on the beaches of Flor-Ri-Da."

We geared back up, making some necessary changes, and roared back onto the highway. The scenery wasn't as pretty as hitchhiking season, as all the leaves had fallen from the trees. We circled the beltways around Baltimore and Washington and entered Virginia. Each state line marker we approach kicked off a mini-celebration of furious pointing and blaring horns, and I convinced myself it was warming, and it probably was; a little anyway.

Around Fredericksburg, we cut off the highway for more scenic local roads toward Charlottesville. The reduced speed made a vast difference in cold and comfort, and the riding became more enjoyable. A little after lunchtime, we found the address that Damon had given me and rolled up in front of it. As we were freeing our packs from the luggage racks, he came out to greet us. I was happy to see him back to his enthusiastic self.

"What's up, fellas! C'mon in! Let's party! Damn, two white boys coming up in this neighborhood on tour. Cops'll be here soon, for sure. Whites don't come around except to collect rent or post eviction notices. Come on in, X-Men! I'll fire up the bong!"

We settled in and met his new girlfriend, Wanda. She was just eighteen, a dark-haired white girl who was so small and thin she was barely there beneath her sweatpants and a too-large AC/DC T-shirt.

Damon made us sandwiches and brought beer from the fridge. He was a storyteller, often embellishing for effect, and told grand tales about "Carl Day," our homelessness, the fight with the rednecks, and other events that had transpired when we were last together. Wanda made up a punch of grain alcohol and fruit juice, and served it up in Mason jars full of ice.

We eased through the day smoking weed, talking and watching college football bowl games with the TV silent and music on their audio system. Wanda played DJ as she and Damon fought between blues requests and her preferred newer rock styles. We outvoted her every time, but occasionally showed mercy and rolled our eyes at each other at some of the punk stuff she played. Dinnertime came, and a deliveryman brought pizza to the door. It was nothing like Jersey pizza, but we downed it in celebration. It was good to be back in the vibe of that college town, and I almost wished we could have stayed longer than one night.

After dinner, the talk turned to the Coal Mine. We'd told Shayne all about it, and he was eager to check it out. Wanda pushed back, as she detested beer and wasn't old enough to drink hard liquor.

"Don't worry, I'll order your screwdrivers and pass them over," Shayne assured her, to settle the argument.

We all took turns cleaning up in the lone bathroom, with Damon and Wanda showering together first, allegedly to save hot water. They defeated the goal as they took longer than they would have individually, as Shayne turned up the stereo to drown out their noise.

We crammed into Wanda's 1960s Volkswagen beetle and merrily made our way to the bar. As we pulled up, we all spotted the marquee at the same time—Muddy Waters Live Tonight.

"Check this out," Damon said. "Am I tripping or some shit? Muddy? For real?"

"Oh, damn, bro, how could you *not* know this?" Shayne shouted.

We all slapped each other on the shoulders as we got out of the tiny car. As we reached the door, the bouncer eyed us suspiciously. I wondered if he'd remembered us from when Carl had flipped the table over and caused a ruckus.

"Show's sold out," he said, after asking us for tickets we didn't have.

Damon hung his head in defeat. "Figures," he said, turning to walk away.

"Hold up, hold up," Shayne said, pushing ahead of us to talk to the doorman.

"Listen, that guy with us is Muddy's nephew. He drove here last minute from Memphis, drove for hours, to surprise him and see the show. Muddy kept telling him since he was a kid, 'Come on out when you're old enough, I'll get you in.' Go ask Mr. Waters, please," Shayne bluffed with a smile.

The dude didn't look too bright, and an impatient line was forming behind us. "Come on, show's gonna start," someone yelled. "Let them in, let's go," a woman called out.

"Please," Shayne said again, pushing cash into the doorman's hand as he shook it.

That sealed the deal, and we paid our cover charge and went in.

"We're on the road tomorrow," Shayne cautioned me. "Let's take it easy."

"Roger that," I replied. "Someone's off to the races, though."

Damon was already at the bar ordering drinks and Muddy's band was in full swing, but he had yet to take the stage.

"Hey, you," someone called as we made our way through the crowd. I turned to see Jolene dancing on a bench against the wall. I pushed my way through to her, picked her up, and carried her to the dance floor.

Because there was a blues legend on the bill, the audience was far more racially mixed than normal. The night was a rare sociological experiment as the crowd mixed, excited, alive, joyous. Black men danced with white women, white men danced with black women, and nobody gave it a thought—a rare thing in the south, even for those more modern times. It gave me hope that maybe someday the world would be like that; in every workplace, in the criminal justice system, people treating each other humanely and fairly.

Late in the night, the band introduced Muddy, and the man walked onto the stage. Everyone stopped what they were doing and stood in awe. He and his music were the foundation for modern rock and roll. He was a legend, despite all the obstacles he'd endured along the way to that stage from a Mississippi slave plantation.

"Thank you," he said, leaning into the mic. "Now don't just stand there, people, let's party!" He counted the band in and they launched into a fiery blues song. We all began to shake and shimmy at once. We had no choice; our bodies would not be denied.

We stayed until the last set wound down and we'd cheered him as he waved and left the stage. The band carried on, but we made our way outside, worn out from the long day and night. I took Jolene's hand and led her around the corner. We kissed deep, condensation flowing from our mouths and noses as we stopped to catch our breath in the night's cold.

"So," she began slowly, "I never had time to ask you in there. Why are you back? Did you decide to become a stayer, farawayer?"

"No, I'm sorry. We're on the way to Florida on our bikes. Want to come?"

"Won't work for me," she said. "I've got a job and a little one. You know that."

I felt bad for asking. I wanted to go home with her, to her comfortable, simple apartment, and spend the night, maybe my life. She was straightforward and undramatic about things, and it was refreshing. I knew it wouldn't happen, and I didn't want to hurt her again or have another sad goodbye in the morning.

"Well, we'll stop here on the way back up north. Maybe I'll be a stayer then."

"Somehow, I doubt that," she said. She laughed and pushed me away playfully. "Goodnight, Levi. Be careful on the bike, OK?"

I wondered why she had found no one and remembered it was harder with a kid. I walked her to her car, told her goodnight, and began searching the lot for my group. Shayne had a girl pushed against a car. They were laughing and making out. Damon and Wanda waited by her car a short distance away.

"Yo, you coming with us?" I shouted to Shayne. He looked at the girl and they said something to each other and laughed.

"Apparently not. She says she's kidnapping me," he shouted back.

We waved, got back into the Beetle, and left. There was only one bedroom, so I grabbed the couch and laid out my sleeping bag, covered by Diego's serape. Wanda brought me a pillow, and I passed out immediately.

Morning came with the clang of pans and silverware. Damon was cooking something at the stove. Shayne snored on a nearby overstuffed chair, having made his way back somehow. I got up and lifted the blinds to see both bikes covered in snow.

"Oh, shit, this isn't good," I said.

Shayne stirred. "Yeah, I got in a few hours ago. It was snowing like hell."

He went right back to sleep, and I joined Damon in the kitchen.

"What're you guys going to do?" he asked. "We only get a little of that stuff down here. They got no snowplows, so you got to wait until it melts. Probably won't take long, soon as the sun warms it."

I looked over at Shayne, who had grabbed my spot on the couch and was back to snoring.

"I guess we're not going anywhere for a while."

We ate in the kitchen, played some soft Gil-Scott Heron music, and enjoyed the time together. We wondered what Diego was doing and talked with some envy about him settling down. Then we spoke about how good it was to be free again, out of the military, as we had dreamed about together for years.

While Wanda and Shayne slept, we went outside and cleaned the snow off the bikes, then went for a walk in the quiet, white morning. They lived in a neat neighborhood of small houses and duplexes that comprised the lives of the families they contained, and would likely be all they would ever know for generations. It was hard to break through the class divisions, despite how hard people tried to make a better life for their children. We weren't too far from the abandoned building we had lived in, and neither of us wanted to visit it. The pain of that time was too recent.

When we got back to the house, Shayne was sitting up on the couch, rubbing his eyes. Wanda was at the stove, cooking a second round of eggs and bacon.

"Oh, *damn*, what a night, huh?" he asked with his usual exuberance.

"Better for some than others," I teased.

He peeped out the window. "We're late," he said.

"Bullshit, there's no such thing. We're free. What's the hurry?"

He agreed as Wanda handed him a plate of food and silverware. They both had work later in the day, having scheduled around our visit. After Shayne had finished his meal and we'd finished a few cups of coffee, we packed up our gear and started assembling it onto the bikes. The sun was up and clumps of melted snow fell from the trees, roofs, and power lines overhead. We pulled on waterproof pants and boot coverings to avoid getting soaked from the inevitable spray from our wheels.

We said our goodbyes. I could tell they were sad to see us go and wanted to join us, just like everyone else we encountered. Everyone wanted an escape from the cycle of their lives, at least temporarily. What they didn't know was how much they'd miss it. Snow and ice patched the roads, causing us to pick our way around the slippery spots on our way to the highway.

We treated ourselves by heading west instead of east, and picked up the Blue Ridge Parkway, a legendary motorcycling road we'd long dreamed about tackling. It was well out of the way, but we took it on with glee, challenging each other on the hairpin turns and switchbacks, pushing the loaded bikes to their limits. I had hitched through it in slow-motion on my earlier trip, but it was nothing like the thrill of high speed on two wheels. The views were breathtaking, and the challenge of navigating it caused a continual flow of adrenaline until we pushed down to Lynchburg and cut back across to I-95.

Taking I-64 back to I-95, we picked our way through Richmond and were once again heading south. The road became dryer, and the weather warmed up as we progressed until we could remove a layer of clothing at the next gas stop after crossing into North Carolina. The seasons were once again reversing; gray became green. Now fully awake, the border-crossing gaiety resumed. *Back on the road.*

Progress became marked by the garish, Latin-stereotype road signs for the South of the Border tourist trap. They marked off the miles with amusing phrases.

Fill up yo' trunque weeth Pedro's junque! 95 miles to go to South of the Border!

I enjoyed the solitude, yet companionship that traveling by motorcycle provided. Soothing acoustic rock played through my headphones. I stretched my legs out on the highway pegs and leaned back against my sleeping bag and bedroll as the bright afternoon sun shone and warmed off to the left.

Finding myself lost in thought, my mind wandered to the past. I pushed away from it and toward the present, then drifted to the future. What was my goal? Did I want to do this forever? Was it even possible? Would I regret it, as an old man, having done nothing significant with my life, possibly destitute, and having hurt so many along the way? I had imagined a life with Carla, Sarah, Mary, Starr, and Jolene at various points in the last few years, and realized something was pulling at me. *Life. Normalcy. The wheel.*

A blast from Shayne's loud after-market horn shook me back to the present. He'd pulled alongside and was pointing at a Welcome to South Carolina sign. I nodded and gave a thumbs-up. Hours had passed without notice.

We hit an exit and ate a small lunch, our stomachs still unsettled from grain alcohol the night before. *This life takes a toll.* Dehydrated from the booze, we were drinking a lot of water, and by necessity stopping more often to relieve ourselves, often pulling over briefly by the side of the road to do so.

During a stop, we discussed the signs we'd seen for Charleston and considered taking a detour to visit the beach there. We agreed there were plenty of beaches in Florida, and we pushed on toward our goal.

We crossed into Georgia in the early evening, horns honking, and pulled off the highway near Savannah. As soon as I removed my helmet, I realized the air was different there—thick with humidity, and sweet. It smelled wonderful.

It was getting dark, and we both admitted to exhaustion. After eating a full meal of fast-food burgers, shakes, and fries, I felt it even more. We pulled off the road into a wooded area and camped next to the bikes. We had one more day of riding ahead, and didn't see how pushing it would have much benefit.

After consulting our atlases by flashlight, we found a suitable space in a small clearing and set up our beds for the night, deciding to skip setting up Shayne's tent to sleep under the stars. It was finally warm and comfortable, no trace of winter remained. We had found where summer lived while we all froze in the northeast for months.

Shayne rambled on various topics in the dark, and the last I remembered of the night was staring up into the stars. I wondered if somewhere Sarah was looking at them, too. I wondered if she still thought about me until I also recalled the last time I'd talked to her. *She's moved on, you've lost her too.*

At dawn's light, we rolled up our bedding and hopped back on the bikes in the early morning fog and chill. We had agreed to not stop for gas or food until we'd crossed the border into the Sunshine State. The idea of it excited us both. We were almost there.

The ocean was close enough to smell as we rolled along the coast, past exits for wonderful sounding places.

Sea Island, St Simon Island, Amelia Island, Blue Hammock Island.

We crossed the border two hours later, and rather than the horn-honking celebration, we pulled over. We yanked off our helmets next to the Welcome to Florida sign, threw our hands up in the air, and began peeling off layers of clothing to make the rest of the trip in just T-shirts and jeans.

Now even closer to the sea, we took detours off the highway to roll through towns like old St. Augustine and Daytona Beach (where we hoped to attend Bike Week in March). The last stretch took us through West Palm Beach and finally to our destination, Fort Lauderdale. It was urban enough to find plenty of work, close enough to Miami for the big-city excitement, far enough south for warm weather, and home to great beaches. *We made it!*

19 KOA

The guy in the KOA campground office checked us in while we looked over a map of the sites. We booked a week to start off.

"You'll want to be over in this section," he said, pointing to an area on the paper.

"It's way in the back," Shayne commented. "Is it swamp?"

"Trust me fellas, that's where you want to be."

We looked at each other and took him at his word, but let him know we'd be back if it wasn't suitable.

"Have fun," he said as we left the office.

We rode slow through the campground with our helmets impaled on the tall sissy bars behind us. Families gathered around picnic tables outside their campers, eating breakfast. The rumble of our bikes attracted the attention of little kids, who pointed with excitement as their parents held them back from the long-haired, bearded menace they perceived in us.

It went on for rows and blocks, until we reached the rear area of the campground, segregated by a small bridge over a stream. After we crossed it, we saw the clerk's logic and smiled at each other as we rode. Rather than families and shiny new campers, a multi-color collage of ratty tents of all sizes filled the area. Young people just like us milled around, half-naked, yawning and stretching. *Free, like us.*

We pulled into our site, a small patch of ground with a picnic table and tree for shade. A neighbor approached as we sat at the table, taking it all in.

"Welcome to Woodstock South," he said, stretching out his hand. "I'm Jeremy. New York."

He sat and filled us in. The section comprised snowbirds like us, college students and young migrant workers down for the winter or just traveling around the country. It was a small society of fellow bohemians with no rules other than respect for others.

"Yeah!" Shayne stood shouting. "These are our people!" His outburst attracted the attention of two tanned, sun-bleached blond girls in cut-off Daisy Duke shorts and bikini tops at a nearby tent. They smiled and waved as they laughed at him. "I think I'm gonna like it here," he whispered.

Jeremy left us to set up camp, and we went about unpacking our gear. I rode back up to the office to grab a few cold sodas from the machine while Shayne assembled the tent. As I pulled back into the site, he stood next to a small pup tent, gesturing like a game-show host. It would barely fit us both.

"Are you fucking kidding me?" I asked, laughing. "That's big enough for you. What about me? People are gonna talk, bro!"

"Don't worry, calm down. We'll make it work," he said in his often dismissive way.

After switching to swim trunks and flip-flops, we headed toward the pool with towels slung over our shoulders. It was a slow journey, as Shayne made it a point to stop and talk to every fellow resident we passed.

We spent a particular amount of time with the two bikini blondes—Brandy and Donna, from Mattituck, NY, out on the end of Long Island. They were college students who were on a winter break from school. Their tent was a large, worn out military surplus job that sagged off to one side.

"Your tent needs work," I said to Brandy.

"Yeah, we just got here yesterday and don't have it figured out yet," she replied.

"I'm familiar with these. I'm a vet. They're a little tricky, but I'll fix it up for you later."

Shayne invited them to join us at the pool, and they agreed. The girls packed a cooler with snacks and a big thermos of orange juice and vodka. We settled in, sitting on the edge of the pool with our legs in the water, leaning back to let the sun wash over us as children screamed and played in the shallow end.

"Oh, man," Shayne sighed. "What the hell have we been doing up north all our lives?"

We all laughed and agreed. "We're thinking of taking a semester off and staying," Brandy said. She sat next to me and touched my leg for emphasis.

"Our parents are going to be pissed when we tell them," Donna added. "My dad actually called it before we left. He knows me well."

We passed the thermos between ourselves, noting the occasional glares from jealous young parents. "I'm dying to get to the beach," Shayne said after a while. We all agreed and went back to the campsites to pack some things.

The day was glorious, as we alternated between napping on our towels on the sand, playing volleyball, and splashing in the ocean waves. Brandy had expressed a lifelong fear of sharks, so I waited until she was distracted in chest-high water and swam to her beneath the surface, grabbing her thigh.

Her shriek pierced the air as I came up to breathe, laughing. She chased me with faux anger. After I let her catch me, she grabbed my ponytail and pulled me to her, kissing me as a wave washed over us. Salt water mixed with the vodka on her breath and I lifted her above the next wave to save her from it.

We left the surf hand-in-hand and made our way toward Shayne and Donna, who huddled close together on the beach, giggling together and sharing a joint. We helped them finish it as the sun set, then headed off toward the bikes to go home. *Home.*

Back at the KOA, darkness had fallen, and campfires had sprung up throughout our little commune. Residents wandered from site to site, drinks in hand, joining in conversations. Some sites featured a guitar player and singer or two, lit up by the fire, sparks flying as the firewood popped and crackled.

Jeremy and two of his friends shared a camper, the only one in our section. We sat around its small table for a while, talking and telling jokes, Brandy on my lap, allegedly because of the lack of space. We all glistened with sweat in the warm night, our eyes shining, and her skin felt good against mine.

"Not a bad first day, huh bru?" Shayne asked, slurring.

"Not bad at all," I answered, smiling and squeezing Brandy's hand.

We left and went back to our campsites. I began shoring up the girls' tent as promised. Shayne and Donna went to sit at our picnic table. After Brandy and I got their tent to stand straight and tall, we looked over toward my site. The picnic table was empty, and our tent was moving about, shaking, guide ropes straining against the stakes.

"I guess they're getting along OK," I said. "I'm homeless."

"Let's go for a swim," she suggested.

"Pool's closed."

"So?" she said with a wink. We snuck off into the dark and surveyed the area. It was well after midnight by that time, and all was quiet in the family area of the campground where the pool sat. It shone in the moonlight, beckoning us, tempting us. I struggled to keep Brandy quiet. She'd had a lot of vodka throughout the day and night and was pretty out of it.

I helped her over the fence and then scaled it myself, shushing her laughter. We entered at the steps in the shallow end and made our way across. When we were waist deep, she removed her bikini top and flung it to the pool deck. The lines of her dark tan were sharp against the brilliant white of her breasts, her small nipples erect in the cool water. The braids of her hair dipped into the water.

She reached down and slipped off her bottom, tossing it to join the top, and then swam under the water to the deeper end, the moonlight shimmering and water creating a rippled distortion of her body as she moved gracefully, a vision of pure beauty. I removed my swimsuit and swam to meet her. We moved to the back corner of the pool, where it was darker. Using a small ledge to brace ourselves, we embraced and made love as quietly as we could, the water splashing rhythmically as we moved together in the pool in the night.

Back at her tent, we grabbed some soap and went to the bathhouse to clean up. She was without fear, and joined me on the men's side. We showered together, washing each other, exploring our bodies, until it was too much and we made love again against the tiled wall as the water ran over us. We toweled each other off and went back to her tent to nuzzle together in her over-sized sleeping bag. As Shayne and Donna hadn't returned, we had the place to ourselves. The last thing I remembered of the night was the familiar smell of that old military canvas and her hair against my face, our naked bodies pressed together.

20 Florida

We fell into our new Florida life. On days we felt like working, we'd get up early and go to the day labor office in town and wait to be picked for roofing crews or other construction. It was hard work in the scorching sun, particularly on the roofs, working with the sickly smelling hot black tar.

The trade-off was worth it. We reminded each other of the weather up north and our good fortune, as we frequented the beach after work and on every day off. Nights in Woodstock South were a party, no matter the day of the week. It was a Utopian tent village. Everyone was young, thankful, respectful, and happy.

Shayne and I avoided the tent problem by alternating nights in the girls' tent, and I grew to prefer the nights that Brandy and I slept in the smaller one, nowhere to go but against each other. We played a game where we tried to synchronize our breathing to see if we'd still be in sync when we woke, and checked to make sure. Our occasional late-night stealth visits to the pool and showers were our secret. We didn't want the others turning it into something ugly. It was a ceremony we looked forward to very much, but made sure we didn't ruin it by going too often. We didn't want any part of life scheduled. *This is freedom, doing what you want to do every day.*

I found myself happier than I'd been in a long time, the guilt, fear, and dark memories surfacing less frequently, although still there, below the surface. I got picked up by a local chain-link fence company because of my experience with my uncle, and was thankful to be away from the tar. Digging post holes in the sandy soil was like a hot knife through butter compared to the hard, rocky north.

A MONTH FLEW BY AND we found ourselves in February, which would go by even faster. Members of our commune had drifted back north, back to obligations, school, jobs, family. *Responsibilities.* Some were just there for a break, a brief adventure. It wasn't their real life. Brandy and Donna fought often with their parents, who were putting pressure on them to get back home and to school, and had stopped sending money.

"Think about your *future* is all they say!" Donna often complained. "We're young! What about our *present*?"

We knew it couldn't last forever, and eventually, their parents won out. That's what happens when someone else controls you with their money and influence, paying for your education, car insurance, food, life. The morning came when they had to leave. We disassembled their big, ratty tent, rolled it up, and put it in their trunk.

After helping to pack the car, Brandy and I walked hand-in-hand to the pool and leaned over the fence we'd climbed over so many times to reach the ecstasy that waited for us in the water. We imagined ourselves there, back in the corner of the deep end, lost in rapture, caring about nothing else in life but that moment.

We cried together and made promises, more promises, and walked back to their site for the last time. Shayne and I waved as their car crossed the bridge back to the real world.

"Well, that sucks," he said.

"Yeah. Especially since I have to sleep in that thing with you now," I replied, trying to laugh.

I took to sleeping outside the tent, having fashioned a lean-to for cover. I didn't need to do that for long, because Shayne fell in with a big biker dude at one of the job sites who offered to let him crash on his couch for rent money. Shayne said he'd let them get comfortable with him, and then work me into the situation somehow.

I found myself alone again. Everything had changed so fast, and that old feeling of karma, the energy turning negative, the guilt and bad dreams reemerging, slowly crept back. With more time on my hands, I made calls back home, and to Sarah to see how she and the baby were doing.

On the way to work one morning, drowsy, a car in front of me braked hard, and I slid on the sandy road, my wheels locked up. I avoided a front-end hit and almost missed him completely. My left exhaust pipe barely touched his fender, but it was enough to rip it away from the bike's engine. It was rideable, but incredibly loud, attracting too much attention. After a few warnings from cops, I had to park it until I could save enough to get it fixed, as it was difficult to repair. I resorted to hitchhiking to work, relying on my thumb again.

A week later, on a Saturday night, I received an invitation to join Shayne and his new friends at their place. Shayne came over to give me a ride. It was a pretty nice condo close to our campground. We settled in at the kitchen table with Brock, the biker. He wore his sleeveless leather vest with colors and patches for his group, the Warlocks.

We drank and smoked and listened to biker music, getting to know one another. Shayne was more low key than normal.

"What do you do?" I asked Brock.

He laughed and motioned down the length of his vest. "This is what I do. It's all I do. Vice is good money. And I manage my old lady's career."

I waited for clarification. "She's a dancer," he said. "She's at work now. When she gets home, the fun starts." Shayne smiled at the comment, but looked down.

It wasn't a loose vibe like Woodstock South. Brock brought an intimidating menace to the air, challenging us to do shots and keep up with him. I had learned to pace myself as I got older. More consumption meant a worse outcome, after a certain point, as I'd well learned. I felt that if I said no, it would lead to a nasty fight, and I didn't want that. I didn't want to offend the host or fight him, so I obliged, to my regret. Sleeping in the dirt had gotten old, and I was interested in a roof over my head.

At some point, well after midnight, we heard a car horn blaring outside. I was already woozy, my mind fogged and out of my comfort zone. We peered out of the window to see Brock's girlfriend Ella climbing out of a big, shiny Mercedes Benz luxury car.

"Let's get this party started!" she yelled. The neighboring apartment lights blinked on as the other residents investigated the noise. One of them yelled for quiet.

She looked up in the direction it came from. "Fuck you, and you, and you!" she screamed, pointing at each balcony, then laughed.

"That's my girl," Brock said. "Now the party starts for real, as stated, as promised."

We went back to the table, and she emerged through the door, a big girl but curvaceous and not afraid to show it off. She wore a loose, low cut midriff silk top and tight jean shorts with tall cowboy boots and lots of tattoos.

"What's up with the car?" Brock asked her.

She laughed. "I talked some rich asshole into letting me borrow it. These idiots will do anything I ask after a lap dance. I put 'em under my spell."

"What did Santa bring?" Brock asked. "Show daddy the goodies."

She reached in her purse and unloaded the drugs and cash she'd received in tips for a few hours of work that night. The table filled with rumpled bills of all denominations. It had to be hundreds of dollars, tax-free. She sorted the cellophane bags like a child with their Halloween candy.

There were several small bags of white coke, a few with prime-looking weed, one with tiny mescaline microdots, and a last one with a brown substance I knew was heroin. I tried to find a way out, but my mind wouldn't work.

Brock started into the treasure, first rolling a hundred-dollar bill up to snort a line of the coke, which he'd dumped on the table and sorted into four piles. After he'd done his, he passed the rolled-up bill, with snot on the end, to me. I justified it would give me some clarity and diffuse the alcohol, so I flipped it over, snot-side down, and took my hit. I passed it over to Shayne. After Ella snorted the last line, she licked the snot-end, which was by then caked with coke. They laughed about it and chain-smoked cigarettes.

Brock then poured four shots of scotch, plopped one orange mescaline pill in each, and counted down until we'd downed them. The psychedelic would also bring clarity, but no relief from the wicked hangover I knew I'd have the next day.

As the drugs kicked in, I became more and more uncomfortable. Brock and Ella began a violent argument over his accusation that she'd traded sex for the use of the car. He shoved her down on a couch and she got back up and slapped him. He threw her right back where she was, and she stayed, crying. Shayne shook his head and whispered that this was how it was.

Ella got up and sat back down at the kitchen table. She produced a short rubber hose, a spoon, and a syringe from a drawer and began cooking up some of the heroin. I knew Brock would try to force it on us. It was a bridge I'd vowed never to cross, but at the moment, I gave it consideration. I watched as Ella put the needle in her arm, released the hose, then leaned back in her chair with the most relaxed and euphoric expression I'd ever seen on a person. It would be nice to be on a cloud, high above the demons that tormented me. *Give me shelter from the storm.*

I closed my eyes and faces came into view. *Sarah. Leah. Mom. Dad. My sisters.* I thought about all the love they'd given me, and then having to attend my funeral. *A funeral for a stupid junkie.* "Don't do it," I said to Shayne. "We always promised." He nodded gravely and I could tell he was concerned, too.

Brock joined us back at the table. I excused myself to use the bathroom, then slipped out the door without saying goodbye. Happy to be out of the smoky, loud apartment, I struggled to remember the way back to the campground. I walked fast, afraid they'd call me back or chase me down in the Mercedes. I became nauseous and vomited several times along the way, spending the last few bouts in futility, retching an empty stomach. *Is this the life you want? How long until you're a junkie, dead or in jail for life?*

Hours later, as the first hints of the sun appeared, I found the KOA and walked through it to the little bridge to what had been our utopia. A few families rustled about, getting a sober early start on their day of fun ahead. Woodstock South was desolate and quiet, with just a few tents left and everyone asleep.

The alcohol had faded from my system, but I was still tripping. I walked to the pool and climbed the fence, taking a seat with my feet in the water I'd shared with Brandy. I closed my eyes and replayed our happy, blissful moments there. *Nothing lasts forever.* I imagined her at home, maybe back at school, dating some spoiled rich preppy college asshole, and wondered if she still thought about me and our time together.

The manager showed up for work and chased me out of the closed pool area. I went to where Brandy's tent was and stood on the vacant site, trying to conjure it up, make everything go back the way it was. *Nothing lasts forever. You can't go back, only forward.*

I crawled into the little pup tent so nobody would bother me and tried to still my mind so I could sleep. Eventually, I was successful. I woke several times sweating with a sick stomach as the sun came up and roasted me. The morning ticked by, and I forced myself back to sleep. Starr's words about recognizing when the energy was changing rang in my throbbing head. *Is this the life you want? Don't fight karma, it'll only get worse. It will punish you until you align.*

Around mid-day I couldn't take the heat anymore and inched out of the tent. Shayne was laying under my lean-to, gripping his head with both hands. "I can't say I like your new friends," I said.

"It wasn't like that at the beginning." He sighed and sat up, his long hair a tangled mess.

"It takes a while to learn who people are. What are you going to do? You stay there and it'll end badly. You can take that to the bank, brother."

He acknowledged, and we talked about the vibe and energy changing. "Daytona Bike week is in two weeks. How about we pack up shop, head up there, settle in, find some work, another campground, meet some girls? I'm sure the party has started."

"A change of scenery would be good. This place had run its course, I think. Too many memories of what was. I'm in."

The new plans got us excited again. We spent the day on the beach plotting with the waves crashing around us. He had met a welder that said he could fix my bike. Shayne moved back to the KOA to save some money, and we worked as much as possible. It took two weeks to get my bike done, and we hit the road again, leaving the once-utopian KOA behind.

THE TRIP UP THE COAST was only a few hours, but it was the recipe I needed. A fresh start, nothing behind and the unknown ahead. The wind and the rumble of the bike engines side by side, harmonizing, my music playing and nobody to ruin it with talking. I had only my own thoughts to deal with.

As we approached Daytona, we began pulling off at each campground marked by roadside signs. They were all full, and we became more anxious with every rejection. They were jammed with bikes and bikers running around with bandannas wrapped around their heads, some women wearing them as tops, not leaving much to the imagination. We wanted badly to be a part of it, but were getting shut out, not free to join in the festivities. Neither of us enjoyed being told *no*.

We stopped at a gas station to regroup and sat on the bikes watching revelers carry out cases of cold beer. They were all just arriving, free from whatever drudgery their lives were up north. They were us, just a few months ago. *Remember, you fuckers, nothing lasts forever.*

"I guess we could have planned this better," I sniped in frustration.

"That's my fault?" Shayne answered.

"Did I say that, bro? I said *we* didn't I?"

After all we'd experienced together, we were finally turning on each other. It felt dark and ugly for the first time, and shouldn't have been since we'd both dreamed of attending this event. We were hot and sweaty in the intense humidity and nowhere to get relief from it. It was getting late in the day, and we had nowhere to stay.

Regrouping, we changed some bills in the store and used the pay phones outside to call every campground and hotel in the area. We stood side by side at the booths and each opened a huge phone book affixed by a chain. "You take A through M," I said. "I'll take N through Z."

"Ready? Go!" He shouted. The new challenge brought us back to life. As we started the calls, our tone was hopeful as we spoke to the reservation clerks. Shayne was using his natural influence, and I tried to mimic his persuasive technique. Our coins dropped into the slots with musical clinks. It sounded like we were two grannies playing the slots in Atlantic City.

As time and our pile of dimes both diminished, the mood backslid again. We exhausted our lists and Shayne worked the store patrons as they exited, with no success.

"I'm beat. Let's just boondock camp," he said. "We have no other option. We've done it before. Fuck it."

"I guess we'll be able to find something as soon as Bike Week is over and everyone is gone," I agreed. "But it's gonna be a tough week living in the woods. We'll save money, though."

We rode off and searched the back roads until we found a spot in a clearing down a dirt path. It was at the base of an electrical tower, with a fenced-in area containing a huge voltage step-down transformer that hummed ominously. The grass was thick, rough, sharp-bladed, and full of weeds and crawling insects.

"Damn, are you sure we're not going to glow after sleeping here?" I asked.

"Fuck it," he said again as he set up the tent and his bedroll in the diminishing light.

We were spent, so I followed his lead and unstrapped my gear. Something had been nagging at me, joining the two constant big things that were always below the surface, Tennessee and Sarah. Something was wrong, and I couldn't put my finger on it, but it kept getting worse, pulling, tugging.

Finally, it hit me in one blinding second. I reached back to pat my back pocket where I kept my wallet. It was flat. Terror flowed through me as I pulled everything off the bike, frantically searching through each pocket, nook, and cranny.

"What the fuck are you doing?" he asked, laying on his sleeping bag.

"Nothing, nothing," I answered.

"It's something; I can tell," he said.

I stopped for a moment and tried to calm my racing mind. I'd used the wallet to get change at the service station. Then I remembered placing it on top of the phone booth as I made my calls. *Stupid.* I had always been diligent about things like that, not leaving matters to chance, but I had fucked up. Every dollar I had was in that wallet, and all my ID.

"Be right back," I said, hopping on the bike and firing it up. I left in a spray of dirt and grass, down the access road, then hit a deep rut and dropped the bike in my haste. After assessing the damage and brushing the dirt from my scraped-up legs and cut-off shorts, I remounted and continued.

I locked my brakes at the phone booths, sliding my tires, just begging for another rough dismount. I threw down the kickstand, jumped off, and ran to the phone I'd used. The wallet wasn't there. I ran into the store and asked the clerk if anyone had turned in a wallet. *Hopefully, a good samaritan. Some people are good. Please, God.*

"Nope," she said. I told her what had happened and scribbled my name and my home phone number on some paper.

"I hate to rain on your parade," she said. "But a few good old boys came in, bought some beer, then went out to use the phones and came back and bought a lot more. Said they'd just won the lottery."

I thanked her and left. Sitting on the bike in the night humidity, sweating, I questioned every stupid idea and decision I'd made in my quest for freedom. I wanted to call home and ask for help, but I didn't even have a dime. I thought about calling collect and then thought about adding more stress and worry to my family. All I'd done was give them more to worry about. *You failed in the military and in essentially everything you've tried to do since.*

I wasn't sure how I could go back and face Shayne, or what we'd do about it. I had no money for gas to get anywhere. His family was well-to-do, his father a finance guy in Manhattan, but a good, grounded Irishman. The whole family had small dirt bikes they rode at a family property in

Pennsylvania, something I'd dreamed about as a kid. He'd taught Shayne about money and avoiding debt, things I felt inferior and insecure about whenever the subject came up, because I didn't understand the concepts as well. My family relied on debt to get by, and it was a constant battle to stay ahead of the bills. I was embarrassed and afraid to tell him what had happened, but I had no choice.

I pulled up to the power station campsite, defeated, the bike waking him from a nap.

"What's up, bro?" he asked.

"My wallet's gone. All my money. Stolen, back at that gas station."

He was quiet for a while, and I had nothing to say. Then he blamed me, and we argued about it. My legs were bleeding from the spill and itching badly. I poured some water from my canteen over them and dried them with my beach towel, smearing it with blood.

"I'll spot you," he finally said. "I think I have enough. We'll find work right away—day labor again starting tomorrow. We can fix this." Like a loyal friend, he put aside the concern he must have felt, and likely anger at me for being so stupid, and was trying to uplift me.

"I don't even have a license or ID."

"Fuck it. Just drive carefully."

I agreed, but told him I didn't want him to miss Bike Week. Over the next few days, I found work to pull a few bucks together while he went to the festivities. I had to buy gas and lunch with his money, and it upset me to have to do that, to have to be reliant on someone else for charity. It hurt me very much to have to do so.

He bought us tickets for the big road race, the motorcycle week grand finale. I was grateful, and we splurged that day, forgetting our problems, really my problems, for just a little while. We sat in the stands at a hairpin corner, behind a protective chain-link fence, with hot dogs and cold sodas. The race started and the professional riders, the best in the world, flew past us at incredible speed, leaning the bikes almost flat, dragging their knees, then bolted upright and sped up, gone like a shot. The legend Kenny Roberts was there on his big yellow Yamaha, challenged by young Freddie Spencer.

"It must be unbelievable to be that good at something," I marveled, transfixed. "The best in the world. Damn, how that must feel." I thought about the discipline and commitment it had to take them. They weren't off fucking around wasting their life, they were dedicating every day to their dream and truly working on it, not making excuses.

Nothing stood in the way of that one thing, that one passion, that drove them. *That's how you get to be the best.* I wanted to be that, as a writer, to write things that would inspire or take people away from their lives temporarily, long after I was gone. I thought I was just a dreamer, and it was no way to support a family, as I'd heard countless times. *And you might already have a family.*

The short, protective bubble of that day ended, and we found ourselves back at the campsite feeling fulfilled from it—a good day, finally.

"Alright, that was fucking great!" Shayne exclaimed. "Right, bru?"

"Damn right," I agreed. "Thank you for buying those tickets. I'll pay you back. I won't forget it."

"Don't worry about it. Listen, everyone clears out tomorrow. We'll be able to hit a campground, finally, and get out of this shit hole."

I fetched the towel, found an area that didn't have dried blood on it, and started dabbing at my wounds. The scrapes on my legs weren't healing. They oozed green-yellow puss, as did new minor cuts I'd received at the day labor jobs. I'd been hiding them under long pants and gauze from my small med kit, hoping they'd heal, but they were only getting worse.

I showed the wounds to Shayne with a flashlight. "Jesus," he said. "That's a staph infection. You need antibiotics. Penicillin. It's in your bloodstream. That shit can fuck you up, even kill you."

I took my bike to a nearby town to find an open pharmacy and buy some antibiotic cream and dressings, wishing I'd kept a few of Jesse's blank prescription forms for some penicillin. On the way out, I noticed a phone booth and stopped to call home collect.

"Levi!" my mom exclaimed as she answered. "Thank God you called. We've been trying to reach you at that campground. They said you left. Your father has been hurt badly at work. He's in the hospital."

The words rained down on me like the drops had back when I lay in the woods after crashing my bike in New Jersey. A profound and immediate sadness washed over me. "What happened? Will he be OK?" I asked, choking back sobs.

"A lathe broke at work when he was using it. A part came off and went through his chest. He had surgery, and he's in intensive care, the ICU. The doctor's not sure, Levi..."

I told her I'd be home as soon as possible. On the way back to the campsite, I thought about all that man had sacrificed for us to have a better life. He wasn't worried about his freedom; only worried about his family. He had done the right thing. *You can't fight karma. It will only get worse. It will take what you love until you obey it.*

I pulled back into the site, and Shayne was fast asleep. After smearing the antibiotic on my wounds and dressing them, I crashed, but woke suddenly during the night. Fire ants had sought out the smell of blood, puss, and decay and crawled into my sleeping bag, causing me to bolt out of it, wounds burning and covered with the biting insects. It was a pain like no other. I was drenched in sweat despite the night having cooled considerably, and used the thermometer in my med kit to take my temp. "Through the roof," I reported to myself. "Fuck."

Shayne woke and laid out an optimistic plan to get to a clinic the next day, and then we'd find a campground and better jobs. We had been living in the dirt for over a week, and hadn't showered the entire time, as well as barely eating. The weight of it all had become as heavy as my pack after a long day of hitchhiking the highways. Each person I'd hurt, each hardship to endure, became another brick added to that load. *A person can only carry so much weight before breaking.* In that moment, I pulled the medallion from my shirt and pressed it to my lips, making my final and most resolute promise to the patron saint of travelers. *It's time to pay the toll. The path is clear now.*

"I'm done, brother," I told him. "I'm going home tomorrow. You didn't cause this mess, you don't need to come with me. I'll be fine."

He paused, and I could tell he was thinking of a strategy to talk me out of it. He was eyeing me and seemed to understand I would not change my mind. It was over. I told him about my father, tears rolling down my face.

"No way you're going alone. You're sick. I won't let you. It's fine, we're in mid-March now, and it's almost time for me to get back to the landscaping job, anyway. I promised I'd be back for spring." I knew he had his heart set on staying until late April. It had been the plan all along, and it was still cold and snowy up north. The trip back would be hard. This was a thing that friends who loved one another did for each other.

We settled it. I was excited for it to be done, once again, and see my family, my home. *The people who love me, unconditionally.* I slept little during the night, my stomach and heart aching along with the pain from my wounds.

21 Return

At dawn, we silently packed our things and loaded the bikes. I was still sweating and in extreme discomfort, just wanting to teleport myself home, for it to be over, to get medical help and relief and, most of all, to see my father. *Please don't die on me, Dad. I love you.* We checked our maps, confirmed our route, pissed in the woods, and said a grateful goodbye to the humming transformer.

We found ourselves part of a long caravan of returnees, along with the folks who had come down for Bike Week. Traffic was bad. We moved in fits and starts, creeping along, and the air-cooled bikes overheated. Shayne pointed at the lines of pickup trucks pulling bike trailers and gave a thumbs-down. Most of the tough bikers couldn't weather the trip on their actual bikes as we did, choosing the comfort of a heated cab instead. *Fucking posers. Real tough guys.* I secretly wished that one of them had room for us.

The trip was unremarkable, as the joy we had on the way down had left us. I could feel Shayne's disappointment and concern for me, as we dispensed with breaks to make the fastest time possible. Sweat rolled down my face inside the helmet and soaked my clothes. I had no appetite, so I didn't eat at our stops, saving my money for gas so I wouldn't have to beg from Shayne again. I kept a running tally of every dollar I had borrowed from him in my notebook.

We retraced our route from the way down, hugging the coast on I-95, the exotic beach exit signs holding no magic for us this time. My cassette player, headphones, and tapes were silent, buried inside my backpack.

We stopped when we reached Fayetteville, NC, in the early evening. It was about halfway home. After eating, we counted our remaining money and treated ourselves to a cheap truck-stop motel for the night. Shayne had insisted, and I knew it was for my benefit. He took care of the check-in and we rushed to the room, eager for a chance to clean up.

Upon entering, it smelled of mildew and cleaning solutions, the thin carpet stained in patches, but the two neatly made beds adorned with plump pillows looked like twin oases. It reminded me of the motels we'd stayed in during that trip to Michigan with my grandfather long ago. Shayne unloaded both bikes as I chose a bed and sat on it, peeling off my clothes.

I looked down at my legs and found the pus had leaked through my jeans and hardened in the wind, caked on them in several places, gluing the pants to my skin. Cursing myself for neglecting to wrap them in my haste to leave the campsite, I went to the bathroom and frightened myself by looking in the mirror, realizing why Shayne had shown such concern. My eyes looked hollow and sunken in and my skin appeared jaundiced. Pieces of debris from the campsite dotted my tangled beard and hair, and I had an oozing lesion on my forehead. I gagged on the smell of myself in the small, closed room. *What brought you to this point? Freedom?*

I pulled back the flimsy vinyl curtain, exposing a rust-stained tub, and ran the shower, keeping the water cool. I stepped in with my jeans still on, in order to soften the fabric and scabs to more easily remove them. Sitting on the tub rim, I slowly peeled the legs down, ripping off the scabs and causing searing pain as the water ran against the open wounds. Blood and yellow-green pus ran in thin rivers down my legs and into the rusted drain.

I opened a small packet of soap and lathered my hands, then scrubbed my hair, scalp, and worked my way down my body. When the soap hit the wounds, it made the pain far worse. Cursing myself, I tried to shut it out, then welcomed it, begging for more, rubbing the soap directly into the wounds. *Take that, you fucker.*

When I had finished my self-flagellation, I grabbed a stiff, coarse, dingy towel from the bar on the wall and treated myself to more pain. I finished drying; the towel stained with blood and yanked my comb through my hair until it pulled through smoothly. I put on the one semi-clean piece of clothing I had left, an old pair of high school gym shorts. The colors and logo momentarily reminded me of Carla. I pushed the memory of her away and vowed to throw the shorts out when I reached home.

Shayne had already laid out my military med kit on the bed when I finally stepped out of the bathroom.

"Damn, boy. It sounded like you were dying in there," he said. "You OK?"

I nodded, not realizing I had made any noise. The pain had put me in another place. It differed from the old ice hockey, football, fight, and bike accident injuries. I blotted the wounds until they stopped bleeding and oozing, then wrapped them with the last of my fresh gauze. Shayne went to the bathroom for his turn and I lay back on the pillows. Everything still hurt, but I felt a cleanliness, a freshness that I hadn't felt in a long time. *A new start.*

I woke, sweating, a few times during the night. Shayne was on the other bed, eating snacks from the vending machine and watching old Western shows on the TV. Each time, I went right back to sleep. Nightmares came. I dreamed of the greasy, lecherous predator taunting me from hell, telling me I'd join him soon, where I belonged. He said we did not differ from one another, each selfishly leaving the wreckage of other people's lives in our wake.

I rose at dawn to Shayne's snoring and went to the bathroom to check things over. Pus had leaked through the gauze and the bandage on my forehead. Our clothes were out of the packs and neatly folded on the dresser. I picked them up and smelled them. He'd gone to the laundry room and washed them. I dressed and began packing, letting him rest.

When I had finished, I left the room to find food. A skunk had sprayed somewhere nearby during the night, and I closed my eyes and stopped for a moment to travel back to that first night with Mary. I thought about how every relationship seemed to go through seasons like the weather; spring when it's blooming, summer when it's hot, fall when it becomes the normal you swore would never allow to happen, and finally winter when it becomes cold as ice and dies.

The office had laid out donuts, coffee, and juices for their trucker patrons, so I loaded up and brought a bounty back to the room. Shayne was up, and we enjoyed the feast before checking out. I was happy to eat something, but didn't want to push it with the long trip ahead. We sat across from each other on the small, rumpled beds, eating quietly for a time.

"So, what's next?" he said, breaking the silence.

I realized I hadn't thought much about it. It felt like the gravitational pull of destiny was guiding me toward something. I just didn't know what—or maybe I couldn't admit it to myself yet. "I'll sign up at the county college, I guess. Computers."

"I thought you wanted to be a writer?"

"It doesn't pay. Can't feed a family that way." It felt horrible to say. It was that moment you become cognizant that reality is taking a lifelong dream away.

He chewed and stared at me. "What family? You're not giving in, are you?"

"No... I dunno. I guess I'll have one at some point."

We packed and saddled up again, going about our work, navigating toward home. I felt dizzy and Shayne caught me drifting to the side of the highway. Each time, he signaled to ask if I was OK, then motioned to pull over. Each time I refused. We were on the home stretch, and I wanted to get to the hospital to see my father.

It became colder by the mile and reached a point where it overtook the other pains. I struggled to focus and keep the bike on the road. State welcome signs passed without fanfare, each one a greater relief. Without the music for a distraction, I spent the trip lost in thought, rehashing old logic and reforming it with the wisdom of experience and maturity. I tried to stay awake and upright.

The time and quiet allowed me to think about my life and my goals, and I thought hard about those things. It helped keep the pain at bay. I thought about what freedom really meant—the ability to do what you enjoy each day with the people that made you happy. It wasn't about constantly running away. In doing so, I had been like a petulant child who did things simply to show he could. I'd found that true happiness came from helping others, making them happy. The times I had done so, whether it was cleaning the house for Diane, fixing Brandy's tent for her, and other good deeds, were the ones that had made me feel best. *Freedom is the ability to choose, and maybe I choose to stay.*

The idea of it filled me with joy, and I knew I'd finally found my answer. Sometimes you don't see yourself truly until many experiences (and mistakes) later. I felt comfortable with the new vision of who I was, and who I wanted to become with each new sunrise; a new day and a new, better person one step closer to his goals and security.

Finally, the Welcome to the Garden State sign appeared, and this time Shayne resumed the horn honks and peg stand, turning to me with a big grin inside his helmet shield and thumbs-up again. I nodded and focused, determined to get through the last stretch.

An hour later, we took the Lake Sussex exit and rolled through town. I saw the same old cars parked outside the Bivouac as we passed it. The bridge felt like an epiphany as we crossed, and within a few minutes, we had pulled up at my parents' house.

Mom burst forth at the racket from the bikes. It was a weekday, so girls were at school. She ran to us with her arms open as we dismounted the bikes and began unfastening our chin straps.

"Oh, thank God..." she said, stopping as I removed my helmet. She looked at Shayne with fear in her eyes, as if I wasn't there. "What happened to him?" she demanded, pointing at me.

"He needs a doctor. He's dehydrated, and he has staph infection."

"Dear Lord, dear Lord," she kept repeating, crying.

We went in and Shayne used the bathroom, wished me luck, embraced me. He said he'd meet me later at the hospital to see my dad, but wanted to give us some time first and go home to unpack. And then he was gone, heading home to his family.

Mom and I rushed to the hospital and Dad's room. He was awake, but with a lot of equipment attached and he looked like hell. I gripped his hand and told him how much I loved him. He whispered the same back in a weak voice and told me I looked like shit.

A nurse came in and Mom explained my condition to her. A doctor followed soon after and wanted to admit me. I refused and insisted I wouldn't leave my father's side. After some debate, they agreed to treat me right there in the chair next to him. They hooked me up to a saline drip for my dehydration and another IV with antibiotics, and we sat there together through the night.

The nurse came back to attend to us and told me how close I'd come to losing my dad. It horrified me to think I would have missed saying goodbye to him, having been out there doing my thing. It would have been one more thing to regret for the rest of my days. *More wreckage from the road.*

I went home the next morning, and Dad followed a few days later. After a few courses of antibiotics, I was on the mend. Scabs were finally forming over my wounds. Days and then weeks went by. The scabs finally fell away, leaving scars that would always remind me of the price paid for the experiences I'd had. Spring came, and the weather warmed. I shaved the beard and took the job with my father, enrolling in night classes at the community college under my GI bill. *Renew, refresh, rebuild, rebirth yourself.*

Sarah called, and I filled her in on my dad's status. They had always hit it off since he liked women that could keep up with him at the bar. She told me that Jean had married Buck, and they got divorced a month later. Then she said that Barry had contracted AIDS and died. I thought about Reagan's inaction and amusement as the epidemic decimated the gay population, but held my anger at bay to not disrupt our conversation with politics.

"How are you and Leah doing?" I asked.

"We're doing great. You wouldn't believe how fast she's growing! The pictures I send are always behind. I won't say she looks like you more every day, though. I know you don't like to hear it, Levi."

"I have eyes, Sarah." My admission surprised me. I had been studying the pictures more and more, secretly hoping to see myself in them and finally get an answer to the question. *Closure.*

"I want you to be happy, Levi, because I love you. I know you wouldn't be happy with us, and that's why it wouldn't work. You want to be free. You're a farawayer, remember?"

Her words hurt me, and it hurt me to imagine them there, alone. The thought of any child without a father had always bothered me, whether it was Mary's or Jolene's, but most of all, Sarah's.

"What about the milkman? I'm sure he's making you happy." Just saying it upset me.

"I broke that off a while ago. He was so good with Leah, but I realized I was only doing it for her. I need to be happy, too. And he wasn't like you, Levi. I have found no one like you, and I still love you. I'd rather be alone than with a substitute; it wouldn't be fair to the substitute either. We'll be fine. I love being a mom, and Leah is my world."

"I feel kind of the same..." I choked on the words.

"Well, if you want, we could do one of those tests."

I thought about it and realized the idea brought out the conflict within me. I took a moment to think, and as always, she respected that. A negative result would make me feel worse for the both of them, and I might never want to see her again. She might want to go find the father. It would crush Sarah, and she'd been so good to me, so patient. A positive result would determine my fate, and I might forever regret having my direction in life determined by some damn medical test. The decision had to be made for a bigger, more important reason—that I loved her and wanted us all to be a family, regardless of the paternity.

"I don't think so, Sarah. They're not that accurate, so it wouldn't bring closure. They're damn expensive, too." We left it at that, and I told her I still loved her before I hung up. It was the first time I'd said those words to her in a long time, and I had said it to no other girl since. It felt good to say, like an exorcism of everything bad that had happened since I had left her behind. I realized in that moment that of all the girls I'd fallen for in the past years on the road, she was the sum of the best parts of all of them.

Love is like a soap bubble drifting on a light summer breeze. You have to fight to keep it afloat, encouraging it upward with gentle motions, because allowing it to land might be disastrous. Like anything else, it could only last so long, but by fighting hard, you could keep it alive.

MY JOURNEY HAD ENDED, and I spent a lot of time in thought, doing postmortem analysis, wondering if and how I had failed in my quest. Maybe that kind of freedom was just an illusion, something in books and movies. As Starr had reminded me, it hadn't ended well for Kerouac and others who had pursued it. Modern society wasn't designed for what I had been trying to do. It made it hard to go against that grain. As you got older, reality crept in, pursued you, and set around your restless legs like the cement I had helped to bag at the concrete plant. It could be done, I was sure, but only at substantial cost—more so depending on how many people out there cared about you, and whom you cared about. *A good life for sociopaths, maybe.*

Once I had freed myself from the dream of reuniting with Carla, I realized it had been just a way to believe I could go back to the past, back to my happy teenage years, get my grandfather back, and that could no longer happen. The whole time, I hadn't been so much yearning for her, but for that magical time in my life. My traveling had been an attempt to freeze time and prevent moving forward, and further away from that part of my life. Now I was free to move ahead. *Free, finally.* I resolved to be happy I'd had those times, rather than regret I couldn't go back to them.

As we get older, the instinct to wander and explore wanes, displaced by the need for survival. Safety becomes a priority, and the need to build a home, reproduce, extend the species takes precedence in our psyche. The body and mind begin their gradual decline early in life. You learn the value of a chosen spot and build a nest there. And yet, the road still called, still nagged from the perimeter of the subconscious. But those thoughts were fading, like the memory of Carla.

Perhaps the idea of freedom, people dreaming of doing the things I had done, was only meant to sustain them through the hardship of doing what they needed to do in life. Dreams of summer vacations get us through the tough winters. Dreams of palm trees in retirement get us through decades of hard work. Maybe I had fought against some unseen force, or broken some unwritten code, by trying to achieve it without earning it.

Throughout history, the young and upcoming generations have been idealists—as yet unencumbered by the problems that will later corrupt their clear and pristine view of the world. Their focus is love, and the good of humanity. But then out of love, the will to survive, and the desire to make those they love comfortable and happy, those views die, finally quashed under the weight of submission. They change their view as the focus shifts to how changes will impact the value of their home, the company's wellbeing, bonuses, salaries, and career progression.

There would be no closure on the matter in Tennessee. I resolved that I'd likely carry the burden of it with me forever, and alternate between believing the man had lived and justifying his death and removal from society. I wondered if it would be my final thought someday, as I took my last breath, and whether I'd see him after that and apologize. The people I'd hurt in my travels, figuratively and literally, had created a great weight on me, and a person can only carry so much weight.

I often thought back on my experiences. I had learned the intrinsic power of *home*, the one place that was yours and would always be yours. Anywhere else you went, you were a stranger, a misfit. You were in someone else's home and they would resent you for it. You were the *other*, and to a smaller extent, subject to the same discrimination as anyone else who dressed differently, spoke differently, or worshipped differently. There is nothing like the familiar comfort and embrace of home, the familiar back roads and bars that fit you like a glove, filled with people just like you.

It was the one place you belonged. Your people were there—friends and cousins, siblings and aunts and uncles. Those who loved you were there to celebrate together every significant moment in your life and theirs. In hard times, they would be there for you, to help you no matter what.

Home would always change along with you. Being absent from that gradual shift, you came out of sync with it. Those things weren't tentacles, as I had imagined. They were the loving embrace of so many arms. I realized that even though they all envied me and my freedom, out there on the road, I also envied them for having the courage to stay.

I resisted the urge to go back to that life, thinking maybe I could make it the traditional way and do the good things I'd dreamed about. Maybe get Dad that Corvette, help set Damon up with a business, have a nice place and maybe even a home and boat for my family on the beautiful, sparkling lake. That would be real freedom, to write and to spend time out there on the water in summer and the ice of winter, teaching my kids to skate and play hockey as I had long ago in my happy childhood in Lake Sussex. Maybe that's how you finally get to reclaim the past, by reliving it with new and improved versions of yourself.

I called Sarah more often as I caught up with the pictures and letters she'd sent in my absence. I looked at each photograph again and again, sometimes holding them next to my reflection in the bedroom mirror; beholding the fatherless child and my lost and lonely self. Leah smiled at me from them, and she had my eyes. *Yes, she certainly has my eyes.*

The End

We shall not cease from exploration
And the end of all our exploring
Will be to arrive where we started
And know the place for the first time.
~ T. S. Eliot

About the Author

Billy DeCarlo is an American author of novels and short stories. He grew up camped out at the corner newsstand, reading as many comic books as he could before the owner would throw him out. He writes out of love and in hope to change the world, or at least a few minds. He still believes there are superheroes, and sees evidence of them sometimes on the news. And villains, lots of villains.

The most rewarding thing a writer can receive is a review from those who enjoyed the work. The most constructive thing a writer can receive is a private message with anything that can help to improve his or her work.

Please sign up for the newsletter at the website so you hear about future books, editions, and other news.

Reviews are the currency of the craft. If you enjoyed this book, please take time to write a review.

Other Books by Billy DeCarlo
Road Warrior (sequel to Farawayer) coming in 2023!
DroidMesh Trilogy (All Ages Sci-Fi)

Sped-Bot

Love-Bot

War-Bot

DroidMesh Trilogy Boxed Set

Vigilante Angels (Noir Crime Fiction)

The Priest

The Cop

The Candidate

Vigilante Angels Boxed Set

Stand-alone Works

Farawayer (Literary Travel Fiction)

Rambles and Daydreams (Short Stories)

Thank you for reading!

Read more at https://billydecarlo.com.

Made in the USA
Middletown, DE
07 July 2023

34697954R00177